ult

ANCIENT LIGHT

ANCIENT LIGHT

John Banville

WINDSOR
PARAGON

First published 2012
by Viking
This Large Print edition published 2013
by AudioGO Ltd
by arrangement with
Penguin Books Ltd

Hardcover   ISBN: 978 1 4713 5040 5
Softcover   ISBN: 978 1 4713 5041 2

British Library Cataloguing in Publication Data available

Printed and bound in Great Britain by
T J International Limited

in memoriam
Caroline Walsh

The Bud is in flower. Mud is Brown. I feel as fit as a Flea. things can go wrong.
Catherine Cleave, in childhood

I

Billy Gray was my best friend and I fell in love with his mother. Love may be too strong a word but I do not know a weaker one that will apply. All this happened half a century ago. I was fifteen and Mrs. Gray was thirty-five. Such things are easily said, since words themselves have no shame and are never surprised. She might be living still. She would be, what, eighty-three, eighty-four? That is not a great age, these days. What if I were to set off in search of her? That would be a quest. I should like to be in love again, I should like to fall in love again, just once more. We could take a course of monkey-gland injections, she and I, and be as we were fifty years ago, helpless in raptures. I wonder how things are with her, assuming she is still of this earth. She was so unhappy then, so unhappy, she must have been, despite her valiant and unfailing cheeriness, and I dearly hope she did not

11

continue so.

What do I recall of her, here in these soft pale days at the lapsing of the year? Images from the far past crowd in my head and half the time I cannot tell whether they are memories or inventions. Not that there is much difference between the two, if indeed there is any difference at all. Some say that without realising it we make it all up as we go along, embroidering and embellishing, and I am inclined to credit it, for Madam Memory is a great and subtle dissembler. When I look back all is flux, without beginning and flowing towards no end, or none that I shall experience, except as a final full stop. The items of flotsam that I choose to salvage from the general wreckage — and what is a life but a gradual shipwreck? — may take on an aspect of inevitability when I put them on display in their glass show-cases, but they are random; representative, perhaps, perhaps compellingly so, but random nonetheless.

There were for me two distinct initial manifestations of Mrs. Gray, years apart. The first woman may not have been she at all, may have been only an annunciation of her, so to speak, but it pleases me to think the two were one. April, of course. Remember what April was like when we were young, that sense of liquid rushing and the wind taking blue scoops out of the air and the birds beside themselves in the budding trees? I was ten or eleven. I had turned in at the gates of the Church of Mary Our Mother Immaculate, head down as usual — Lydia says I walk like a permanent penitent — and the first presage I had of the woman on the bicycle was the fizzing of tyres, a sound that seemed to me excitingly erotic when I was a boy, and does so even yet, I do not know why. The church stood on a rise, and when I looked up and saw her approaching with the steeple beetling at her back it seemed thrillingly that she had come swooping down out of the sky at just that moment, and that what I had heard was not the sound of tyres on the tarmac but of rapid wings beating the air. She was almost upon me, freewheeling, leaning back relaxedly and steering with one hand. She wore a gaberdine raincoat, the tails of it flapping behind to right and left of her like, yes, like wings, and a blue jumper over a blouse with a white collar. How clearly I see her! I must be making her up, I mean I must be making up these details. Her skirt was wide and loose, and now all at once the spring wind caught it and lifted it, laying her bare all the way up to her waist. Ah, yes.

Nowadays we are assured that there is hardly a jot of difference between the ways in which the sexes experience the world, but no woman, I am prepared to wager, has ever known the suffusion of dark delight that floods the veins of a male of any age, from toddler to nonagenarian, at the spectacle of the female privy parts, as they used quaintly to be called, exposed accidentally, which is to say fortuitously, to sudden public view. Contrary, and disappointingly I imagine, to female assumptions, it is not the glimpsing of the flesh itself that roots us men to the spot, our mouths gone dry and our eyes out on stalks, but of precisely those silken scantlings that are the last barriers between a woman's nakedness and our goggling fixity. It makes no sense, I know, but if on a crowded beach on a summer day the swimsuits of the female bathers were to be by some dark sorcery transformed into underwear, all of the males present, the naked little boys with their pot bellies and pizzles on show, the lolling, muscle-bound lifeguards, even the hen-pecked husbands with trouser-cuffs rolled and knotted hankies on their heads, all, I say, would be on the instant transformed and joined into a

14

herd of bloodshot, baying satyrs bent on rapine.

I am thinking particularly of those olden days when I was young and women under their dresses — and which of them then did not wear a dress, save the odd golfing girl or spoilsport film star in her pleated slacks? — might have been fitted out by a ship's chandler, with all sorts and shapes of rigging and sheeting, jibs and spankers, sheers and stays. My Lady of the Bicycle, now, with her taut suspenders and pearly-white satin knickers, had all the dash and grace of a trim schooner plying fearlessly into a stiff nor'wester. She seemed as startled as I by what the breeze was doing to her modesty. She looked down at herself and then at me and raised her eyebrows and made an O of her mouth, and gave a gurgling laugh and smoothed the skirt over her knees with a careless sweep of the back of her free hand and sailed blithely past. I thought her a vision of the goddess herself, but when I turned to look after her she was just a woman rattling along on a big black bike, a woman with those flaps or epaulettes on the shoulders of her coat that were fashionable then, and crooked seams in her nylons, and boxy hair just like my mother's. She slowed prudently in the gateway, her front wheel wobbling, and gave a chirrup on her bell before proceeding out into the street and turning left down Church Road.

I did not know her, had never seen her before, so far as I knew, though I would have thought that by then I had seen everyone in our tight little town at least once. And did I in fact see her again? Is it possible that she was indeed Mrs. Gray, the same one who four or five years later would irrupt so momentously into my life? I cannot summon up the features of the woman on the bike clearly enough to say for sure if she truly was or was not an early sighting of my Venus Domestica, though I cling to the possibility with wistful insistence.

What affected me so in that encounter in the churchyard, besides the raw excitement of it, was the sense I had of having been granted a glimpse into the world of womanhood itself, of having been let in, if only for a second or two, on the great secret. What thrilled and charmed me was not just the sight I got of the woman's shapely legs and fascinatingly complicated underthings, but the simple, amused and generous way that she looked down at me, doing that throaty laugh, and the negligent, backhanded grace with which she subdued her ballooning skirt. This must be another reason why she

16

has become merged in my mind with Mrs. Gray, why she and Mrs. Gray are for me the two faces of the one precious coin, for grace and generosity were the things I treasured, or should have treasured, in the first and, I sometimes disloyally think — sorry, Lydia — only real passion of my life. Kindness, or what they used to call loving-kindness, was the watermark discernible in Mrs. Gray's every gesture towards me. I think I am not being overly fond. I did not deserve her, I know that now, but how could I have known it then, being a mere boy, callow and untried? No sooner have I written down those words than I hear the weaselly whine in them, the puling attempt at self-exculpation. The truth is I did not love her enough, I mean I did not love her as I had it in me to do, young as I was, and I think she suffered for it, and that is all there is to say on the subject, though I am sure that will not stop me from saying a great deal more.

Her name was Celia. Celia Gray. It does not sound quite right, does it, that combination? Women's married names never sound right, in my opinion. Is it that they all marry the wrong men, or at any rate men with the wrong surnames? *Celia* and *Gray* make altogether too languid a coupling, a slow hiss followed by a soft thud, the hard *g* in Gray not half hard enough. She was not languid, anything but. If I say she was buxom that fine old word will be misunderstood, will be given too much weight, literally and figuratively. I do not think she was beautiful, at least not conventionally so, although I suppose a boy of fifteen could hardly have been called on to award the golden apple; I did not think of her as beautiful or otherwise; I fear that, after the initial gloss had gone dull, I did not think of her at all, but took her, however gratefully, for granted.

A memory of her, a sudden image coming back unbidden, was what set me stumbling off down Memory Lane in the first place. A thing she used to wear, called a half-slip, I believe — yes, undergarments again — a slithery, skirt-length affair in salmon-coloured silk or nylon, would leave, when she had taken it off, a pink weal where the elastic waistband had pressed into the pliant, silvery flesh of her belly and flanks, and, though less discernibly, at the back, too, above her wonderfully prominent bum, with its two deep dimples and the knubbled, slightly sandpapery twin patches underneath, where she sat down. This rosy cincture encircling her middle stirred me deeply, suggestive as it was of tender punishment, exquisite suffering — I was thinking of the harem, no doubt, of branded houris and the like — and I would lie with my cheek resting on her midriff and trace the crimpled line of it with a slow fingertip, my breath stirring the shiny dark hairs at the base of her belly and in my ear the pings and plonks of her innards at their ceaseless work of transubstantiation. The skin was always hotter along that uneven, narrow track left by the elastic, where the blood crowded protectively to the surface. I suspect, too, I was savouring the blasphemous hint that it gave of the crown of thorns. For our doings together were pervaded throughout by a faint, a very faint, sickly religiosity.

I pause to record or at least to mention a dream I had last night in which my wife had left me for another woman. I do not know what this might signify, or if it signifies anything, but certainly it has left an impression. As in all dreams the people in this one were plainly themselves and at the same time not, my wife, to take the principal player, appearing as short, blonde and bossy. How did I know it was she, looking so unlike herself as she did? I, too, was not as I am, but corpulent and ponderous, sag-eyed, slow-moving, a kind of an old walrus, say, or some other soft, lumbering water-going mammal; there was the sense of a sloped back, leathery and grey, disappearing slidingly around a rock. So there we were, lost to each other, she not she and I not I.

My wife harbours no sapphic inclinations, so far as I know — though how far is that? — but in the dream she was cheerfully, briskly, butch. The object of her transferred affections was a strange little man-like creature with wispy sideburns and a faint moustache and no hips, a dead ringer, now that I think of it, for Edgar Allan Poe. As to the dream proper I shall not bore you, or myself, with the details. Anyway, as I think I have already said, I do not believe we retain details, or if we do they are so heavily edited and censored and generally fancified as to constitute a new thing altogether, a dream of a dream, in which the original is transfigured, as the dream itself transfigures waking experience. This does not prevent me from crediting dreams with all sorts of numinous and prophetic implications. But surely it is too late in the day for Lydia to leave me. All I know is that this morning I woke in the pre-dawn hour with an oppressive sense of loss and deprivation and all-pervading sadness. Something seems set to happen.

■ ■ ■ ■

I think I was a little in love with Billy Gray
before I was a lot in love with his mother.
There is that word again, love; how easily it
trips off the pen. Strange, thinking of Billy
like this. He would be my age now. That is
hardly remarkable — he was my age then
— yet it gives me a shock. I feel as if I have
suddenly taken a step up — or is it a step
down? — into another phase of ageing.
Would I know him if I met him? Would he
know me? He was so upset when the scandal
broke. I am sure I felt the shock of public
disgrace as much as he did, or more so, I
should think, but all the same I was taken
aback by the passion with which he repudi-
ated me. After all, I would not have minded
if he had been sleeping with my mother,
difficult though that would have been to
imagine — I found it difficult to imagine
anyone sleeping with Ma, the poor old
thing, which was how I thought of her, as
poor, and old, and a thing. That surely was
what so troubled Billy, having to contem-
plate the fact that his mother was a woman
whom someone desired, and furthermore
that the someone was me. Yes, it must have
been all kinds of agony for him to picture

the two of us rolling naked in each other's arms on that filthy mattress on the floor in Cotter's place. He had probably never seen his mother without her clothes on, or not that he could remember, anyhow.

It was he who first stumbled on the Cotter house, and I used to worry that one day he would stumble on his mother and me at our love-play there. Was she aware that Billy knew the place? I cannot remember. If she was, my worry would have been as nothing compared to her terror at the thought of discovery by her only son as she was being made love to by his best friend in the midst of ancient squalor on a dirty, leaf-littered floor.

I recall the day I first saw the house. We had been in the little hazel wood along by the river, Billy and I, and he had brought me up to a ridge and pointed out the roof among the treetops. From the height on which we stood only the roof was visible, and at first I could not make it out, for the slates were covered with moss as green as the surrounding foliage. That must have been why it remained hidden for so long, and why presently it would make such a secure trysting-place for Mrs. Gray and me. I wanted to go down and break in straight away — for we were boys, after all, and still young enough to be on the look-out for what we would have called a club-house — but Billy was reluctant, strangely, as it seemed to me, since he had discovered the place and had even been inside it, or so he said. I believe he was a little afraid of that house; perhaps he had a premonition, or thought it haunted, as indeed it soon would be, not by ghosts but by the Lady Venus and her sportive boy.

It is odd, but I see our pockets that day filled with hazel nuts we had collected down in the wood and the ground around us plated with the hammered gold of fallen leaves, yet it was April, it had to have been April, the leaves green and still on the trees and the hazel nuts not even formed yet. Try as I will, however, I see not spring but autumn. I suppose we straggled away, then, the two of us, through the green not golden leaves, with our pockets not full of nuts, and went home, leaving Cotter's place undisturbed. Something in me had been struck, though, by the look of that sagging roof among the trees, and I went back the very next day, led by love the necessitous and ever-practical, and discovered in the tumbledown house just the place of shelter Mrs. Gray and I were in need of. For, yes, we were by that time already intimate, to put it as delicately as I may.

Billy had a sweetness to his nature that was very attractive. His features were nice, though his skin was poor, somewhat pitted, like his mother's, I am afraid, and prone to pimples. He had his mother's eyes, too, of a liquid umber shade, and wonderfully long fine eyelashes, each lash perfectly distinct, so that I thought, or think now, of that special paintbrush that miniaturists use, the business end a single filament of sable. He walked with a curious bow-legged rolling gait, swinging his arms in a hooped fashion that made it seem as if he were gathering invisible sheaves of something out of the air before him as he went along. That Christmas he had given me a manicure set in a neat pigskin case — yes, a manicure set, with a pair of scissors and nail clippers and a file, and a polished ivory stick, shaped at one end like a tiny flattish spoon, which my mother examined doubtfully and pronounced either a cuticle-pusher — a *cuticle-pusher*? — or more prosaically an implement for prising dirt from under the nails. I was puzzled by this girlish gift yet accepted it with good if uncertain grace. I had not thought to get him anything; he did not seem to have expected that I would, or to mind that I had not.

I wonder now, suddenly, if it was his mother who bought the manicure set for him to give to me, a coy and secret gift, delivered by proxy, that she thought I might guess had really come from her. This was some months before she and I had become — oh, go on and say it, for God's sake! — before we had become lovers. She had known me, of course, for I had been calling for Billy at the house most days that winter on the way to school. Did I look to her like the kind of boy who would think a manicure set just the thing for Christmas? Billy's own attentions to personal hygiene were less than thorough. He bathed even more infrequently than the rest of us did, as indicated by that intimate, brownish whiff he gave off on occasion; also the pores in the grooves beside his nostrils were blackly clogged, and with a shiver of mingled relish and revulsion I would imagine getting at them with my thumbnails for pincers, after which I would certainly have had need of that elegant little ivory gouge. He wore jumpers with holes in them and his collars seemed never to be clean. He possessed an air rifle and shot frogs with it. He was truly my best friend, and I did love him, in some way or other. Our chumship was sealed one winter eve when we were sharing a clandestine cigarette in the back seat of the family station wagon parked outside the house — this is a vehicle we shall become deeply familiar with presently — and he confided to me that his given name was not William, as he would have the world believe, but Wilfred, and further that his middle name was Florence, after his dead uncle Flor. Wilfred! Florence! I kept his secret, I can say that for myself, which is not much, I know. But, ah, how he wept, for pain and rage and humiliation, the day he met me after he had found out about his mother and me; how he wept, and I the prime cause of his bitter tears.

I cannot remember the first time I saw Mrs. Gray, if she was not the woman on the bike, that is. Mothers were not people that we noticed much; brothers, yes, sisters, even, but not mothers. Vague, shapeless, unsexed, they were little more than an apron and a swatch of unkempt hair and a faint sharp tang of sweat. They were always dimly busy in the background, doing things with baking tins, or socks. I must have been in Mrs. Gray's vicinity numerous times before I registered her in any particular, definite way. Confusingly, I have what is certain to be a false memory of her, in winter, applying talcum powder to the shinily pink inner sides of my thighs where they had become

26

raw from the chafing of my trousers; highly unlikely, since apart from anything else the trousers I was wearing on that occasion were short, which would hardly have been the case if I was fifteen, since we were all in longed-for longers by the age of eleven or twelve at the latest. Then whose mother was that one, I wonder, the talc-applier, and what opportunity for an even more precocious initiation did I perhaps let pass?

Anyhow, there was no moment of blinding illumination when Mrs. Gray herself stepped forth from the toils and trammels of domesticity and came skimming towards me on her half-shell, wafted by the full-cheeked zephyrs of spring. Even after we had been going to bed together for some time I would have been hard put to give a fair description of her — if I had tried, what I would have described would probably have been a version of myself, for when I looked at her it was me that I saw first, reflected in the glorious mirror that I made of her.

Billy never talked to me about her — why would he? — and seemed to pay her no more heed than I did for so long. He was a laggard, and often of a morning when I called for him going to school he was not ready, and I would be invited in, especially if it was raining or icy. He did not do the inviting — remember that suffusion of mute fury and burning shame we experienced when our friends got a glimpse of us *in flagrante* in the naked bosom of our families? — so it must have been she. Yet I cannot recall a single instance of her appearing at the front door, in her apron, with her sleeves rolled, insisting I come in and join the family circle at the breakfast table. I can see the table, though, and the kitchen that it almost filled, and the big American-style fridge the colour and texture of curdled cream, the straw basket of laundry on the draining board, the grocery-shop calendar showing the wrong month, and that squat chrome toaster with a seething gleam of sunlight from the window reflected high on its shoulder.

Oh, the morning smell of other people's kitchens, the cotton-wool warmth, the clatter and haste, with everyone still half asleep and cross. Life's newness and strangeness never seemed more vividly apparent than it did in such moments of homely intimacy and disorder.

Billy had a sister, younger than he, an unnerving creature with the look of a pixie, with long, rather greasy plaits and a narrow sharp stark white face the top half of which was blurred behind enormous horn-rimmed spectacles with circular lenses as thick as magnifying glasses. She seemed to find me irresistibly amusing and would wriggle inside her clothes with malignant hilarity when I appeared in the kitchen with my schoolbag, shuffling in like a hunchback. She was called Kitty, and indeed there was something feline in the way she would slit her eyes when she smiled at me, compressing her lips into a thin, colourless arc that seemed to stretch all the way between her intricately voluted, translucent, prominent pink ears. I wonder now if she, too, might have been sweet on me and all the snuffly amusement were a means of hiding the fact. Or is this just vanity on my part? I am, or was, an actor, after all. There was something the matter with her, she had some condition that was not spoken of that made her what in those days was called delicate. I found her unnerving, and was I think even a little afraid of her; if so, it was prescient of me.

Mr. Gray, the husband and father, was long and lean, and myopic, too, like his daughter — he was an optician, as it happens, a fact the high irony of which is unlikely to be lost on any of us — and wore bow-ties and sleeveless Fair Isle jumpers. And of course there were, presently, those two short stubby horns sprouting just above his hairline, the cuckold's mark, which I regret to say were my doing.

Was my passion for Mrs. Gray, at the outset, at any rate, anything more than an intensification of the conviction we all had at that age that our friends' families were so very much nicer, more gracious, more interesting — in a word, more desirable — than our own? At least Billy had a family, whereas there was only me and my widowed mother. She kept a boarding-house for travelling salesmen and other transients, who did not so much lodge in the place as haunt it, like anxious ghosts. I stayed out as much as I could. The Grays' house was often empty in the latter part of the afternoons and Billy and I would lounge about there for hours after school. Where did the others, Mrs. Gray and Kitty, for instance, where did they get to at those times? I can still see Billy, in his navy-blue school blazer and grubby white shirt from the collar of which he had just yanked one-handedly a stained school tie, standing in front of the fridge with the door open, gazing glassy-eyed into its lighted interior as if he were watching something engrossing on television. In fact there was a television set in the upstairs living room, and sometimes we would go up there and sit slumped in front of it with our hands plunged in our trouser pockets and our feet on our schoolbags, trying to watch the afternoon horse-racing from exotic-sounding places on the other side of the sea, such as Epsom, or Chepstow, or Haydock Park. Reception was poor, and often all we would see would be phantom riders cocked astride their phantom mounts, floundering blindly through a blizzard of static interference.

In the desperate idleness of one of those afternoons Billy hunted out the key to the cocktail cabinet — yes, the Grays possessed such an exotic item, for they were among the town's more well-to-do folk, though I doubt anyone in the house ever actually drank a cocktail — and we broke into a precious bottle of his father's twelve-year-old whiskey. Standing at the window, cut-glass tumbler in hand, my pal and I felt like a pair of Regency rakes looking down in high disdain upon a drably sober world. It was my first drink of whiskey, and although I would never develop a liking for the stuff, that day the sullen, bitter reek of it and the scald of it on my tongue seemed portents of the future, a promise of all the rich adventures that life surely had in store for me. Outside in the little square the wan sunlight of early spring was gilding the cherry trees and making the black, arthritic tips of their branches glisten, and old Busher the rag-and-bone man on his cart went grinding past, a wagtail scurrying out of the way of the frilled hoofs of his horse, and at the sight of these things I felt a sharp sweet ache of yearning, objectless yet definite, like the phantom pain in an amputee's missing limb. Did I see, or sense, even then, away down the tunnel of time, tiny in the distance yet growing steadily more substantial, the figure of my future love, chatelaine of the House of Gray, already making her abstracted, dallying way towards me?

What used I call her, I mean how did I address her? I do not remember saying her name, ever, though I must have. Her husband sometimes called her Lily, but I do not think I had a pet-name, a love-name, for her. I have a suspicion, which will not be dismissed, that on more than one occasion, in the throes of passion, I cried out the word *Mother*! Oh, dear. What am I to make of that? Not, I hope, what I shall be told I should.

Billy took the whiskey bottle into the bathroom and topped up the telltale gap with a gill of water from the tap, and I dried and polished the glasses as best I could with

32

my handkerchief and put them back where they had been on the shelf in the cocktail cabinet. Partners in crime, Billy and I were suddenly shy of each other, and I took up my schoolbag hurriedly and made my getaway, leaving my friend slumped on the sofa again, watching the unwatchable racers pounding through the electric snow.

I would like to be able to say it was that day, because I remember it so particularly, that I came face to face with Mrs. Gray for the first, real, time, at the front door, perhaps, she coming in as I was going out, her face flushed from the thrilling air of outdoors and my nerves tingling still after the whiskey; a chance touch of her hand, a surprised, lingering look; a thickening in the throat; a soft jolt to the heart. But no, the front hall was empty except for Billy's bicycle and an unpartnered roller-skate that must have been Kitty's, and no one met me in the doorway, no one at all. The pavement when I stepped on to it seemed farther away from my head than it should be, and tended to tilt, as though I were on stilts and the stilts had squashy springs attached to the ends of them — in short, I was drunk, not seriously so, but drunk nevertheless. Just as well, then, that I did not encounter Mrs. Gray, being in such a state of soggy euphoria, for there is no telling what I might have done and thereby ruined everything before it had even started.

And look! In the square, when I come out, it is, impossibly, autumn again, not spring, and the sunlight has mellowed and the leaves of the cherry trees have rusted and Busher the rag-and-bone man is dead. Why are the seasons being so insistent, why do they resist me so? Why does the Mother of the Muses keep nudging me like this, giving me what seem all the wrong hints, tipping me the wrong winks?

My wife just now climbed all the way up here to my eyrie under the roof, unwillingly negotiating the steep and treacherous attic stairs that she hates, to tell me that I have missed a telephone call. At first, when she put her head in at the low door — how smartly I encircled this page with a protective arm, like a schoolboy caught scribbling smut — I could hardly understand what she was saying. I must have been concentrating very hard, lost in the lost world of the past. Usually I hear the phone ringing, down in the living room, a far-off and strangely plaintive sound that makes my heart joggle anxiously, just as it used to do long ago when my daughter was a baby and her crying woke me in the night.

The caller, Lydia said, was a woman, whose name she did not catch, though she was unmistakably American. I waited. Lydia was looking dreamily beyond me now, out through the sloped window in front of my desk, to the mountains in the distance, pale blue and flat, as if they had been painted on the sky in a weak wash of lavender; it is one of the charms of our city that there are few places in it from which these soft and, I always think, virginal hills are not visible, if one is prepared to stretch. What, I asked gently, had this woman on the phone wished to speak to me about? Lydia with an effort withdrew her gaze from the view. A film, she said, a movie, in which it seems I am being offered a leading part. This is interesting. I have not acted in a film before. I enquired as to the movie's title, or what it is to be about. Lydia's look grew vague, I mean more vague than it had been up to now. She did not think the woman had told her what the title is. Apparently it is to be a biopic, but of whom she is not sure — some German, it seems. I nodded. Had the woman perhaps left a number so that I might call her back? At this Lydia lowered her head and frowned at me from under her eyebrows in solemn silence, like a child who has been asked a difficult and onerous question the answer to which she does not know. Never mind, I said, no doubt the woman would phone again, whoever she was.

My poor Lydia, she is always a little dazed like this after one of her bad nights. Her name, by the way, is really Leah — Lydia is a mishearing of mine that stuck — Leah Mercer *as was,* as my mother would have said. She is large and handsome, with broad shoulders and a dramatic profile. Her hair these days is a two-tone shade of what used to be called salt-and-pepper with, in the undergrowth, a few uncertain sallow low-lights. When I met her first her hair had the lustre of a raven's wing, with a great silver streak in it, a flash of white fire; as soon as the silver began to spread she allowed herself to succumb to the blandishments of Adrian at Curl Up and Dye, whence she returns hardly recognisable after her monthly appointment with this master col-ourist. Her glossy, kohl-black eyes, those eyes of a desert daughter, as I used to think them, have lately taken on a faded, filmy aspect, which makes me worry about the possibility of cataracts. In her young days her figure had the ample lines of one of In-gres's odalisques but now the glory has fallen and she wears nothing but loose, billowing garments in muted hues, her camouflage, as she says with a sad laugh. She drinks a little too much, but then so do I; our decade-long great sorrow simply will not be drowned, tread it though we will below the surface and try to hold it there. Also she smokes heavily. She has a sharp tongue of which I am increasingly wary. I am very fond of her, and she, I believe, is fond of me, despite our frictions and occasional tight-lipped disagreements.

We had a dreadful night, the two of us, I with my dream of having been replaced in Lydia's affections by an androgynous writer of Gothic tales, and Lydia suffering one of those nocturnal bouts of mania that have beset her at irregular intervals over the past ten years. She wakes, or at least leaps from the bed, and goes dashing in the dark through all the rooms, upstairs and down, calling out our daughter's name. It is a kind of sleepwalking, or sleeprunning, in which she is convinced our Catherine, our Cass, is still alive and a child again and lost somewhere in the house. I get up groggily and follow her, only half awake myself. I do not try to restrain her, heeding the old wives' caution against interfering in any way with a person in that state, but I keep close in case she should trip over something and I might be able to catch her before she falls and save her from injuring herself. It is eerie, scurrying through the darkened house — I do not dare switch on the lights — in desperate pursuit of this fleeting figure. The shadows throng us round like a silent chorus, and at intervals a patch of moonlight or the radiance from a street-lamp falling in at a window will seem a dimmed spotlight, and I am reminded of one of those tragic queens in the Greek drama, raging through the king her husband's palace at midnight shrieking for her lost child. Eventually she tires herself out, or comes to her senses, or both, as she did last night, sinking down on a step of the stairs, all in a heap, shedding terrible tears and sobbing. I hovered about her helplessly, not knowing quite how to get my arms around her, so amorphous a shape did she appear, in her sleeveless black nightdress, her head hanging and her hands plunged in her hair that in the dark looked as black as it was the first time I saw her, walking out into summer through the revolving door of her father's hotel, the Halcyon of happy memory, the tall glass panels of the door throwing off repeated, glancing bursts of blue and gold — yes, yes, the crest of the wave!

The worst part, for me, of these extrava-
ganzas of anguished hue and cry comes at
the end, when she is all contrition, berating
herself for her foolishness and begging to
be forgiven for waking me so violently and
causing such needless panic. It is just, she
says, that in her sleepwalking state it seems
to her so real a thing that Cass is alive, her
living daughter, trapped in one of the rooms
of the house, terrified and unable to make
herself heard as she calls for help. Last night
she was so ashamed and angry that she
swore at herself, using horrible words, until
I hunkered down beside her and held her in
an awkwardly simian embrace and made her
lay her head in the hollow of my shoulder,
and at last she grew quiet. Her nose was
running and I let her wipe it on the sleeve
of my pyjamas. She was shivering, but when
I offered to fetch her dressing-gown or a
blanket she clung to me the more tightly
and would not let me leave her. The faintly
stale smell of her hair was in my nostrils
and the ball of her bare shoulder was chill
and smooth as a marble globe under my
cupped hand. Around us the hall furniture
stood dimly in the gloom like shocked and
speechless attendants.

I think I know what it is that torments
Lydia, besides the unassuageable grief she

has been nursing in her heart throughout the ten long years since our daughter died. Like me, she was never a believer in any of the worlds to come, yet I suspect she fears that through a cruel loophole in the laws of life and death Cass did not fully die but is somehow existing still, a captive in the land of the shades and suffering there, half of the pomegranate seeds still unswallowed in her mouth, waiting in vain for her mother to come and claim her back to be among the living again. Yet what is now Lydia's horror was once her hope. *How could anyone die who was so much alive?* she demanded of me that night in the hotel in Italy where we had come to claim Cass's body, and so fierce was her tone and so compelling her look that for a moment I, too, thought that a mistake might have been made, that it might be someone else's unrecognisable daughter who had smashed herself to death on those wave-washed rocks below the bare little church of San Pietro.

As I have said, we had not ever believed in the immortal soul, Lydia and I, and would smile in gentle condescension when others spoke of their hopes of some day seeing again departed loved ones, but there is nothing like the loss of an only child to soften the wax of sealed convictions. After

Cass's death — to this day I cannot see those words written down without a disbelieving shock, they seem so unlikely, even as I grave them on the page — we found ourselves venturing, tentatively, shamefacedly, to entertain the possibility not of the next world, exactly, but of a world next to this one, contiguous with it, where there might linger somehow the spirits of those no longer here and yet not entirely gone, either. We seized on what might be signs, the vaguest portents, wisps of intimation. Coincidences were not now what they had been heretofore, mere wrinkles in the otherwise blandly plausible surface of reality, but parts of a code, large and urgent, a kind of desperate semaphoring from the other side that, maddeningly, we were unable to read. How we would begin to listen now, all else suspended, when, in company, we overheard people speaking of having been bereaved, how breathlessly we hung on their words, how hungrily we scanned their faces, looking to see if they really believed their lost one not entirely lost. Certain dispositions of supposedly chance objects would strike us with a runic force. In particular those great flocks of birds, starlings, I think they are, that gather out over the sea on certain days, amoebically swooping and swirling, switching direction in perfect, instantaneous co-ordination, seemed to be inscribing on the sky a series of ideograms directed exclusively at us but too swiftly and fluidly sketched for us to interpret. All this illegibility was a torment to us.

I say us, but of course we never spoke of these pathetic hopes of a hint from the beyond. Bereavement sets a curious constraint between the bereaved, an embarrassment, almost, that is not easy to account for. Is it the fear that such things if spoken of will take on an even greater weight, become an even heavier burden? No, that is not it, not quite. The reticence, the tactfulness, that our mutual grieving imposed on Lydia and me was at once a measure of magnanimity, the same that makes the gaoler tiptoe past the cell in which the condemned man on his last night is asleep, and a mark of our dread of stirring up and provoking to even more inventive exercises those demonic torturers whose special task it was, is, to torment us. Yet even without saying, each knew what the other was thinking, and, more acutely, what the other was feeling — this is a further effect of our shared sorrow, this empathy, this mournful telepathy.

I am thinking of the morning after the

very first one of Lydia's nocturnal rampages when she had started up from the pillow convinced our recently dead Cass was alive and in the house somewhere. Even when the panic was over and we had dragged ourselves back to bed we did not get to sleep again, not properly — Lydia doing hiccuppy after-sobs and my heart tom-tomming away — but lay on the bed on our backs for a long time, as if practising to be the corpses that one day we shall be. The curtains were thick and drawn tightly shut, and I did not realise the dawn had come up until I saw forming above me a brightly shimmering image that spread itself until it stretched over almost the entire ceiling. At first I took it for an hallucination generated out of my sleep-deprived and still half-frantic consciousness. Also I could not make head or tail of it, which is not surprising, for the image, as after a moment or two I saw, was upside-down. What was happening was that a pinhole-sized opening between the curtains was letting in a narrow beam of light that had turned the room into a camera obscura, and the image above us was an inverted, dawn-fresh picture of the world outside. There was the road below the window, with its blueberry-blue tarmac, and, nearer in, a shiny black hump that was part of the roof of our car, and the single silver birch across the way, slim and shivery as a naked girl, and beyond all that the bay, pinched between the finger and thumb of its two piers, the north one and the south, and then the distant, paler azure of the sea, that at the invisible horizon became imperceptibly sky. How clear it all was, how sharply limned! I could see the sheds along the north pier, their asbestos roofs dully agleam in the early sunlight, and in the lee of the south pier the bristling, amber-coloured masts of the sailboats jostling together at anchor there. I fancied I could even make out the little waves on the sea, with here and there a gay speckle of foam. Thinking still that I might be dreaming, or deluded, I asked Lydia if she could see this luminous mirage and she said yes, yes, and reached out and clutched my hand tightly. We spoke in whispers, as if the very action of our voices might shatter the frail assemblage of light and spectral colour above us. The thing seemed to vibrate inside itself, to be tinily atremble everywhere, as if it were the teeming particles of light itself, the streaming photons, that we were seeing, which I suppose it was, strictly speaking. Yet surely, we felt, surely this was not entirely a natural phenomenon, for which there would be a perfectly simple scientific explanation, preceded by a soft little cough and followed by an apologetic hum — surely this was a thing given to us, a gift, a greeting, in other words a sure sign, sent to comfort us. We lay there watching it, awestruck, for, oh, I do not know how long. As the sun rose the inverted world above us was setting, retreating along the ceiling until it developed a hinge at one edge and began sliding steadily down the far wall and poured itself at last into the carpet and was gone. Straight away we got up — what else was there to do? — and started our dealings with the day. Were we comforted, did we feel lightened? A little, until the wonder of the spectacle to which we had been treated began to diffuse, to slip and slide and be absorbed into the ordinary, fibrous texture of things.

It was by the coast, too, that our daughter died, another coast, at Portovenere, which is, if you do not know it, an ancient Ligurian seaport at the tip of a spit of land stretching out into the Gulf of Genoa, opposite Lerici, where the poet Shelley drowned. The Romans knew it as Portus Veneris, for long ago there was a shrine to that charming goddess on the drear promontory where now stands the church of St. Peter the Apostle. Byzantium harboured its

45

fleet in the bay at Portovenere. The glory is long faded, and it is now a faintly melancholy, salt-bleached town, much favoured by tourists and wedding parties. When we were shown our daughter in the mortuary she had no features: St. Peter's rocks and the sea's waves had erased them and left her in faceless anonymity. But it was she, sure enough, there was no doubting it, despite her mother's desperate hope of a mistaken identity.

Why Cass should be in Liguria, of all places, we never discovered. She was twenty-seven, and something of a scholar, though erratic — she had suffered since childhood from Mandelbaum's syndrome, a rare defect of the mind. What may one know of another, even when it is one's own daughter? A clever man whose name I have forgotten — my memory has become a sieve — put the poser: What is the length of a coastline? It seems a simple enough challenge, readily met, by a professional surveyor, say, with his spyglass and tape measure. But reflect a moment. How finely calibrated must the tape measure be to deal with all those nooks and crannies? And nooks have nooks, and crannies crannies, *ad infinitum,* or *ad* at least that indefinite boundary where matter, so called, shades off seamlessly into thin air.

Similarly, with the dimensions of a life it is a case of stopping at some certain level and saying this, *this* was she, though knowing of course that it was not.

She was pregnant when she died. This was a shock for us, her parents, an after-shock of the calamity of her death. I should like to know who the father was, the father not-to-be; yes, that is something I should very much like to know.

The mysterious movie woman called back, and this time I was first to get to the phone, hurrying down the stairs from the attic with my knees going like elbows — I had not been aware I was so eager, and felt a little ashamed of myself. Her name, she told me, was Marcy Meriwether, and she was calling from Carver City on the coast of California. Not young, with a smoker's voice. She asked if she was speaking personally with Mr. Alexander Cleave the actor. I was wondering if someone of my acquaintance had set me up for a hoax — theatre folk have a distressing fondness for hoaxes. She sounded peeved that I had not returned her original call. I hastened to explain that my wife had not caught her name, which prompted Ms. Meriwether to spell it for me, in a tone of jaded irony, indicating either

47

that she did not believe my excuse — it had sounded limp and unlikely even to me — or just that she was tired of having to spell her mellifluous but faintly risible moniker for people too inattentive or dubious to have registered it properly the first time round. She is an executive, an important one, I feel sure, with Pentagram Pictures, an independent studio which is to make a film based on the life of one Axel Vander. This name, too, she spelled for me, slowly, as if by now she had decided she was dealing with a half-wit, which is understandable in a person who has spent her working life among actors. I confessed I did not know who Axel Vander is, or was, but this she brushed aside as of no importance, and said she would send me material on him. Saying it, she gave a dry laugh, I do not know why. The film is to be called *The Invention of the Past,* not a very catchy title, I thought, though I did not say so. It is to be directed by Toby Taggart. This announcement was followed by a large and waiting silence, which it was obvious I was expected to fill, but could not, for I had never heard of Toby Taggart either.

I thought that by now Ms. Meriwether would be ready to give up on a person as ill-informed as I clearly am, but on the contrary she assured me that everyone

48

involved in the project was very excited at the prospect of working with me, very excited, and that of course I had been the first and obvious choice for the part. I purred dutifully in appreciation of this flattery, then mentioned, with diffidence but not, I judged, apologetically, that I had never before worked in film. Was that a quick intake of breath I heard on the line? Is it possible a film person of long experience as Ms. Meriwether must be would not know such a thing about an actor to whom she was offering a leading part? That was fine, she said, just fine; in fact Toby wanted someone new to the screen, a fresh face — mark, I am in my sixties — an assertion that I could tell she no more believed in than I did. Then, with an abruptness that left me blinking, she hung up. The last I heard of her, as the receiver was falling into its cradle, was the beginning of a bout of coughing, raucous and juicy. Again I wondered uneasily if it was all a prank, but decided, on no good evidence, that it was not.

Axel Vander. So.

Mrs. Gray and I had our first — what shall I call it? Our first encounter? That makes it sound too intimate and immediate — since after all it was not an encounter in the flesh — and at the same time too prosaic. Whatever it was, we had it one watercolour April day of gusts and sudden rain and vast, rinsed skies. Yes, another April; in a way, in this story, it is always April. I was a raw boy of fifteen by then and Mrs. Gray was a married woman in the ripeness of her middle thirties. Our town, I thought, had surely never known such a liaison, though probably I was wrong, there being nothing that has not happened already, except what happened in Eden, at the catastrophic outset of everything. Not that the town came to know of it for a long time, and might never have found out had it not been for a certain busybody's prurience and insatiable nosiness. But here is what I remember, here is

50

what I retain.

I hesitate, aware of a constraint, as if the prudish past were plucking at my sleeve to forestall me. Yet that day's little dalliance — there is the word! — was child's play compared with what was to come later.

Anyway, here goes.

Lord, I feel fifteen again.

It was not a Saturday, certainly not a Sunday, so it must have been a holiday, or a holyday — the Feast of St. Priapus, perhaps — but at any rate there was no school, and I had called at the house for Billy. We had a plan to go somewhere, to do something. In the little gravelled square where the Grays lived the cherry trees were shivering in the wind and sinuous streels of cherry blossom were rolling along the pavements like so many pale-pink feather boas. The flying clouds, smoke-grey and molten silver, had great gashes in them where the damp-blue sky shone through, and busy little birds darted swiftly here and there or settled on the ridges of the roofs in huddled rows, fluffing up their feathers and carrying on a ribald chattering and piping. Billy let me in. He was not ready, as usual. He was half dressed, in shirt and pullover, but still had on striped pyjama bottoms and was barefoot, and gave off the woolly odour of an unfresh bed. He led the way upstairs to the living room.

In those days, when no one but the very rich could afford to have central heating, our houses on spring mornings such as this one had a special chill that gave a sharp, lacquered edge to everything, as if the air had turned to waterglass overnight. Billy went off to finish dressing and I stood in the middle of the floor, being nothing much, hardly even myself. There are moments like that, when one slips into neutral, as it were, not caring about anything, often not noticing, often not really *being*, in any vital sense. My mood that morning was not one of absence, however, not quite, but of passive receptivity, as I think now, a state of not quite conscious waiting. The metal-framed oblong windows here, all shine and sky, were too bright to sustain my gaze, and I turned from them and cast idly about the room. How quick with portent they always seem, the things in rooms that are not ours: that chintz-covered armchair braced somehow and as if about to clamber angrily to its feet; that floor-lamp keeping so still and hiding its face under a coolie's hat; the upright piano, its lid greyed by an immaculate coating of dust, clenched against the wall with a neglected, rancorous mien, like a large ungainly pet the family had long ago ceased to love. Clearly from outside I could hear those lewd birds doing their wolf-whistles. I began to feel something, a vague, flinching sensation down one side, as if a weak beam of light had been trained on me or a warm breath had brushed my cheek. I glanced quickly towards the doorway, but it was empty. Had there been someone there? Was that a skirl of fading laughter I had caught the end of?

I crossed quickly to the door. The corridor outside was empty, although I seemed to detect the trace of a presence there, a wrinkle in the air where someone had been a moment before. Of Billy there was no sign — perhaps he had gone back to bed, I would not have been surprised. I ventured along the corridor, the carpet — what colour, what colour was it? — muffling my tread, not knowing where I was going or what I was looking for. The wind was whispering in the chimneys. How the world talks to itself, in its own dreamy, secretive fashion. A door was halfway open, I did not notice it until I had almost passed by. I see myself there, glancing sideways and back, and everything slowing down suddenly with a sort of a lurch and a bump.

That carpet, now I remember: it was a

pale blue or bluey-grey strip, what is called a runner, I think, and the floorboards at the sides were varnished an unpleasant dark shade of brown and glistened like sucked, sticky toffee. See what can be called up, all manner of thing, when one concentrates.

Time and Memory are a fussy firm of interior decorators, though, always shifting the furniture about and redesigning and even reassigning rooms. I am convinced that what I looked into through that open door-way was a bathroom, for I recall distinctly the chilly gleam of porcelain and zinc, yet what caught my gaze was the kind of looking-glass that dressing-tables in women's bedrooms had in those days, with a curved upper edge and wings at the sides and even — can this be right? — little triangular flaps set atop the wings that the lady seated at her toilet could draw forwards at an angle to give her a view of herself from above. More confusingly still, there was another mirror, a full-length one, fixed to what would have to have been the outwards-facing side of the inwards-opening door, and it was in this mirror that I saw the room reflected, with at its centre the dressing-table, or whatever it was, with its own mirror, or I should say mirrors. What I had, therefore, was not, strictly speaking, a view of the bathroom, or bedroom, but a reflection of it, and of Mrs. Gray not a reflection but a reflection of a reflection.

Bear with me, through this crystalline maze.

So there I am, paused outside that doorway, gaping at an angle into the full-length looking-glass fixed, improbably, to the outside of the door that stood opened inwards. I did not register at once what it was I was seeing. Up to then the only body I had known at close quarters was my own, and even with that still evolving entity I was not on particularly intimate terms. What I would have expected a woman with no clothes on to look like I am not sure. No doubt I had pored hotly over reproductions of old paintings, ogled this or that old master's pink-thighed frump fighting off a faun or classical matron enthroned in pomp among, in Madame Geoffrin's happy formulation, a fricassee of children, but I knew that even the nakedest of these strapping figures, with their tundish breasts and perfectly bald and grooveless deltas, gave a far from naturalistic representation of woman in the raw. Now and then in school an antique dirty postcard would be passed from hand to fumbling hand under the desks, but as often as not the daguerreotyped cocottes showing off bare bits of themselves would be obscured behind smeared thumbprints and a filigree of white creases. In fact, my ideal of mature womanhood was the Kayser Bondor lady, a foothigh, cut-out cardboard beauty propped on the hosiery counter of Miss D'Arcy's haberdashery shop at the near end of our Main Street, arrayed in a lavender gown and showing off an excitingly chaste fringe of petticoat above a pair of lovely and impossibly long legs sheathed in fifteen-denier nylon, a svelte sophisticate who came swishing imperiously into many a nocturnal fantasy of mine. What mortal woman could match up to such presence, such stately poise?

Mrs. Gray in the mirror, in the mirrored mirror, was naked. It would be more gallant to say she was nude, I know, but naked is the word. After the first instant of confusion and shock I was struck by the grainy look of her skin — I suppose she must have had gooseflesh, standing there — and by the dull glimmer of it, like the sheen on a tarnished knife-blade. Instead of the shades of pink and peach that I would have expected — Rubens has a lot to answer for — her body displayed, disconcertingly, a range of muted tints from magnesium white to silver and

56

tin, a scumbled sort of yellow, pale ochre, and even in places a faint greenishness and, in the hollows, a shadowing of mossy mauve.

What was presented to me was a triptych of her, a body as it were dismembered, or I should say disassembled. The mirror's central panel, that is, the central panel of the mirror on the dressing-table, if that is what it was, framed her torso, breasts and belly and that smudge of darkness lower down, while the panels at either side showed her arms and her elbows, oddly flexed. There was a single eye, somewhere at the top, fixed on me levelly and with the hint of a challenge, as if to say, *Yes, here I am, what do you make of me?* I know very well this jumbled arrangement is unlikely, if not impossible — for one thing, she would have needed to be positioned close up to and directly in front of the mirror, with her back turned to me, for me to be able to see her reflected like that, but she was not there, only her reflection was. Could she have been standing some way away, at the opposite side of the room, and hidden from me in the angle of the open door? But in that case she would not have bulked so large in the mirror, would have appeared more distant and much smaller than she did. Unless the

57

two mirrors, the one on the dressing-table in which she was reflected and the one on the door reflecting her reflection, produced in combination a magnifying effect. I do not think so. Yet how can I account for all these anomalies, these improbabilities? I cannot. What I have described is what appears in my memory's eye, and I must say what I see. Later, when I asked her, Mrs. Gray herself denied such a thing had ever happened, and said I must take her for a fine rawsie — her word — if I thought she would show herself off in that fashion to a stranger in the house, and a boy, at that, and her son's best friend. But she lied, I am convinced of it.

That was all there was, that briefest glimpse of a fragmented woman, and at once I passed on along the corridor, stumblingly, as if I had been given a hard push in the small of the back. What? you will cry. Call that an encounter, call that a dalliance? Ah, but think of the boiling storm in a boy's heart after such licence, such accommodation. And yet, no, not a storm. I was not as shocked or inflamed as I should have expected to be. The strongest sensation I had was one of quiet satisfaction, as an anthropologist might feel, or a zoologist, who by happy chance, all unexpectedly, has glimpsed a creature the aspect and attributes of which confirm a theory as to the nature of an entire species. I knew now something I could never unknow, and if you scoff and say that after all it was knowledge only of what a naked woman looks like, you show that you do not remember what it was to be young and yearning for experience, yearning for what is commonly called love. That the woman had not flinched under my gaze, had not run to slam the door shut or even put up a hand to cover herself, seemed to me neither heedless nor brazen, but odd, rather, very odd, and a matter for deep and prolonged speculation.

The thing did not end without a fright, however. When on reaching the head of the stairs I heard rapid footsteps behind me I would not turn for fear it might be she, sprinting after me like a maenad, still without a stitch on and driven by who knew what wild design. I felt the skin at the back of my neck pucker as if in expectation of being set upon violently, by hands, clutching fingers, teeth, even. What could she want of me? The obvious was not the obvious — I was only fifteen, remember. I was torn between the impulse to plunge headlong down the stairs and flee the house, never to darken its doorstep again, and an opposite urge to stand my ground, and turn, and open wide my arms and receive into them this lavish and unlooked-for gift of womanhood, naked as a needle, in Piers the Ploughman's happy formulation, all breathless and a-flutter and drooping with desire. The person behind me was not Mrs. Gray, however, but her daughter, Billy's sister, the unnerving Kitty, all pigtails and specs, who squeezed past me now, wheezing and tittering, and went clattering down the stairs, at the bottom of which she stopped and turned and cast up at me a hair-raisingly knowing smirk, and then was gone.

After taking a deep and for some reason painful breath I, too, descended, circumspectly. The hall was empty, with Kitty nowhere to be seen, for which I was relieved. I opened the front door quietly and stepped out into the square, my gonads humming like those pretty porcelain insulators, little fat doll-like things, that there used to be on the arms of telegraph poles, that the wires went through, or around — remember? I knew that Billy would wonder what had become of me but I did not think that in the circumstances I could face him, not for now, anyway. He bore a strong resemblance to his mother, have I mentioned that? Oddly, though, he never did speak of my having flown the house, not when I met up with him next day, not ever, in fact. I sometimes wonder — well, I do not know what it is I wonder. Families are strange institutions, and the inmates of them know many strange things, often without knowing that they know them. When Billy eventually found out about his mother and me, did I not think his rage, those violent tears, a mite excessive, even in a case as provocative as the one in which we all suddenly found ourselves mired? What do I imply? Nothing. Move on, move on, as we are directed to do at the scene of an accident, or a crime.

Days passed. Half the time I spent in contemplation of Mrs. Gray reflected in the mirror of my memory and the other half imagining I had imagined everything. It was a week or more before I saw her again. There was a tennis club outside the town, by the estuary, where the Grays had a family membership, and where I went sometimes with Billy to knock a ball about, feeling horribly conspicuous in my cheap plimsolls and threadbare singlet. Ah, but the tennis clubs of yore! My heart haunts still those enchanted courts. Even the names, Melrose, Ashburn, Wilton, The Limes, bespoke a world more graceful far

61

than the dingy backwater where we lived. This one, out by the estuary, was called Courtlands; I imagine the pun was unintentional. I had seen Mrs. Gray playing there only once, partnering her husband in a doubles match against another couple who in my memory are no more than a pair of white-clad phantoms bobbing and dipping in the ghostly soundlessness of a lost past. Mrs. Gray played the net, crouching menacingly with her rear end in the air and springing up to slash at the ball like a samurai slicing an enemy diagonally in half. Her legs were not as long as the Kayser Bondor lady's, were in fact more sturdy than anything else, but nicely tanned, and shapely enough at the ankle. She wore shorts rather than one of those boring skirtlets, and there were damp patches at the armpits of her short-sleeved cotton shirt.

That day, the day of the incident — the incident! — that I wish to record, I was walking homewards alone when she overtook me in the car and stopped. Was it the day of the doubles match? Cannot remember. If it was, where was her husband? And if I was coming from the club, where was Billy? Detained, the pair of them, by the amatory goddess, delayed, diverted, locked in the lavatory and shouting in vain to be let out — no matter, they were not there. It was evening and the sunlight was watery after a day of showers. The road, patterned with fragrant patches of damp, ran beside the railway line, and beyond that the estuary was a shifting mass of turbulent purple, and the horizon was fringed with a boiling of ice-white clouds. I had slung my jumper over my shoulders and knotted the sleeves loosely in front, like a real tennis player, and carried my racquet in its press at a negligent angle under my arm. When I heard the motor slowing behind me I knew, I do not know how, that it was she, and my heartbeat, too, seemed to slow, and developed a syncopated catch. I stopped, and turned, frowning in feigned surprise. She had to stretch all the way across the passenger seat to roll down the window. The car was not a car in fact but a station wagon, of a flat grey shade and somewhat battered; she had left the motor running and the big ugly hump-backed thing gasped and trembled on its chassis like an old horse with a chill, coughing out blue smoke at the back. Mrs. Gray leaned low with her face tilted up towards the open window, smiling at me quizzically, reminding me of the amiably sardonic heroines of the screwball comedies of an earlier day, who made rapid-fire wisecracks and bullied their beaux and gaily spent their gruff fathers' countless millions on sports cars and silly hats. Did I say her hair was of an oaken shade and cut in a nondescript style, and that there was a curl at one side that she was always pushing behind her ear, though it would never stay put? "I think, young man," she said, "we are both going the same way." And so we were, although it turned out not to be the way home.

She was an impatient driver, apt to lose her footing on the pedals, and given to swearing under her breath and yanking violently at the gear stick, which was mounted on the steering column, her left arm working like the articulated handle of a pump. Did she smoke a cigarette? Yes, she did, darting it frequently at the gap where her window was open an inch at the top, though each time most of the ash blew back in again. The front seat had no armrest in the middle and was as wide and as plumply upholstered as a sofa, and when she trod on the brakes or clashed the gears we jounced a little on it in unison. For a long time Mrs. Gray said nothing, frowning out at the road ahead, her thoughts seemingly elsewhere. I sat with my hands resting in my lap, the fingers touching at their tips. What was I thinking of? Nothing, that I recall; I was just waiting, again, for what would happen to happen, as I waited that day in the Grays' living room before the encounter in the mirror, but more excitedly, more breathlessly, this time. She had changed out of her tennis whites into a dress made of some light stuff with a pattern of pale flowers. Now and then I caught a faint whiff of her mingled fragrances, while a dribble of cigarette smoke from her lips drifted sideways and went into my mouth. I had never been so sharply conscious of the presence of another human being, this separate entity, this incommensurable not-I; a volume displacing air, a soft weight pressing down on the other side of the bench seat; a mind working; a heart beating.

We skirted the town, following a sun-dappled back road beside a dry-stone wall and a wood of glimmering birches. It was a part of the town's hinterland I rarely found myself in; odd, how in a place so narrowly circumscribed as ours there were parts where one tended not to go. The evening was waning but the light was still strong, the sun racing through the trees beside us, those trees which as I see them now are much too lushly leaved, it being only April, for the seasons are shifting yet again. We crested a low hill where the wood fell back, and were afforded an unexpectedly panoramic view across garishly lit uplands to the sea, then we plunged down into a shadowed dell and suddenly at a muddy bend Mrs. Gray with a grunt spun the steering wheel and slewed the car to the left and we shot off the road on to an overgrown woodland track and she took her foot off the accelerator and the car bumped drunkenly over a few yards of uneven ground and came to a groaning, swaying stop.

She switched off the engine. Birdsong invaded the silence. With her hands still resting on the steering wheel she leaned forwards to peer up through the slanted windscreen into the tracery of ivory and brown branches above us. "Would you like to kiss me?" she asked, still with her eye canted upwards.

It had seemed less an invitation than a general enquiry, something she was simply curious to know. I looked into the brambled gloom beside the car. What was surprising was not to be surprised by any of this. Then, in the way of these things, we both turned our heads at the same moment and she set a first down between us on the soft seat to brace herself and with one shoulder lifted she advanced her face, tilted sideways at a slight angle, her eyes closed, and I kissed her. It was really a very innocent kiss. Her lips were dry and felt as brittle as a beetle's wing. After a second or two we disengaged, and sat back, and I had to clear my throat. How piercingly the birds' voices rang through the hollow wood. "Yes," Mrs. Gray murmured, as if confirming something to herself, then started up the engine again and twisted about to look through the rear window, the tendons of her neck drawn tight at the side and an arm laid along the back of the seat, and crunched the gears into reverse and joggled us backwards along the track and out on to the road.

I knew precious little about girls — and consequently the little I knew was precious indeed — and next to nothing about grown women. At the seaside for a summer when I was ten or eleven there had been an auburn beauty of my own age whom I had adored at a distance — but then, who in the honeyed haze of childhood has not adored an auburn beauty by the seaside? — and a redhead in town one winter, called Hettie Hickey, who despite her less than lovely name was as delicate as a Meissen figurine, who wore multiple layers of lace petticoats and showed off her legs when she danced the jive, and who on three consecutive and never to be forgotten Saturday nights consented to sit with me in the back row of the Alhambra cinema and let me put a hand down the front of her dress and cup in my palm one of her surprisingly chilly but excitingly pliable, soft little breasts.

These glancing hits of the love god's shafts, along with that vision of the bicyclist in the churchyard laid bare by a breeze — a playful god at work there, too, surely — had formed the total of my erotic experience to date, aside from solitary exercises, which I do not count. Now, after that kiss in the car, I seemed to myself not to be living, quite, but suspended in a state of quivering potential, blundering through my days and tossing at night on a sweaty and reeking bed, wondering did I dare — ? and would she dare — ? Such schemes I devised to meet her again, to be alone with her again, to verify what I hardly could hope would be true, that if I pressed my advantage she might — well, that she might what? Here was the point where all grew vague. Often I could not tell which was more urgent, the longing to be allowed to delve into her flesh — for after that kiss my formerly passive intentions had moved on to the stage of active intent — or the need to understand what exactly such delving and doing would entail. It was a confusion between the categories of the verb to know. That is, I was more or less familiar with what would be required in order for me to do and for her to be done to, but inexperienced though I was, I felt certain that the mere mechanics of the thing would be the least of it.

What I was certain of was that what seemed promised by my two encounters with Mrs. Gray, the one on the far side of that nexus of looking-glasses and the one on this side, in the station wagon under the trees, would be of an entirely new order of experience. My feelings were a giddily intensified mixture of anticipation and alarm, and a beady determination to take with both hands, and whatever other extremities might be called on, anything that should prove to be on offer. There was an avid throb now in my blood that startled me, and shocked me, too, a little, I think. And, yet, all the while, despite this passion, these pains, there lingered an odd sense of disengagement, of not registering fully, of being there and not being there, as if everything were still taking place in the depths of a mirror, while I remained outside, gazing in, untouched. Well, you know the sensation, it is not unique to me.

That brief moment of contact in the birch

wood was followed by another week of silence. At first I was disappointed, then incensed, then sullenly disheartened. I thought I was deceived and that the kiss, no more than the exhibition in the mirror, had meant next to nothing to Mrs. Gray. I felt an outcast, alone with my humiliation. I avoided Billy and walked to school on my own. He seemed not to notice my coolness, my new wariness. I watched him covertly for any sign that he might know something of what had occurred between his mother and me. In my darker moments I would have myself convinced that Mrs. Gray was playing an elaborate prank and making mock of me, and I burned for shame at being so easily duped. I had a hideous vision of her regaling the tea-table with an account of what had occurred between us — "And then he did, he kissed me!" — and the four of them, even glum Mr. Gray, shrieking and hilariously shoving each other. My distress was such that it even roused my mother from her chronic lethargy, though her murmurs of enquiry and half-hearted concern only infuriated me, and I would give her no answer, but would stump out of the house and slam the door shut behind me.

When at last at the end of that second, tormented, week I met Mrs. Gray in the street by chance, my first impulse was not to acknowledge her at all, but to display a cutting hauteur and walk straight past her without a word or a sign. It was a spring day of wintry gales and spitting sleet, and we were the only two abroad in Fishers Walk, a laneway of whitewashed cottages that ran under the high granite wall of the railway station. She was struggling against the wind with her head down, the bat-wings of her umbrella snapping, and it would have been she who passed me by, seeing nothing of me above the knees, had I not halted directly in her path. Where did I find the courage, the effrontery, to take such a bold stand? For a second she did not recognise me, I could see, and when she did she seemed flustered. Could she have forgotten already, or have decided to pretend to forget, the display in the mirror, the embrace in the station wagon? She had no hat and her hair was sprinkled with glittering beads of melted ice. "Oh," she said, with a faltering smile, "look at you, you're frozen." I suppose I must have been shivering, not from the cold so much as the miserable excitement of encountering her accidentally like this. She wore galoshes and a smoke-coloured transparent plastic coat buttoned all the way up to her throat. No one wears

71

those coats any more, or galoshes either; I wonder why. Her face was blotched from the cold, her chin raw and shiny, and her eyes were tearing. We stood there, buffeted by the wind, helpless in our different ways. A foul gust came to us from the bacon factory out by the river. Beside us the wet stone wall glistened and gave off a smell of damp mortar. I think she would have sidestepped me and walked on had she not seen my look of need and desolate entreaty. She gazed at me for a long moment in surmise, measuring the possibilities, no doubt, calculating the risks, and then at last made up her mind.

"Come along," she said, and turned, and we walked off together in the direction whence she had come.

It was the week of the Easter holidays, and Mr. Gray had taken Billy and his sister to the circus for the afternoon. I thought of them huddled on a wooden bench in the cold with the smell of trodden grass coming up between their knees and the tent flapping thunderously around them and the band blaring and farting, and I felt superior and more grown-up than not only Billy and his sister but than their father, too. I was in their home, in their kitchen, sitting at that big square wooden table drinking a mug of milky tea that Mrs. Gray had made for me, watchful and wary, it is true, but sheltered, and warm, and quivering like a gun-dog with expectancy. What were acrobats to me, or a dreary troupe of clowns, or even a spangled bareback rider? From where I sat I would have happily heard that the big top had collapsed in the wind and smothered them all, performers and spectators alike. An iron wood-stove in one corner sparked and hissed behind a sooty window, its tall black flue trembling with heat. Behind me the big refrigerator's motor shut itself off with a heave and a grunt, and where there had been an unheard hum was suddenly a hollow quiet. Mrs. Gray, who had gone off to shed her raincoat and her rubber over-shoes, came back chafing her hands. Her face that had been blotched was glowing pink now, but her hair was still dark with wet and stood out in spikes. "You didn't tell me there was a drop on the end of my nose," she said.

She had an air of faint desperation and at the same time seemed ruefully amused. This was uncharted territory, after all, for her, surely, as much as for me. Had I been a man and not a boy, perhaps she would have known how to proceed, by way of banter, sly smiles, a show of reluctance betokening its opposite — all the usual — but what was she to do with me, squatting there toad-like at her kitchen table with the rain-wet legs of my trousers lightly steaming, my eyes determinedly downcast, my elbows planted on the wood and the mug clutched tight between my hands, struck dumb by shyness and covert lust?

In the event she managed with an ease and briskness that I had not the experience to appreciate properly at the time. In a cramped room off the kitchen there was a top-loading washing machine with a big metal paddle sticking up through its middle, a stone sink, an ironing board standing tensed and spindly as a mantis, and a metal-framed camp bed that could have doubled as an operating table had it not been so low to the ground. But, come to think of it, was it a bed? It might have been a horsehair mattress thrown on the floor, for I seem to recall cartoon convict stripes and rough ticking that tickled my bare knees. Or am I confusing it with the subsequent mattress on the floor at the Cotter house? Anyway, in this place of lying down we lay down together, on our sides at first and facing each other, still in our clothes, and she pressed herself against me full-length and kissed me on the mouth, hard, and for some reason crossly, or so it seemed to me. Casting up a quick glance sideways past her temple towards the ceiling so high above, I had the panicky sensation of lying among sunken things at the bottom of a deep cistern.

Above the bed and halfway up the wall there was a single window of frosted glass, and the rain-light coming through was soft and grey and steady, and that and the laundry smell and the smell of some soap or cream that Mrs. Gray had used on her face seemed all to be drifting up out of the far past of my infancy. And indeed I did feel like an impossibly overgrown baby, squirming and mewling on top of this matronly, warm woman. For we had progressed, oh, yes, we had made rapid progress. I suspect she had not intended we should do more than lie there for a certain time chaste enough in our clothes, grinding ourselves against each other's lips and teeth and hip bones, but if so she had not reckoned with a fifteen-year-old boy's violent single-mindedness. When I had writhed and kicked myself free of trousers and underpants, the air was so cool and satiny against my naked skin that I seemed to feel myself break out all over in a foolish smile. Did I still have my socks on? Mrs. Gray, putting a hand to my chest to stay my impatience, got to her feet and took off her dress and lifted her slip and slithered out of her underthings, and then, still in her shift, lay down again and suffered me to re-fasten my tentacles around her. She was saying *No* over and over in my ear now, *no no no nooo!* though it sounded to me more like low laughter than a plea that I should stop what I was doing.

And what I did turned out to be so easy, like learning without effort how to swim. Frightening, too, of course, above those unplumbed depths, but far stronger than fear was the sense of having achieved, at last and yet so early on, a triumphant climacteric. No sooner had I finished — yes, I am afraid it was all very quick — and rolled off Mrs. Gray on to my back to lie teetering on the very rim of the narrow mattress with one leg flexed while she was wedged against the wall than I began to puff up with pride, even as I laboured for breath. I had the urge to run and tell someone — but whom could I tell? Not my best friend, that was certain. I would have to be content to hug my secret close to me and share it with no one. Though I was young I was old enough to know that in this reticence would lie a form of power, over myself as well as over Mrs. Gray.

If I was in fear, frantically swimming

there, what must she have felt? What if there
had indeed been a catastrophe at the circus
so that the show had to be stopped and
Kitty had come running in to tell how the
young man on the flying trapeze had lost
his grip and plummeted down through the
powdery darkness to break his neck in a
cloud of sawdust in the dead centre of the
ring, only to find her mammy engaged in
half-naked and incomprehensible acrobatics
with her brother's laughable friend? I stand
in amazement now before the risks that
Mrs. Gray took. What was she thinking of,
how did she dare? Despite the pride of my
accomplishment, I had no sense that it was
for the sole sake of me that she was willing,
more than willing, to put so much at peril. I
should say that I did not imagine myself so
treasured, I did not think myself so loved.
This was not from diffidence or a lack of a
sense of my own significance, no, but the
very opposite: engrossed in what I felt for
myself, I had no measure against which to
match what she might feel for me. That was
how it was at the start, and how it went on,
to the end. That is how it is, when one
discovers oneself through another.

Having had of her what I had most grievously desired, I now faced the tricky task of
disengaging from her. I do not mean I was

not appreciative or that I felt no fondness for her. On the contrary, I was adrift in a daze of tenderness and incredulous gratitude. A grown-up woman of my own mother's age but otherwise as unlike her as could be, a married woman with children, my best pal's ma, had taken off her dress and unhooked her suspenders and stepped out of her drawers — white, ample, sensible — and with one stocking still up and the other sagging to the knee had lain down under me with her arms open and let me spill myself into her, and even now had turned on her side again with a fluttery sigh of contentment and pressed her front to my back, her slip bunched around her waist and the fuzz at her lap wiry and warm against my backside, and was caressing my left temple with the pads of her fingers and crooning in my ear what seemed a softly salacious lullaby. How could I not think myself the town's, the nation's — the world's! — most favoured son and lavishly blest boy?

I still had the taste of her in my mouth. My hands still tingled from a certain cool roughness along her flanks and the outsides of her upper arms. I could still hear her rasping gasps and feel the way that she seemed to be falling and falling out of my arms even as she arched herself violently against me. Yet she was not I, she was wholly another, and young though I was and new to all this, I saw at once, with merciless clarity, the delicate task that I had now of thrusting her back into the world among the countless other things that were not myself. Indeed, I was gone from her already, was already sad and lonely for her, though still clasped in her arms with her warm breath on the back of my neck. I had once seen a pair of dogs locked together after mating, standing end to end and facing away from each other, the hound casting about in a bored and gloomy fashion, the female hanging her head dejectedly, and God forgive me but this was what I could not keep myself from thinking of now, poised like a spring on the edge of that low bed, yearning to be elsewhere and remembering this lavish, astonishing, impossible quarter of an hour of happy toil in the embrace of a woman-sized woman. So young, Alex, so young, and already such a brute!

At last we got up gropingly and fastened ourselves away into our clothes, bashful now as Adam and Eve in the garden after the apple was eaten. Or no, I was the bashful one. Although I thought I must surely have injured her insides with all my plunging and gouging, she was quite collected, and even seemed preoccupied, thinking perhaps what to make for tea when her family came home from the circus, or, prompted by our surroundings, wondering if my mother would notice telltale stains on my underwear next wash-day. First love, the cynic observes, and afterwards the reckoning.

I, too, had my distractions, and wanted for instance to know why there should be a bed, or even a bare mattress, if that was what it was, in the laundry room, but feared it would be indelicate to ask — I never did find out — and perhaps the suspicion crossed my mind that I had not been the first to lie down there with her, though if it did the suspicion was unfounded, I am sure of that, for she was anything but promiscuous, despite all that had just occurred, and all that was yet to occur, between her and me. Also, I was unpleasantly sticky in the region of my groin, and I was hungry, too, as what young chap would not be after such exertions? The rain had stopped a while before but now another shower began to tinkle against the window above the bed, I could see the wind-driven ghostly drops shiver and slide on the greyly misted glass. I thought with what felt like sorrow of the wetted boughs of the cherry trees outside glistening blackly and the bedraggled blossoms falling. Was this what it was to be in love, I asked myself, this sudden plangent gusting in the heart?

Mrs. Gray was fastening a suspender, the hem of her dress lifted high, and I pictured myself falling to my knees in front of her and burying my face between the bare and very white tops of her legs, plumped up a little and rounded above the tightness of her stockings. She saw me looking and smiled indulgently. "You're such a nice boy," she said, straightening, and giving herself a shimmy from shoulder to knee to settle her garments into line, a thing that, I realised with a qualm of dismay, I had often seen my mother do. Then she reached out a hand and touched my face, cupping her palm along my cheek, and her smile turned troubled and became almost a frown. "What am I going to do with you?" she murmured, with a helpless little laugh, as if in happy amazement at everything. "— You're not even shaving yet!"

I thought her quite old — she was the same age as my mother, after all. I was not sure what to feel about this. Should I be flattered that a woman of such maturity, a respectable wife and mother, had found me, maculate, ill-barbered and far from fragrant though I was, so overpoweringly desirable that there was nothing for it but to take me to bed while her husband and her children all unknowing were splitting their sides at the antics of Coco the clown or gazing up in anxious admiration as petite Roxanne and her blue-jawed brothers cavorted flat-footedly on the high-wire? Or had I been simply a diversion, a plaything of the moment, to be toyed with by a bored housewife in the dull middle of an ordinary afternoon and then unceremoniously sent packing, while she turned back to the business of being who she really was and forgot all about me and the transfigured creatures we had both seemed to be when she was thrashing in my arms and crying out in ecstasy?

By the by, I do not fail to notice how persistently the theme of the circus, with its gaud and glitter, has intruded on proceedings here. I suppose it is an apt background to the hectic spectacle Mrs. Gray and I had just put on, although our only audience was a washing machine, an ironing board and a box of Tide, unless of course the goddess and all her starry fays were present, too, unseen.

I left the house gingerly, drunker than I had been that other time on Billy's father's whiskey, my knees as rickety as an old man's and my face on fire still. The April day that I stepped out into was, of course, transfigured, was all flush and shiver and skimming light, in contrast to the sluggishness of my sated state, and as I moved through it I felt that I was not so much walking as wallowing along, like a big slack balloon. When I got home I avoided my mother, for I was sure the livid marks of a lust so lately, if only temporarily, satisfied would be plainly visible in my burning features, and I went straight to my room and threw myself, fairly threw myself, on the bed and lay on my back with a forearm shielding my shut eyes and replayed on an inner screen, frame by frame, in maniacally slow slow-motion, all that had taken place not an hour past on that other bed, gaped upon in awe and astonishment by a gallery of innocent domestic appliances. Down in the drenched garden a blackbird began to rinse its throat with a cascade of song and as I listened to it hot tears welled in my eyes. *"O Mrs. Gray!"* I cried out softly, *"O my darling!"* and hugged myself for sweet sorrow, suffering the while from the stabs of a stinging prepuce.

I had no thought that she and I would ever do again what we had done that day. That it had happened once was hard enough to credit, that it should be repeated was inconceivable. It was essential therefore that every detail be fetched up, verified, catalogued and stored in memory's lead-lined cabinet. Here, however, I experienced frustration. Pleasure, it turned out, was as difficult to relive as pain would have been. This failure was no doubt part of the price for being shielded from the imagination's re-enactive powers, for had I been allowed to feel again with the same force, every time I thought of it, all that I had felt as I was bouncing up and down on top of Mrs. Gray, I think I should have died. Similarly, of Mrs. Gray herself I was unable to call up a satisfactorily clear and coherent image. I could remember her, certainly I could, but only as a series of disparate and dispersed parts, as in one of those old paintings of the Crucifixion in which the implements of torture, the nails and hammer, spear and sponge, are laid out in a close-up and lovingly executed display while off to the side Christ is dying on the cross in blurred anonymity — dear God, forgive me, compounding bawdry with blasphemy as I do. I could see her eyes of wet amber, unnervingly reminiscent of Billy's, brimming under half-closed lids that throbbed like a moth's wings; I could see the damp roots of her hair that was drawn back from her forehead, already showing a greying strand or two; I could feel the bulging side of a plump and polished breast lolling against my palm; I could hear her enraptured cries and smell her slightly eggy breath. But the woman herself, the total she, that was what I could not have over again, in my mind. And I, too, even I, there with her, was beyond my own recall, was no more than a pair of clutching arms and spasming legs and a backside frenziedly pumping. This was all a puzzle, and troubled me, for I was not accustomed yet to the chasm that yawns between the doing of a thing and the recollection of what was done, and it would take practice and the resultant familiarity before I could fix her fully in my mind and make her of a piece, in total, and me along with her. But what does it mean when I say in total and of a piece? What was it I retrieved of her but a figment of my own making? This was a greater puzzle, a greater trouble, this enigma of estrangement.

I did not want to face my mother that day, not solely because I thought my guilt must be writ plain all over me. The fact was, I would not look at any woman, even Ma, in quite the same way ever again. Where before there had been girls and mothers, now there was something that was neither, and I

85

hardly knew what to make of it.

As I was leaving the house that day Mrs. Gray had stopped me on the front-door mat and quizzed me as to the state of my soul. She was herself devout in a hazy sort of way and wished to be assured that I was on good terms with Our Lord and, especially, with his Holy Mother, for whom she had a particular reverence. She was anxious that I should go to confession without delay. It was apparent she had given the matter some consideration — had she been thinking it over when we were still grappling on that improvised bed in the laundry room? — and said now that while certainly I must lose no time in confessing the sin I had just committed, there would be no need to reveal with whom I had committed it. She, too, would confess, of course, without identifying me. While she was saying these things she was briskly straightening my collar and combing my horrent hair with her fingers as best she could — I might have been Billy being seen off to school! Then she put her hands on my shoulders and held me at arms' length and looked me up and down with a carefully critical eye. She smiled, and kissed me on the forehead. "You're going to be a handsome fellow," she said, "do you

86

know that?" For some reason this compliment, although delivered with an ironical cast, straight away set my blood throbbing again, and had I been more practised, and less worried about the imminent return of the rest of the family, I would have hustled her backwards down the stairs to the laundry room and pulled off her clothes and mine and pushed her on to that pallet-bed or mattress and started all over again. She mistook my suddenly louring aspect for a scowl of resentful scepticism, and said she had truly meant it, that I was good-looking, and that I should be pleased. I could think of no reply, and turned from her in a tumult of emotions and stumbled off swollenly into the rain.

I did go to confession. The priest I settled on, after much hot-faced agonising in the church's Saturday-evening gloom, was one I had been to before, many times, a large asthmatic man with stooped shoulders and a doleful air, whose name by happy chance, though perhaps not so happy for him, was Priest, so that he was Father Priest. I worried that he would know me from previous occasions, but the burden I was carrying was such that I felt in need of an ear that I was accustomed to, and that was accustomed to me. Always, when he had slid back the little door behind the grille — I can still hear the abrupt and always startling clack it used to make — he would begin by heaving a heavy sigh of what seemed long-suffering reluctance. This I found reassuring, a token that he was as loath to hear my sins as I was to confess them. I went through the pre-scribed, singsong list of misdemeanours — lies, bad language, disobedience — before I ventured, my voice sinking to a feathery whisper, on the main, the mortal, matter. The confessional smelt of wax and old varnish and uncleaned serge. Father Priest had listened to my hesitant opening gambit in silence and now let fall another sigh, very mournful-sounding, this time. "Impure actions," he said. "I see. With yourself, or with another, my child?"

"With another, Father."

"A girl, was it, or a boy?"

This gave me pause. Impure actions with a boy — what would they consist of? Still, it allowed of what I considered a cunningly evasive answer. "Not a boy, Father, no," I said.

Here he fairly pounced. "— Your sister?"

My *sister,* even if I had one? The collar of my shirt had begun to feel chokingly tight. "No, Father, not my sister."

"Someone else, then. I see. Was it the bare

skin you touched, my child?"

"It was, Father."

"On the leg?"

"Yes, Father."

"High up on the leg?"

"Very high up, Father."

"Ahh." There was a huge stealthy shifting — I thought of a horse in a horse-box — as he gathered himself close up to the grille. Despite the wooden wall of the confessional that separated us I felt that we were huddled now almost in each other's arms in whispered and sweaty colloquy. "Go on, my child," he murmured.

I went on. Who knows what garbled version of the thing I tried to fob him off with, but eventually, after much delicate easing aside of fig leaves, he penetrated to the fact that the person with whom I had committed impure actions was a married woman.

"Did you put yourself inside her?" he asked.

"I did, Father," I answered, and heard myself swallow.

To be precise, it was she who had done the putting in, since I was so excited and clumsy, but I judged that a scruple I could pass over.

There followed a lengthy, heavy-breathing silence at the end of which Father Priest cleared his throat and huddled closer still. "My son," he said warmly, his big head in three-quarters profile filling the dim square of mesh, "this is a grave sin, a very grave sin."

He had much else to say, on the sanctity of the marriage bed, and our bodies being temples of the Holy Ghost, and how each sin of the flesh that we commit drives the nails anew into Our Saviour's hands and the spear into his side, but I hardly listened, so thoroughly anointed was I with the cool salve of absolution. When I had promised never to do wrong again and the priest had blessed me I went up and knelt before the high altar to say my penance, head bowed and hands clasped, glowing inside with piety and sweet relief — what a thing it was to be young and freshly shriven! — but presently, to my horror, a tiny scarlet devil came and perched on my left shoulder and began to whisper in my ear a lurid and anatomically exact review of what Mrs. Gray and I had done together that day on that low bed. How the red eye of the sanctuary lamp glared at me, how shocked and pained seemed the faces of the plaster saints in their niches all about! I was supposed to know that if I were to die at that moment I would go straight to Hell not only for having done such vile deeds but for entertaining such vile recollections of them in these hallowed surroundings, but the little devil's voice was so insinuating and the things he said so sweet — somehow his account was more detailed and more compelling than any rehearsal I had so far been capable of — that I could not keep myself from attending to him, and in the end I had to break off my prayers and hurry from the place and skulk away in the gathering dusk.

On the following Monday when I came home from school my mother met me in the hall in a state of high agitation. One look at her stark face and her under-lip trembling with anger told me that I was in trouble. Father Priest had called, in person! On a weekday, in the middle of the afternoon, while she was doing the household accounts, there he was, without warning, stooping in the front doorway with his hat in his hand, and there had been no choice but to put him in the back parlour, that even the lodgers were not permitted to enter, and to make tea for him. I knew of course that he had come to talk about me in light of the things I had told him. I was as much scandalised as frightened — what about the much vaunted seal of the confessional? — and tears of outraged injury sprang to my eyes. What, my mother demanded, had I been up to? I shook my head and showed her my innocent palms, while in my mind I saw Mrs. Gray, shoeless and her feet bleeding and her hair all shorn, being driven through the streets of the town by a posse of outraged, cudgel-wielding mothers shrieking vengeful abuse.

I was marched into the kitchen, the place where all domestic crises were tackled, and where now it quickly became clear that my mother did not care what it was I had done, and was only angry at me for being the cause of Father Priest's breaking in upon the tranquillity of a lodgerless afternoon while she was at her sums. My mother had no time for the clergy, and not much, I suspect, for the God they represented either. She was if anything a pagan, without realising it, and all her devotions were directed towards the lesser figures of the pantheon, St. Anthony, for instance, restorer of lost objects, and the gentle St. Francis, and, most favoured of all, St. Catherine of Siena, virgin, diplomatist and exultant stigmatic whose wounds, unaccountably, were invisible to mortal eyes. "I couldn't get rid of him," she said indignantly, "sitting there at the table slurping his tea and talking about the Christian Brothers." At first she had

92

been at a loss and could not grasp his import. He had spoken of the wonderful facilities on offer at the Christian Brothers' seminaries, the verdant playing fields and Olympic-standard swimming pools, the hearty and nutritious meals that would build strong bones and bulging muscles, not to mention, of course, the matchless wealth of learning that would be dinned into a lad as quick and receptive as he had no doubt a son of hers was bound to be. At last she had understood, and was outraged.

"A vocation, to the Christian Brothers!" she said with bitter scorn. "— Not even the priesthood!"

So I was safe, my sin undisclosed, and never again would I go for confession to Father Priest, or to anyone else, for that day marked the onset of my apostasy.

The material, as Marcy Meriwether called it — making it for some reason sound, to my ear, like the leftovers from a post-mortem — arrived today, by special delivery, all the way from the far sunny side of America. Such a fuss attached to its coming! A clatter of hoofs and a fanfare on the post-horn would not have been out of place. The courier, who bore himself like a Balkan war criminal, with a shaved head and dressed all in shiny black and wearing what looked like commando boots laced halfway up his shins, was not content to ring the bell but immediately set to pounding on the door with his fist. He refused to hand over the big padded envelope to Lydia, insisting that it could only be received by the named recipient, in person. Even when I ventured down from my attic roost, summoned exasperatedly by Lydia, he demanded that I produce photographic identification of myself. I thought this supererogatory at the least, but he was not to be moved — obviously his notion of himself and his duties is crazily deluded — and in the end I fetched my passport, which he pored over for fully half a minute, breathing hard down his nostrils, then for the other half scanned my face with a doubting eye. So cowed was I by his unwarranted truculence that I think my hand shook as I signed my name to the form on his clipboard. I suppose I shall have to get used to this kind of thing, I mean special deliveries and dealing with thugs, if I am going to be a film star.

I tried to open the envelope by tearing at it with my nails but it was sealed into an impenetrable plastic sheath, and I had to take it into the kitchen and put it on the table and go at it with the breadknife, while Lydia looked on in amusement. When I got it open at last a sheaf of papers gushed out of it and spilled across the tabletop. There were newspaper cuttings and offprints of magazine essays and lengthy book reviews in small print by people I have vaguely heard of, with striking and often difficult names — Deleuze, Baudrillard, Irigaray and, for some reason my favourite, Paul de Man — all of them considering and for the most part taking violent issue with the work and opinions of Axel Vander.

So he was a literary figure, this Vander, a critic and a teacher and, it is clear, a gleeful stirrer-up of controversies. Hardly an obvious subject for a major motion picture, I would have thought. I have spent the morning at my desk wading through what his opponents and detractors had to say of him — he seems to have had few friends — but I did not succeed in making much headway. Vander's is the kind of arcane and coded specialism — the word *deconstruction* crops up frequently — that my daughter, Cass, would have known all about. Along with the loose leaves there came not a film script but, instead, a thick volume, *The Invention of the Past* — so that is where they got their title — which with commendable cheek proclaims itself to be the unauthorised biography of Axel Vander. I put it aside for later consideration. I shall have to take a very deep breath before plunging into that muddied well of facts and, I have no doubt, fictions, since all biographies are necessarily if unintentionally mendacious. He seems a slippery specimen, this Vander — whose name, by the way, looks very like an anagram, to me. Also, it is faintly familiar, and I wonder if Cass might indeed have spoken to me of him.

In the evening Marcy Meriwether called yet again — I imagine the telephone, from years of usage, grafted into her hand, like Orpheus's lyre — to make sure that *the material* had arrived. She tells me she is also sending a person to see me, one of her scouts, as she describes him. He is called Billy Striker. An odd name, but at least it breaks the tiresomely alliterative series of Marcy Meriwether and Toby Taggart and Dawn Devonport — yes, Dawn Devonport: Did I mention that I am to play opposite her in *The Invention of the Past*? You are impressed. I confess the prospect of working with such a lustrous star is alarming. I shall surely shrivel up in the glare of her celebrity.

To take my mind off these unsettlingly exciting matters I have been doodling in the margin here, making a small calculation. That first tryst with Mrs. Gray, under the aegis of the ironing board, took place one week before her birthday, which fell, and still falls, if she is living still, on the last day of April. That means that our whatever-to-call-it — affair? infatuation? reckless frolic? — endured in all for just short of five months, or one hundred and fifty-four days and nights, to be exact. Or, no, there were

97

only one hundred and fifty-three nights, since by the night of the last day she was gone from me for ever. Not, for that matter, that we had any nights together, not a single one or even part of one, for where would we, could we, have spent it? It is true I daydreamed of the Grays all going away together to stay somewhere overnight and of Mrs. Gray sneaking back and letting me into the house and leading me upstairs to her bedroom and keeping me passionately engaged there until rosy-fingered dawn came creeping under the window-blind to rouse us. It was the kind of fantasy with which I beguiled many a vacant interval away from my darling. A fantasy, of course, for aside from the nice difficulty Mrs. Gray would have had in getting free of her family there was the question of what my mother would have said when she discovered my bed unslept in, not to mention Mr. Gray and what he would have done should he have got suspicious and hurried home and walked in on his wife and her under-age lover energetically defiling the marriage bed. Or what if they all came back together, Mr. Gray and Billy and Billy's sister, and found us at it? I pictured them standing in the bedroom doorway in a lurid wedge of light from the landing, Mr. Gray in the middle with Billy on one side and Kitty on the other, all three clutching tightly to each other's hands and gazing in slack-jawed stupefaction at the guilty lovers, surprised in their stew of shame, untangling themselves hastily from what would be their last lubricious embrace.

At the start, the back seat of the Grays' old station wagon — it was the colour of elephant-hide, I can see it clear — or even the front seat on those occasions when my desire would brook no delay, was a commodious enough bower of bliss for a daemon lover and her lad. I do not say it was comfortable, but what is comfort to a boy when his blood is up? It was on that last day of April that we next met, although I did not know it was her birthday until she told me. Had I been more observant and less impatient to get going on the main business I might have noticed how quiet she was, how thoughtful, how gently sad, even, in contrast to her briskness and gaiety that other, first, time when we had lain down together. Then she told me what day it was, and said she was feeling her age, and gave a great sigh. "Thirty-five," she said, "— think of that!"

The station wagon was parked up the same woodland track where we had stopped that other evening, and she lay asprawl on the back seat, head and shoulders propped awkwardly against a folded picnic-blanket, with her dress pulled up to her armpits and me lying over her, spent for the moment, my left hand paddling in the sopping hot hollow between her thighs. The evening sun was weakly shining, but it was raining, too, and big drops from the overhanging trees were plopping in tinny-sounding syncopation on the metal roof above us. She lit a cigarette — she favoured Sweet Afton, in their nice custard-coloured packet — and when I asked her for one she widened her eyes in feigned shock and said certainly not, and then blew smoke in my face and laughed.

She was not a native of our town — have I said that? — and neither was her husband. They had come from somewhere else, when they were married first and before Billy was born, and Mr. Gray had leased a premises on the corner of the Haymarket and set up his spectacle shop there. The circumstances of her other, ordinary, life, her life away from the two of us and what we were to and in each other, composed a subject I found by turns boring and sorely painful, and when she spoke of them, as she often did, I would give an impatient sigh and attempt to steer her on to other things, to steer her *into* other things. Lying in her arms like this I could make myself forget that she was Mr. Gray's wife, or Billy's mother — I could even forget the cat-like Kitty — and did not wish to be reminded that she had a family firmly in place and that I was, despite all, an interloper.

The town where the Grays had come from — I cannot remember where it was, if I ever bothered to ask — was much bigger and grander than ours, or so she insisted. She liked to tease me by describing its broad streets and fine shops and wealthy suburbs; the people, too, she said, were worldly and polished, not like the people here, where she felt trapped and bitterly discontent. Trapped? Discontent? When she had me? She saw my look and leaned forwards and took my face between her hands and drew me to her and kissed me, breathing laughter and smoke into my mouth. "I never got a better birthday present," she whispered huskily. "My lovely boy!"

Her lovely boy. I do think she thought of me, or made herself think of me, as somehow a sort of long-lost son, a prodigal delightfully returned, feral from his sojourn among the swine and in need of her womanly, indeed matronly, attentions to soothe and civilise him. She indulged me, of course, indulged me beyond an adolescent's maddest imaginings, but she kept a monitoring eye on me, too. She made me promise to bathe more often and more thoroughly and to brush my teeth regularly. I was to wear a clean pair of socks every day, and to ask my mother, though without rousing her suspicions, to buy me some presentable underwear. One afternoon at Cotter's place she produced a suede folder tied in the middle with a leather thong and unwrapped it and laid it out on the mattress to reveal a gleaming set of barber's implements, pairs of scissors and a straight razor and tortoiseshell combs and gleaming silver shears with a superimposed double set of tiny and very sharp teeth. The thing was a sort of older sibling of the manicure set Billy had given me for Christmas. She had once done a hairdressing course, she told me, and at home she cut everyone's hair, even her own. Despite my whines of complaint — how was I to explain this to my mother? — she made me sit on an old cane chair in the sunny doorway and went at my tussocky mop with professional dispatch, singing to herself while she worked. When she was done she let me see myself in the miniature mirror of her powder compact; I looked like Billy. As to my mother, by the way, I need not have worried, for in her usual foggy way she did not even notice my unexplained shorn hair — that was my mother, all over.

I remember suddenly where these things came from, the manicure set and the barber's tool-kit and probably that compact, too: Mr. Gray sold them, in his shop, of course! — how could I forget? So they were got at cost price. The thought of my beloved as a cheapskate is something of a let-down, I must say. How harshly I judge her, even yet.

But no, no, she was generosity itself; I have said that already and I say it again. Certainly she granted me full freedom of her body, that opulent pleasure garden where I sipped and sucked, dazed as a bumble-bee in full-blown summer. Elsewhere there were limits, though, beyond which I was forbidden to stray. For instance, I could talk all I liked about Billy, make fun of him, if I wished, betray his secrets — to these tales told of her suddenly strangered son she listened with unblinking attention as though I were a traveller of old returned with news from fabulous Cathay — but of her delicate Kitty no scathing mention was permitted, or, especially, of her pathetically short-sighted husband. Need I say this made me itch to pour mockery and scorn upon them both in her hearing, though I did not, since I knew what was good for me. Oh, yes, I knew what was good for me, all right.

Looking back now I am surprised at how little I learned about her and her life. Is it that I was not listening? For certainly she loved to talk. There were times when I suspected that a sudden intensification of passion on her part — a rake of her nails across my shoulder-blades, a hot word panted in my ear — was merely a manoeuvre to make me have done more quickly so that she might lie back and set to chatting at her blissful ease. Her mind was littered with all sorts of odds and ends of arcane and curious information, gleaned from her wide reading in *Tit-Bits* and the "Ripley's Believe It or Not!" column in the newspapers. She knew about the dance that bees do when they are harvesting honey. She could tell me what the scribes of old made their ink from. One afternoon at Cotter's place with the sun angling down on us through a high-up cracked pane she explained to me the principle of a householder's right to ancient light — the sky must be visible at the top of a window viewed from the base of the opposite wall, if memory serves — for she had once worked as a clerk in the offices of a company of chartered surveyors. She knew the definition of *mortmain,* could rattle off the signs of the Zodiac in their order. What are glacé cherries made from? Seaweed! What is the longest word that can be typed on the top row of the keys of a typewriter? Typewriter! "You didn't know *that,* did you, smarty-pants?" she would cry, and laugh for delight, and dig me in the ribs with her elbow. But of herself, of what the popular psychologists would have called her inner life, what things did she tell me? Gone, all gone.

Or not all, not quite. I remember what she said one day when I complacently remarked that of course she and Mr. Gray could no longer be doing together what she and I so frequently did. First she frowned, not understanding exactly what I meant, then she smiled at me very sweetly and sadly shook her head. "But I'm married to him," she said, and it was as if this simple statement should tell me all I needed to know about her relations with a man whom I had made it my business to hate and despise. I felt as if I had been delivered a haphazard yet swift, hard blow to the solar plexus. First I sulked, then I sobbed. She held me like a baby to her breast, murmuring *ssh, ssh* against my temple and rocking us both gently from side to side. I endured this embrace for a while — what sweetly vindictive pleasure is masked behind love's pain — then tore myself away in a fury.

We were in Cotter's house, on the mattress on the floor in what had been the kitchen, both of us naked, she sitting tailor-fashion with her ankles crossed — I was not so upset that I did not notice the glinting dewy pearls that I had left sprinkled through the wiry floss between her legs — and I kneeling before her, face contorted in jealous rage and all smeared over with mingled tears and snot, shrieking at her for her perfidy. She waited until I had worn myself out, then made me lie down against her, still sniffling, and began to play distractedly with my hair — what locks, what tresses, I had then, my God, despite those barber's shears she wielded — and after a number of hesitations and false starts, with much sighing and troubled murmuring, she said that I must try to understand how difficult all this was for her, being married and a mother, and that her husband was a good man, a good, kind man, and that she would die rather than hurt him. My sole response to this parroting of the romantic claptrap from the women's magazines she was so partial to was an angrily dismissive wriggle.

She stopped, and was silent for a long while, and her fingers, too, left off worrying my hair. Outside, thrushes were making the woods round about ring with their manic whistling, and the sun of early summer shining through a broken casement was hot on my bare back. We must have made a striking composition there, the two of us, a profane pietà, the troubled woman nursing in her embrace a heartsick young male animal who was not and yet somehow was her son. When she began to speak again her voice sounded far-off, and different, as if she had changed into someone else, a stranger, pensive and calm: in other words, alarmingly, an adult. "I was married young, you know," she said, "barely nineteen — what's that, only four years older than you? I was afraid I'd be left on the shelf." She laughed with bitter rue and I could feel her shaking her head. "And now look at me."

I took this as an admission of profound unhappiness with her married lot, and consented to be mollified.

This is I think the point at which to say a word or two about our secret place of rendezvous. How proud of myself and my resourcefulness I was when I first took Mrs. Gray to see it. I met her on the roadside above the hazel wood as we had arranged, stepping out from under the trees and feeling gratifyingly like a fellow in the pictures who is obviously up to no good. She came driving along in that negligent way that always gave me a thrill to see, one hand loosely gripping the big, worn, polished cream-coloured steering wheel and the other holding a cigarette, her freckled elbow stuck out at the rolled-down window and that curl behind her ear spinning in the wind.

She stopped a little way off from me and waited until another car going in the opposite direction had passed by. It was an overcast May morning with a metallic glare in the clouds. I had not gone to school, but had crept off here, and my schoolbag was hidden under a bush. I told her that I had the day free because of an appointment at the dentist's later. For all that she was technically my lover she was a grown-up, too, and often I found myself fibbing to her like this, as I would to my mother. She was wearing her light, flowered frock with the wide skirt, knowing by now how much I enjoyed watching her take it off — lifting it over her head with her arms straight up and her breasts in their white halter huddling fatly against each other — and a pair of black velvet pumps that she had to slip out

108

of and carry, to save them from the wood-land mire. She had pretty feet, all at once I see them, pale and unexpectedly long and slender, very narrow at the heel and broad-ening gracefully towards the toes, which were quite straight and almost as prehensile as fingers, each one separate to itself, and which she wiggled now as she walked, dig-ging them luxuriantly into the leaf-mould and the wet loam and squealing faintly for pleasure.

I had thought of making her wear a blind-fold, to sharpen the surprise of what I had to show her, but had been afraid she might trip and break something: I had a horror of her suffering an injury when she was with me and of my having to run for help to someone, my mother, say, or even, God forbid, Mr. Gray. She was childishly excited, dying to know what was the surprise that I had for her, but I would not tell, and the more she pressed the more stubborn I grew, and even began to be a little annoyed by her importuning, and strode ahead of her so that she had to hurry at almost a stum-bling run, barefoot as she was, just to keep up with me. The path wound its sombre way under the unleaving trees — see, it has sud-denly become autumn again, impossibly! — and by now I was full of vexed misgiving. I am struck, looking back, by how volatile my temper was when I was with her, how quickly I would fly into a rage over a trifle, or for no reason at all. I seemed permanently suspended over a pit of smouldering, sulphurous fury the fumes of which made my eyes smart and took my breath away. What was the cause of this sullen sense of being put upon and unfairly used that never stopped tormenting me? Was I not happy? I was, but underneath I was angry, too, all the time. Perhaps it was that she was too much for me, that love itself and all it demanded of me was too heavy a burden, so that even as I writhed rapturously in her embrace I longed in my secret heart for the old complacencies, the old and easy ordinariness of things before they had suffered her transforming touch. I suspect that in my heart I wanted to be a boy again, and not whatever it was my desire for her had made of me. What a thing of contradictions I was, poor, addled Pinocchio.

But, oh dear, how her face fell when at last she saw what I had brought her to, I mean Cotter's old house, in the woods. It was a matter of a moment only, her faltering, and at once she rallied and put on her broadest, bravest, head-girl's smile, but in that moment even a creature as self-

110

absorbed and unobservant as I could not have missed the look of sharp distress that crazed the skin of her cheeks and pinched her mouth and drew her eyes down at their corners, as if what she was confronted with, a house once foursquare and handsome now laid waste by time, its walls falling and its paltry timbers all on show, were the very image of all the folly and danger she had indulged in by taking for her lover a boy young enough to be her son.

To distract us both from her dismay she busied herself putting on her absurdly dainty shoes, propping an ankle on a knee and using her index finger for a shoehorn, maintaining her balance by holding on tightly to my arm with a hand that trembled from more than merely the effort of keeping herself upright. Affected by her disillusionment I, too, was disillusioned now, and saw the tumbledown old place for what it was and cursed myself for bringing her there. I freed my arm from her grasp and drew away from her brusquely, and went forwards and gave the mildewed front door a hard, angry push, sending it yawing wildly with a screech on the single hinge that was all that was holding it up, and stepped inside. The walls in places were hardly more than a mesh of laths, stuck in patches here and there with crumbling plaster, and wallpaper most of which hung down in lank strips, like lianas. There was a smell of rotting wood and lime and old soot. The staircase had collapsed, and there were holes in the ceilings, and in the bedroom ceilings above, too, and in the roof above that again, so that when I looked up I could see clear through two storeys and the attic to the sky, glinting in spots through the slates.

Of Cotter I knew nothing except that he must have been long gone, and all the other Cotters with him.

A floorboard creaked behind me. She cleared her throat delicately. Sulking, I refused to turn. We stood there in the dusty hush, amid pallid beams of radiance from above, I facing into the empty house and she at my back. We might have been in church.

"It's a grand place," she said apologetically, in a softly subdued voice, "and you were very clever to find it."

We walked about, with a sober and thoughtful mien, saying nothing and avoiding each other's eye, like a pair of newlyweds dubiously pacing the lines of their prospective first home while the bored estate agent loiters outside on the step smoking a cigarette. We did not so much as kiss, that day.

It was she who on a later day found the lumpy, stained old mattress, folded in two and squashed into a dank and reeking cupboard under the stairs. Together we dragged it out, and to air it we set it over two kitchen chairs under the only window that still had glass in it and where we judged the sun would shine in most strongly. "It'll do," Mrs. Gray said. "I'll bring sheets, next time."

In fact, over the coming weeks she brought all sorts of things: an oil lamp, never to be lit, with a bulbous chimney of marvellously fine spun glass that made me imagine old Muscovy; a teapot and an unmatched pair of teacups and saucers, also never to be used; soap and a bath towel and a bottle of eau-de-Cologne; various foodstuffs, too, including a jar of potted meat and tinned sardines and packages of crackers, "in case," she said with a low laugh, "you might get peckish."

She delighted in this parody of home-making. When she was little, she said, she had loved to play house, and indeed as I watched her producing one toy-like goody after another from her shopping basket and arranging them on sagging shelves about the room she seemed of the two of us by far the younger. I pretended to disdain this feeble simulacrum of domestic bliss that she was assembling piece by piece, but there must have been something in me, an enduring strain of childishness, that would not allow me to hold back but led me forwards, as if by the hand, to join her in her happy games.

Some games. Was she guilty of rape, if only in the statutory sense? Can a woman be a rapist, technically? By taking to bed a fifteen-year-old boy, and a virgin, to boot, I imagine she would have been legally culpable to a serious degree. She must have thought of it. Perhaps her capacity to conceive of imminent disaster was blunted by a constant awareness of the possibility — the inevitability, as it happened — that one day a long time off in the future she would be found out and disgraced not only before her family but in the eyes of the entire town, if not the country. There were occasions when she would go silent and turn away from me and seem to be looking at something approaching that was still far off yet not so distant that she could not make it out in all its awfulness. And on those occasions did I offer solace, try to divert her, draw her away from that dreadful vista? I did not. I went into a huff at being neglected, or made a cutting remark and flung myself from that mattress on the rotted floorboards and stamped off to another part of the house. The whitewashed privy in the back garden with its stained and seatless throne and a century's accumulation of cobwebs in the corners was a favourite perch when I wished to punish her for some misdemeanour by a prolonged and, I trusted, worrying absence. What did I brood on, sitting there in the classic pose with my elbows on my knees and my chin on my hands? We do not need to go to the Greeks, our tragic predicament is written out on rolls of lavatory paper. There was a particular smell from outside, sharp and greenly sour, that came in at the square hole set high up in the wall behind the cistern, that I catch at times still on certain damp days in summer and that makes something struggle to open inside me, a stunted blossom pushing up out of the past.

That she never followed me or tried to coax me back when I had stormed off like this added fuel to my resentment, and when I did return, feigning a cold and stony indifference, I would watch from the corner of my eye for any hint of mockery or amusement — a lip bitten to prevent a smile, or even a gaze too quickly averted, would have sent me marching straight off to the jakes again — but always I would find her waiting with a calm grave gaze and an expression of meek apology, although half the time she must have been bewildered as to what it could be that she was being required to atone for. How tenderly she would hold me, then, and how accommodatingly she would spread herself on that filthy mattress and take inside her all my engorged fury, need and bafflement.

It is extraordinary that we were not lighted upon sooner than we were. We took what precautions we could. At the start we were careful always to make our way to Cotter's place separately. She would park the station wagon in a leafy lane half a mile away and I would hide my bike under a patch of brambles beside the path along by the hazel wood. It was scarily thrilling to strike off through the trees and make my stealthy way down to the hollow where the house was, stopping now and then and cocking an ear, alert as Leatherstocking, to the woodland's restive silence.

I could not decide which I preferred, to get there first and have to wait for her, palms wet and my heart hammering — would she come this time or had she been brought to her senses and decided to have done with me forthwith? — or to find her there before me, crouching anxiously outside the front door as always, for she feared rats, she said, and would not venture inside on her own. In the first minute or two a peculiar constraint would settle between us, and we would not speak, or only stiffly, like polite strangers, and would hardly look at each other, awed by what we were to each other and also, and yet again, no doubt, by the enormity of what we had undertaken together. Then she would contrive to touch me casually in some way, brush her hand as if by chance against mine or trail a strand of her hair across my face, and at once, as if a catch had been released, we would fall into each other's arms, kissing and clawing while she made little moaning sounds of sweet distress.

We became adept at getting out of our clothes, or most of them, without breaking our embrace, and then, her wonderfully cool and slightly granular skin pressed all along mine, we would crabwalk to the makeshift bed and fall over slowly together in a sort of toppling swoon. At first, on the mattress, we would be all knees and hips and elbows, but after a moment or two of desperate scrimmaging all our bones would seem to relax and bend and blend, and she would press her mouth against my shoulder and exhale a long, shuddering sigh, and so we would begin.

But what, you will be asking, of my friend Billy, what was he doing, or not doing, while his mother and I were at our joyous callisthenics? That is a question I myself often asked, with much anxiety. Of course I found it increasingly hard to face him now, to look him in that always relaxed and easy eye of his, for how would he not see the glow of guilt I felt sure I must be giving off? This became less of a difficulty when school ended and the summer holidays began. In the holidays allegiances shifted, fresh interests arose that inevitably involved us with new or at least different sets of companions. There was no question between Billy and me that we were still best friends, only we saw much less of each other now than heretofore, that was all. Away from school, even the best of friends were aware of a slight reserve between them, a shyness, an awkwardness, as if they were afraid, in the new dispensation of endless and untrammelled freedoms, of inadvertently catching each other out in some shaming circumstance, wearing ridiculous bathing-togs, say, or holding hands with a girl. Thus that summer Billy and I, like everyone else, began discreetly to avoid each other, he for the ordinary reasons I have mentioned, and I — well, I for my own, extraordinary reasons.

One morning his mother and I were given a horrible fright. It was a misty Saturday in early summer, the sun struggling whitely through the trees yet bringing the promise of a sweltering day to come. Mrs. Gray was supposed to be shopping and I was supposed to be doing I do not remember what. We were sitting side by side on the mattress with our backs against the powdery wall and our elbows on our knees, and she was letting me have a puff of her cigarette — it was a convention between us that I did not smoke although I was already on ten or fifteen a day, as she was well aware — when suddenly she sprang alert and put a hand fearfully on my wrist. I had heard nothing, but now I did. There were voices on the ridge above us. I thought at once of Billy and me up there that day when he had pointed out to me Cotter's mossy roof camouflaged among the treetops. Could this be him again, come to show the place to someone else? We strained to hear, breathing at the shallowest tops of our lungs. Mrs. Gray was looking at me sideways, the whites of her eyes flashing in terror. The voices coming down through the trees made a hollow, ringing sound, like the sound of steel mallets striking musically on wood — or of Fate, more like, amusedly tapping at his finger-drum. Were they the voices of children or of adults or of both? We could not tell. All kinds of wild fancies darted through my mind. If it was not Billy, it was workmen coming with sledgehammers and crowbars to demolish what remained of the house; it was a search-party looking for a missing person; it was the Guards, dispatched by Mr. Gray to arrest his wanton wife and her precocious inamorato.

Mrs. Gray's lower lip had begun to tremble. "Oh, holy God," she whispered gulpingly. "Oh, dear Jesus."

In a short while, however, the voices faded and there was silence again up on the ridge. Still we dared not stir, still Mrs. Gray's fingers were digging like talons into my wrist. Then abruptly she scrambled up and began to put on her clothes in clumsy haste. I watched her with a mounting sense of alarm, no longer fearful of discovery but of something much worse, namely, that the shock she had got would cause her to take fright finally and flee the place and never come back to me. I demanded to know, my voice cracking, what she thought she was doing, but she did not answer. I could see by her eyes that she was elsewhere already, on her knees, probably, clinging to her husband's trouser legs and desperately begging his forgiveness. I thought of making some large pronouncement, of delivering some solemn admonition — *If you walk out of here now you need never think of . . .* — but I could not find the words, and even if I could have I would not have dared to utter them. I was staring into the abyss that had been there under me all along. If I were to lose her, how would I bear it? I should leap up now, I knew, and put my arms around her, not to reassure her — what did I care for her fear? — but to prevent her by main force from leaving. A peculiar lethargy had come over me, however, the terrified lethargy that is said to come over the skittering mouse when it looks up in dread and sees the hovering hawk, and I could do nothing but sit there and watch as she pulled up her pants under her dress and bent to gather up her velvet shoes. She turned her face to me, bleared with panic. "What do I look like?" she demanded in a whisper. "Do I look all right?" Without waiting for a reply, she ran to her bag for her compact and snapped it open and peered into the little mirror inside it, looking a bit like an anxious mouse herself now, nostrils twitching and the tips

121

of her two slightly overlapping front teeth exposed. "Look at me," she breathed in dismay. "The wreck of the *Hesperus*!"

I began to cry, startling even myself. It was the real thing, a child's raw, helpless blurting. Mrs. Gray stopped what she was doing and turned and stared at me, appalled. She had seen me weep before, but that was in rage or to try to get her to bend to my will, not like this, abjectly, defencelessly, and I suppose it was borne in on her afresh how young I was, after all, and how far out of my depth she had led me. She knelt down on the mattress again and embraced me. It was a shivery sensation to be in her arms naked when she was dressed, and even as I leaned into her and bawled for sorrow I found to my pleased surprise that I was becoming aroused again, and I lay back down and drew her with me and, despite her squirms of protest, got my hands under her clothes, and so we were off again, my sobs of childish fear and anguish now become the familiar, hoarse panting that would rise and rise along its arc to the final, familiar whoop of triumph and wild relief.

I think that was the day I told her of my intention to make her pregnant. I recall a drowsy noontide and the two of us lying quietly together in a tangle of sweat-smeared limbs, a wasp buzzing at the corner of a broken pane and a smoking blade of sunlight from one of the holes in the roof plunged at an angle in the floor beside us. I had been brooding as so often on the painful and unavoidable fact that was Mr. Gray, her inexpungible husband, working myself the while into a fine state of suppressed wrath, and the thought of wreaking what would surely be the ultimate revenge upon him had hardly formed in my mind before I had heard myself announce it aloud and quite as if it were a thing in need only of being accomplished. At first it seemed Mrs. Gray did not understand, could not take in what I had said, and small wonder — it was hardly the kind of thing a woman in the midst of a more than usually perilous affair would expect to hear from the mouth of her under-age lover. When she was taken off-guard or had been told something that she could not absorb at once she had a way, I have noticed it in other women, too, of going very still and quiet on the spot, as if she had found herself suddenly under threat and were lying low until the danger had passed. So she remained for some moments motionless, with her back and her warm behind against my front and one of my arms gone to sleep underneath her. Then she heaved herself over violently on to her other side so that she was facing me. First she stared at me disbelievingly, then she gave me a tremendous, two-handed push in the chest that sent me sliding backwards across the mattress so that my shoulder-blades clattered against the wall. "That's a disgusting thing to say, Alex Cleave," she said, in a low and terrible voice. "You should be ashamed of yourself, so you should."

Was it then that she told me about the child she had lost? A little girl, it was, her last-born after Billy and his sister. The babe was sickly, and died after a day or two of flickering life. The death itself when it came was sudden, however, and it was a torment to Mrs. Gray that the mite had not been baptised and that therefore her soul was in Limbo. It made me uneasy to hear of this creature, who for her mother was a vividly lingering presence, idealised and adored. When Mrs. Gray spoke of her, crooning and lovingly sighing, I thought of the little gilt figurine of the Infant of Prague, with its crown and cape, its sceptre and orb, which reigned in impassive, miniature splendour behind the fanlight over the front door of my mother's house and which I had been afraid of when I was little and found uncanny still. Mrs. Gray's grasp on the finer

124

points of Christian eschatology was not strong, and in her view of it Limbo was not a place of permanent sequester for the souls of the unchristened but a sort of painless Purgatory, a halfway house between earthly life and the rewards and joys of the beatific transcendent, where her babe even now was biding in patient expectation of being one day, perhaps the Last Day, raised up to the presence of her Heavenly Father, where the two of them, mother and child, would be joyfully reunited. "I hadn't even chosen a name for her," Mrs. Gray told me, with a sorrowful gulp, and wiped her nose on the back of her hand. Small wonder my threat of impregnation alarmed and angered her.

Yet I might have suggested to her, that day, that if she and I were indeed to have a little one of our own it would be a replacement down here for the embryonic angel impatiently waiting her turn in line at the Limbic gate. By now, however, what with this talk of dead babies, my enthusiasm for precocious fatherhood had cooled considerably — had turned, in fact, to ashes.

It struck me afterwards that what was remarkable about her response when I stated my intention of putting her in the family way was that she did not seem entirely surprised by it; shocked, naturally, outraged, yes, but not surprised. Perhaps women are never surprised by the prospect of being pregnant, perhaps they live in a constant state of preparedness for just that eventuality; I might consult Lydia on this matter, Lydia, my Lydia, my encyclopydia. Mrs. Gray that day did not even ask why I should want her to have a child, as if she accepted that it would be the most natural and obvious thing that I should want. If she had asked, I would not have known quite how to answer. Should she get pregnant by me it would hurt her husband, yes, and that would be pleasing, but it would hurt us, too, her and me, and grievously. Did I really know what I was saying, and if I did, did I mean it? I am sure I did not — I was hardly more than a child myself, after all — and had said it I am sure only to shock her and attract all her attention on to myself, exclusively, a task to which I devoted much effort and ingenuity. Yet I find myself contemplating now, with a pang of what feels like genuine regret, the possibility that between us we might have produced a fine, bright boy, say, with her eyes and my limbs, or a glowing girl, a miniature version of her, complete with shapely ankles and slender toes and an unruly curl behind her ear. Absurd, absurd. Think of it, my meeting up

126

with him or her now, a son or daughter nearly as old as I am, the two of us tongue-tied with embarrassment before the grotesque and comic predicament into which an accident of love and a boy's spitefulness had thrown us, and from which nothing could extricate us except my death, and even that would not wipe the laughable stain from the record. And yet, and yet. My mind turns in confusion, my heart shrinks and swells. Absurd. Look at me, blundering here on the brink of old age and still wistfully dreaming of generation, of a son who might comfort me, of a daughter whom I could love, and on whom I might one day lean an infirm arm and be led down the last road at the end of which awaits what the Psalmist in his solemn fashion calls my long home.

Of course, I would have preferred a daughter. Yes, definitely a daughter.

It is a wonder, in fact, that Mrs. Gray did not become pregnant, as frequently and as energetically as we went at the business that would have made her so. How did she avoid it? In this land, in those days, there was no available legal means to prevent conception, other than celibacy, and even if there had been she would not have consented to it, out of devotion to her faith. For she did believe in God, not the God of love, I think, but certainly the God of vengeance.

But wait. Maybe she did get pregnant. Maybe that was why she skedaddled so precipitately when our affair was discovered. Maybe she went off and had a baby, a little girl, ours, without telling me. If so, that little girl is a big woman now, fifty years old, with a husband, and children of her own, perhaps — other, unknown, people, bearing my genes! Dear God. What a thing that is to think of. But no, no. By the time I came along, frisky and cocksure, she must have been barren.

The scout from Pentagram Pictures turns out to be Billie, not Billy like my pal, and Stryker, not Striker — yes, it was probably Marcy Meriwether's idea of a joke not to spell these names out for me — and is a woman and emphatically not, as I had assumed, a man. I was up here in my attic as usual when I heard her preposterous little car come whining and coughing into the square and then the doorbell ringing. I paid no heed, thinking it must be someone to see Lydia. And as it happened Lydia did detain her, took her into the kitchen and sat her down and plied her with cigarettes and tea and a biscuit; my wife has a weakness for misfortunates and oddities of all kinds, especially if they are female. What can they have talked about, those two? Afterwards I did not enquire, out of some form of delicacy, or shyness, or misgiving. It was a good twenty minutes before Lydia came up and

129

knocked on my door to tell me I had a visitor. I rose from my desk, ready to accompany her downstairs, but she moved to one side in the narrow doorway and, with the air of a magician producing a very large rabbit from a very small hat, brought the young woman forwards from the narrow stairway and with a gentle push propelled her into the room, and departed.

As well as being a woman, Billie Stryker is not at all what I had expected. What did I expect? Someone smart and snappy and transatlantic, I suppose. Billie, however, is obviously a native of these parts, a short pudgy person in, I judge, her middle to late thirties. She really is of a remarkable shape, and might have been assembled from a collection of cardboard boxes of varying sizes that were first left out in the rain and then piled soggily any old way one on top of another. The general effect was not improved by the extremely tight jeans she was wearing, and the black polo-necked jumper that made her large head look like a rubber ball set squarely atop all those precariously stacked cartons. She has a tiny sweet face inset amid much surplus flesh, and her wrists are dimpled like a baby's and look as if they have been tied round with tight loops of thread at the junctures where her hands are attached to, or inserted into, as it might be, the ends of her arms. There was a purple and yellow shadow under her left eye, the remains of what a week or so ago must have been a real shiner — how or where did she come by that, I wonder?

I wished that Lydia had not brought her up here, for besides the fact that it is my bolthole, the sloped room is small and Billie is not, and as I edged my way around her I felt rather like Alice grown huge and trapped in the White Rabbit's house. I directed her to the old green armchair that is the only piece of furniture there is space enough for in here, along with my desk that I work at — I call it work — and the antique swivel chair that I sit in. When we moved in first Lydia tried to persuade me to make a proper study for myself in one of the downstairs rooms that are empty — the house is large and there are just the two of us — but I am content up here, and do not mind being cramped, except on occasions such as this, which are extremely rare. Billie Stryker sat there, with a decided but inexplicably forlorn air, twiddling her chubby fingers and panting softly and looking at everything except me. She has a special and slovenly way of inhabiting a chair, seeming to sag from it rather than sit in it, perching herself

131

on the front edge of the cushion with her big knees loosely splayed and her runnered feet turned inwards so that the outer sides of her ankles are resting flat on the floor. I sidled to my desk, smiling and nodding, like a lion-tamer making cautiously towards his chair and pistol, and sat down.

She seemed to know no more of why she was here than I did. She is a researcher, if I understood her correctly; are movie researchers known as scouts? I have so much to learn. I asked if she had been researching the life of Axel Vander and she looked at me as if I had made a joke, though not a funny one, and gave a brief and seemingly derisory laugh that sounded as if it had been learned from Marcy Meriwether. Yes, she said, she had done a job on Vander. Done a job, eh? That sounds worryingly strenuous. I was puzzled by her unforthcoming manner and did not know how to proceed, and we sat together in a weighty silence for quite a long time. Idly it occurred to me that since she was a researcher and would know how to go about that sort of thing I might hire her on a freelance basis to track down Mrs. Gray for me. Honestly, the fancies that wander into one's head. All the same, it should not be difficult to trace my lost love's whereabouts. There will be people still in the town who will remember the Grays — it is only fifty years since they left, after all, and the cause of their sudden leaving was surely memorable — and who will be bound to know what became of them. And Billie Stryker, I feel sure, would be a relentless bloodhound were she to be set on the scent.

I put a question or two about the movie project we are both supposedly engaged on, and again she darted at me that quick and, I thought, incredulous glance, though it progressed hardly higher than my knees, and then she went back to gazing morosely at the carpet. This was hard work, and I was beginning to lose patience. Idly I walked my fingers along the desk and, humming, looked out of the window, from which past a corner of the square a glimpse can be had of the canal. This orderly and placid imitation river is as much of water as I can bear these days; after Cass's death we could not go on living by the sea, as we used to; the sight of waves crashing on rocks was not to be borne. Why and to what purpose had Marcy Meriwether sent this taciturn and lumpish creature to me? — and what had Lydia been up to with her in that long interval they had spent together downstairs? There are times when I feel myself caught up in a definite, concerted and yet seemingly aimless conspiracy run by women. "Not everything means something," Lydia likes to say, cryptically, and takes on that slightly swollen look, as if she were sternly but with difficulty forbidding herself to laugh.

I asked Billie Stryker if there was anything I could fetch for her in the way of refreshments, which was when she told me about the tea and biccies that Lydia had pressed on her, down in the kitchen. I should say something about this kitchen. It is Lydia's place, as this attic room is mine. She spends much of her time there these days — I rarely venture beyond the threshold. It is a cavernous chamber with a high ceiling and unclad walls of rough stone. There is a big window over the sink, but it looks directly into a clump of briars that immemorially was a rose tree, so that the daylight hardly penetrates and a brooding dimness reigns in the room. Lydia's desert ancestry is never more plainly apparent, to me, at any rate, than when she is presiding there, at the high square table of scrubbed deal, with her newspapers and her cigarettes, a shawl of circassian purple draped over her shoulders and her dusky forearms hooped with many slender bangles of jingling silver and gold. I should not say so, but I often think that in another age my Lydia might have been taken for a witch. What *did* they talk about down there, she and Billie Stryker?

Billie said now that she would have to be getting on — to what? I wondered — yet she gave no other sign of being ready to depart. I said, though I could not hide my perplexity, that I was glad that she had called, and that I was happy to have met her. This was followed by more silence and slack staring. And then, almost before I knew it, I had begun to talk about my daughter. This was strange, not at all like me. I cannot remember when I last spoke of Cass to anyone, even Lydia. I guard my memories of my lost one jealously, keep them securely under wraps, like a folio of delicate watercolours that must be protected from the harsh light of day. Yet there I was, babbling about her and her doings to this uncommunicative and wary stranger. Of course, I see Cass in every young woman I meet, not Cass as she was when she cut short her own life but as she might be now, these ten years later. She would be about Billie Stryker's age, as it happens, though that, surely, is the extent of what they would have in common.

Yet being reminded of Cass, especially in such a tenuous fashion, was a far cry from talking about her, and so precipitately, at that, so wildly, even. When I think of Cass — and when am I not thinking of Cass? — I seem to sense all about me a great rushing and roaring, as if I were standing directly under a waterfall that drenches me and yet somehow leaves me dry, dry as a bone. This is what mourning has become for me, a constant, parching deluge. I find, too, that a certain shame attaches to being bereft. Or no, it is not quite shame. A certain awkwardness, say, a certain sheepishness. Even in the very earliest days after Cass's death I felt it imperative not to blubber overmuch in public but at all costs to maintain my poise, or the appearance of it; when we wept we wept in private, Lydia and I, smilingly shutting the front door on our departing comforters and immediately falling on each other's neck and fairly howling. However, talking to Billie Stryker now I felt as if I were indeed weeping in some way. I cannot explain it. There were no tears, of course, only the words pouring out of me unstoppably, yet I had that almost voluptuous sense of helpless, headlong falling that one has when one gives in to a really good bawl. And of course when at last I ran out of words I was rueful and abashed all over, as if I had lightly scalded myself. How did

Billie Stryker, seemingly without the least effort, get me to say so much? There must be more to her than meets the eye. As I should hope there is, for what meets the eye is less than prepossessing.

What did I say to her, what did I tell her? I cannot remember. I recall only the babbling, not what it was I babbled. Did I say my daughter was a scholar and that she suffered from a rare disorder of the mind? Did I describe how when she was young and her condition was as yet undiagnosed her mother and I would swing dizzyingly between anxious hope and ashen disappointment as the signs of her malady seemed to diminish only to rise up again more starkly and more unmanageably than ever? How we used to long, in those years, for just one ordinary day, a day when we might get up in the morning and eat our breakfast without caring for anything, reading bits out of the paper to each other and planning things to do, and afterwards take a stroll, and look at the scenery with an innocent eye, and later share a glass of wine, and later still go to bed together and lie at peace in each other's arms and drift into untroubled sleep. But no: our lives with Cass were a constant watching brief, and when she eluded us at last and did her disappearing trick — when she made away with herself, as they so accurately say — we acknowledged even in the midst of our sorrow that the end she had brought to our vigil had been inevitable. We wondered, too, and were aghast to find ourselves wondering it, if our vigilance itself had somehow served to hasten that end. The truth is she had been eluding us all along. At the time of her death we thought she was in the Low Countries deep in her arcane studies, and when word came from Portovenere, far off in the south, the dread word that in our hearts we had known all along would some day come, we felt not only bereaved but in a manner outmanoeuvred, cruelly and, yes, unforgivably outwitted.

But wait, hang on — something has just struck me. I was the one whom Billie Stryker was researching today. That was the point of all that hedging and hesitating on her part, all those ponderous silences: it was all a stalling tactic while she waited patiently for me to start talking, as I inevitably would, into the vacuum she had carefully prepared. How subtle of her, not to say sly, not to say, indeed, underhand. But what did she find out about me, except that I once had a daughter and she died? When I apologised for rambling on for so long about Cass, she

138

shrugged and smiled — she has a very affecting smile, by the way, sad and sweetly vulnerable — and said it was all right, she did not mind, that it was her job to listen. "That's me," she said, "the human poultice."

I think I really will ask her to find Mrs. Gray for me. Why not?

We went downstairs and I escorted her to the front door. Lydia was nowhere to be seen now. Billie's car is an ancient and badly rusted Deux Chevaux. When she had clambered in behind the wheel she leaned out again to inform me, seemingly as an afterthought, that there is to be a read-through of the script, in London, early next week. All the cast will be there, the director, of course, and the scriptwriter. The latter's name is Jaybee, something like that — I have become slightly deaf and it distresses me to have to keep on asking people to repeat what they have said.

Billie drove off in swirling billows of dark-brown exhaust smoke. I stood looking after her until she was gone from the square. I was puzzled and at a loss, and prey to a faint but definite unease. Was it by some sorcery she had got me to speak of Cass, or was I only waiting for the chance? And if this is the sort of person I shall be dealing with in the coming months, what have I let myself in for?

I have spent the afternoon perusing, I think that is the word, *The Invention of the Past,* the big biography of Axel Vander. The prose style was what struck me first and most forcefully — indeed, it nearly knocked me over. Is it an affectation, or a stance deliberately taken? Is it a general and sustained irony? Rhetorical in the extreme, dramatically elaborated, wholly unnatural, synthetic and clotted, it is a style such as might be forged — *le mot juste!* — by a minor court official at Byzantium, say, a former slave whose master had generously allowed him the freedom of his extensive and eclectic library, a freedom the poor fellow all too eagerly availed himself of. Our author — the tone is catching — our author is widely but unsystematically read, and uses the rich tidbits that he gathered from all those books to cover up for the lack of an education — little Latin, less Greek, ha ha — although the effect is quite the opposite, for in every gorgeous image and convoluted metaphor, every instance of cod learning and mock scholarship, he unmistakably shows himself up for the avid autodidact he indubitably is. Behind the gloss, the studied elegance, the dandified swagger, this is a man racked by fears, anxieties, sour resentments, yet possessed, too, of an occasional mordant wit and an eye for what one might call the under-belly of beauty. No wonder he was drawn to Axel Vander for a subject.

This Vander, I may say, was an exceedingly strange bird. For a start, it seems he was not Axel Vander at all. The real Vander, a native of Antwerp, died mysteriously some time in the early years of the war — there were rumours, widespread though hardly plausible, that despite his hair-raisingly reactionary politics he took part in the Resistance — and this other, counterfeit, one, who has no recorded history, simply assumed his name and slipped adroitly into his place. The false Vander carried on the genuine one's career as a journalist and critic, fled Europe for America, married, and settled in California, in the pleasant-sounding town of Arcady, and taught for many years at the university there; the wife died — it appears she was prematurely senile and Vander may in fact have murdered her — and shortly afterwards Vander abandoned his work and moved to Turin, where he was to die himself a year or two later. These are the facts, garnered from the helpful Chronology our author supplies after the Preface, and which he would be scandalised to see me present in such an unadorned and unfiddled-with fashion. The books that Vander wrote in his American years, in particular the collection of essays hermetically entitled *The Alias as Salient Fact: The Nominative Case in the Quest for Identity,* won him a large if contested reputation as an iconoclast and an intellectual sceptic. "A strain of nastiness runs throughout the work," his disenchanted biographer writes, with a palpably curled lip, "and all too often his tone is that of a crabbed and venomous spinster, the kind of person who confiscates footballs that small boys accidentally kick into her garden and spends her evenings writing poison-pen letters on perfumed note-paper to her neighbours in the village." You see what I mean about the style.

And this Vander is the character I have to play. Dear me.

Yet in a way I can see why someone thought there is material for a movie here. Vander's story weaves a certain mephitic spell. Perhaps I am overly suggestible, but as I sat reading in the old green armchair where lately Billie Stryker had perched and panted, the feeling came over me of being surreptitiously seized on and deftly taken hold of. The October sky in the slanted window above me had a floating of copper clouds, and the light in the room was a pale dense gas, and the silence, too, was dense, as if my ears had been stopped up as in an aeroplane, and I seemed to see the shadowy first and valid Axel Vander faltering and falling without a sound and his usurper stepping seamlessly into his place and walking on, into the future, and overtaking me, who will presently in turn become a sort of him, another insubstantial link in the chain of impersonation and deceit.

I shall go out for a walk; perhaps it will restore me to myself.

I like to walk. Or better say, I walk, and leave it at that. It is an old habit, acquired in the early months of grieving after Cass died. There is something in the rhythm and the aimlessness of being out for a stroll that I find soothing. My profession, from which I thought I had retired until Marcy Meriwether summoned me back to the footlights, or the arc-lights, or whatever they are called, has always allowed me the freedom of the daytime hours. There is a certain tepid satisfaction to be had in being abroad and at one's leisure while other folk are penned indoors at work. The streets at mid-morning or in the early afternoon have an air of definite yet unfulfilled purpose, as if something important had forgotten to happen in them. The halt and the lame come out by day to air themselves, the old, too, and the no longer employed, wiling away the empty hours, nursing their losses, probably, as I do. They have a watchful and a slightly guilty manner; perhaps they fear being challenged for their idleness. It must be hard to get used to there being nothing urgent that needs to be done, as I am bound to find out when those arc-lights are extinguished for the last time and the set is struck. Theirs I imagine is a world without impetus. I see them envying the busyness of others, eyeing resentfully the lucky postman on his round, the housewives with their shopping baskets, the white-coated men in vans delivering necessary things. They are the unintended idlers, the ones astray, the at-a-loss ones.

I observe the tramps, too, that is another old pastime of mine. It is not what it used to be. Over the years the tramp, your true tramp, has been diminishing steadily in quality and quantity. Indeed, I am not sure that one can any more speak of tramps as such, in the old, classic sense. No one nowadays rambles the roads, or carries a bundle on a stick or sports a coloured neckerchief, or ties his trouser legs below the knees with twine, or collects cigarette butts from the gutter to keep in a tin. The wandering ones are all drunks now, or on drugs, and care nothing for the traditional ways of the road. The addicts in particular are a new breed, always in a hurry, always on a mission, trotting unswervingly along crowded pavements or weaving heedless through the traffic, lean as prairie dogs, with scrawny behinds and flat feet, the young men dead-eyed and scratchily light of voice, their women staggering behind them clutching stricken-eyed papooses and incoherently screaming.

One vagrant I have been monitoring for some time now I call Trevor the Trinity-man. He is a very superior type, an aristocrat of the species. When I first spotted him, it must be five or six years ago, he was in fine shape, sober and full of pep. It was a glary summer morning and he was crossing one of the bridges over the river, skipping along in the sharp light and swinging his arms, got up in a dark-blue pea-coat and brand-new desert boots of yellow suede with thick crêpe soles. He sported also a particularly jaunty corduroy cap with a peak, and despite the summer warmth he had a Trinity scarf knotted at his neck — hence my nickname for him. His grizzled beard was trimmed neatly to a point, his eyes were clear, his face was ruddy, with only the lightest tracery of broken veins. I am not sure what it was in him that caught my attention. It must have been the look he had of having been brought back from somewhere dreadful and restored to health and vigour, for I am sure he had been in St. Vincent's or St. John of the Cross's drying out; Lazarus probably looked like that after Martha and Mary brought him home from the cemetery and unwound the last of his grave-clothes and got him on his feet and generally smartened him up. I saw him again a couple of times about the streets, still bouncy and bright, and stood behind him one morning in a newsagent's where he was buying the *Times,* and noted his markedly fruity tones.

Then disaster struck. It was early, eight or half past on a misty autumn morn, and I was crossing the same bridge where I had got my first sighting of him, and there he was, scarf, jaunty cap, yellow boots and all, marooned in the stream of hurrying office workers, suspended at an angle, limp as a marionette and precipitously swaying, eyes shut as if he were dozing and his lower lip redly adroop, and clutching in his left hand a big bottle in a brown-paper bag.

It was not the end of him, though, this plunge from grace, not at all. He has clambered back on to the wagon many a time, and although each time he has toppled off again, and although each fall takes a heavier toll on him generally, these repeated resurrections that he pulls off cheer me up, and I find myself breaking out in a smile of welcome when, after another ominous period of absence, he comes bustling towards me in the street, bright of eye, the nap of his suede boots brushed, his Trinners scarf freshly washed and free of drool. He pays me not the slightest heed, of course, and has never once, I am sure, felt the pressure of my eagerly following eye.

When he is drinking he begs. He has honed his performance and is admirably consistent, shuffling up to likely marks with a cupped hand jutting out and crooning piteously, like a tired and thirsty infant, his face all twisted up to one side and his bloodshot eyes swimming with unshed tears. But it is only acting. Feeling extra magnanimous one day, I gave him a tenner — it was after lunch and I had been drinking myself — and at once, startled by this unexpected bounty, he snapped out of character and beamed at me and thanked me warmly in a rich, Woosterish accent. I think if I had allowed it he would have seized my hand in both of his and pressed it in comradely gratitude and affection. As soon as I had passed on, however, he went straight back into his part, mooing and mugging with that hand held out.

On a good day he makes a tidy sum, I should think. I spied him once in the bank, of all unlikely places, at a teller's hatch, exchanging a counterful of copper coins for paper money. How patient the uniformed young woman attending him was, how forbearing and good-humoured, apparently not even minding the breathtaking stink that he gives off. Placidly he watched her count the coins, graciously he accepted the scant pile of notes she gave him in exchange, and stored them in an inner recess of his by now worn and permanently stained pea-coat. "Thank you, my dear, you are very kind," he murmured — yes, I had crept up close enough behind him to catch what he might say — and he touched the back of the young woman's hand lightly in acknowledgement with the merest tip of a filthy finger.

He ranges far and wide in his wanderings, for I have seen him all over the city, even in the outskirts. On the way to take a plane early one icy spring morning I spotted him on the airport road. He was making his determined way towards town, his breath smoking and a drop at the end of his poor old battered nose glinting like a fresh-cut jewel in the pink-tinged, frosty sunlight. What was he doing there, where was he coming from? Is it conceivable that he had been abroad, and had just returned, on a dawn flight? How do I know he is not an internationally renowned scholar, an expert in Sanskrit, say, or a peerless authority on the Noh theatre? The great pragmaticist Charles Sanders Peirce had to beg for bread and even for a time lived on the streets. Anything is possible.

His gait. There must be something wrong with his feet — poor circulation, I would guess — for he moves at a slithering shuffle, a hindered jog-trot, one might call it, though still he makes a surprisingly rapid progress. His hands are bad, too — circulation again — and I notice he has taken to wearing fingerless grubby white woollen gloves that someone must have knitted for him. As he goes along he keeps his arms up, with elbows bent, those gloved paws held out before him, like a punch-drunk boxer going through the slow motions of warming up.

It is a shock to think that he must be my junior by a good twenty years.

I encountered him this afternoon, on my

walk, as I hoped I would, for by now he is a kind of talisman to me. I was down by the dog-racing track, where the skeleton of the old gasometer still stands. That is the kind of neighbourhood, shabby and unassuming, where I prefer to stroll; I am a poor sort of *flâneur* and never took to the grand avenues or the broad sweeps of city parkland. I came upon Trevor of Trinity sitting contentedly on a bit of broken wall opposite the bus depot. He had a clear plastic carton in his lap and was eating something from it that he must have bought from the shop at the filling-station down the road. I thought it would be a pie of some kind, or one of those knobbly sausage rolls that look pre-eaten, but when I drew level with him I saw it was, of all things, a croissant. Good old Trev, ever the upholder of life's little niceties! He had a paper cup of coffee, too — not tea, for I could smell the rich brown aroma of the beans. He was drunk, though, and quite befuddled, and was talking to himself in a mumble while he ate, the flakes of pastry tumbling down his front. I could have stopped and sat down beside him; I even slowed my pace and held back a little, thinking to do so, but then lost my nerve and walked on, regretfully. He was oblivious of me, as usual, too squiffy to notice the grey

150

old faded matinée idol in his good tweed overcoat and strangler's kid gloves skulking past.

I should like to know who he is, or was. I should like to know where he lives. He has shelter, of that I am certain. Someone takes care of him, looks after him, buys him new boots when the old ones have worn out, launders his scarf, delivers him to the hospital to be dried out. I am sure it is a daughter. Yes, a devoted daughter, surely.

Me and the silver screen, now, I know you will want to hear all about that. Not silver any more, of course, but gaudily tinted, which is nothing but a disimprovement, in my opinion. Marcy Meriwether had assured me that I was the first person to have been offered the part of Axel Vander, but I subsequently learned that it was offered to at least three other actors of my vintage, all of whom turned it down, which was when Marcy M. in desperation called me up and invited me to play the old monster. Why did I accept? I was a stage performer all my working life and thought it rather late in my career to be starting on a different tack. I suppose I was flattered — well, yes, I was flattered, of course I was: vanity again, my besetting sin — and could not but say yes. Film acting, as it turns out, seems markedly easy — standing around, mostly, and having one's makeup constantly refreshed and repaired — in comparison with the nightly grind of the stage. Money for jam, really. Or *ham,* did I hear someone say?

The read-through of the script took place in a big, white, eerily empty house on the Thames that had been hired specially for the occasion, near where the new Globe Theatre stands. I confess I was nervous to be venturing into this novel and faintly alarming world. I knew a few of the cast from stage productions we had been in together, and others were so familiar from the various films I had seen them in that I felt I knew them, too. The result was that there was for me something of the atmosphere of a first day back at school after the long summer hols, a new class and new teachers to be coped with, a lot of new faces and the ones remembered from last term all slightly altered, slightly larger, coarser, more threatening. Billie Stryker was there, looking more damply cardboardy than ever today in her bulging jeans and high-necked jumper. She gave me a cautious wave and one of her rare and tentative and wearily melancholy smiles. The sight of her steadied me, which surely shows how much I was in need of reassurance.

The hired house was cavernous and bone-white, like an enormous skull, hollowed out and bleached, with all sorts of passages and cubbyholes and winding stairways throughout which our voices reverberated, joining and clashing in a headache-inducing blare. The weather was strange — it was one of those hectic days that come sometimes in October, when it seems that out of sheer mischievousness the year has reversed itself temporarily and turned back to springtime. The tawny sunlight was hard and without warmth, and a stiff, muscular breeze was barrelling its way up the river and churning the water to mud-brown waves.

Dawn Devonport was the last to arrive, naturally, being the starriest star among us. Her limousine, one of those special sleek black shiny jobs, probably armour-plated, with tinted, opaque windows and a menacing grille, wallowed heavily on its reinforced suspension as it drew up to the door. The driver, spruce in dove-grey and a cap with a shiny peak, hopped out in that burly yet balletic way they do and whisked open the rear door and the lady extricated herself from the deep back seat with practised deftness, affording the merest glimpse of the underside of one long, honey-hued leg. A couple of dozen of her fans had been waiting to greet her, huddled on the pavement in the cutting wind — how did they know where to come to, or am I being naïve? — and now they broke into a ragged round of applause that sounded to my ear more derisive than adoring. As she made her way between them, she seemed not to walk but waft, borne along in the bubble of her inviolable beauty.

Her real name is Stubbs, or Scrubbs, something unsuitably blunt like that, so it is no wonder that she should have hurried to change it — but why, oh, why Devonport? She is known in the trade, inevitably, as the Casting Couch, though I am surprised these youngsters today should know of such a thing, which surely went out with the Metros, the Goldwyns and the Mayers. She truly is a captivating creature. The only flaw in her loveliness that I can detect is a faint, a very faint, greyish down all over her skin that under the camera seems the tremulous bloom of a peach but that in real life makes her look as grimy as a street-urchin. I hasten to say that I find this hint of the slums exciting in a way that I cannot account for, and were I younger — well, were I younger I should imagine myself capable of all sorts of things and probably end up making a great fool of myself. She came into our midst, where we waited for her in the large and draughty hallway of the house, to a chorus of clearings of male throats — we must have sounded like a colony of bullfrogs at the steamy height of the mating season — and glided at once at a seahorse's slight, forwards-leaning incline straight to Toby Taggart, our director, and laid two fingers of one hand on his wrist and did that famous wisp of a smile, glancing blurredly off to the side, and spoke rapidly a breathless word or two meant for him alone to hear.

You will be surprised to learn that she is a slight person, far slighter, certainly, than she appears on the screen, where she looms in huge brightness with all the magnificence and majesty of Diana of the Three Roads herself. She is impossibly thin, as they all have to be these days — "Oh, but I don't eat," she told me, with a tinkly laugh, when we broke for lunch and I gallantly offered to fetch her a sandwich — especially on the inner sides of her upper arms, I notice, which are positively concave, with sinews unpleasantly on display under the pallid skin that makes me think, I am sorry to say, of a plucked chicken. It is hard to tell what the rest of her is like, I mean in real life, for of course there is little of her that has not been bared already to public view, particularly in her earliest roles when she was eager to show the jaded mammoths who run her world just what stuff she was made of, but on the big screen all flesh becomes blanded over and made to seem as suave and densely resistant as plastic. She has something of the flapper about her, an impression which I am sure she fosters deliberately. She favours little pointed, high-sided shoes that button up the front, and old-fashioned stockings with seams, and diaphanous, tunic-like dresses inside which her lithe and seemingly weightless body moves, as though independent of any restraint, to its own sinuous, nervy rhythm. Have you noticed that you do not see her hands in close-up? They are another flaw, although I like them, also. They are large, too large certainly for their delicate wrists, and strongly veined, with big-knuckled, spatulate fingers.

For all the worked-at fragility of the image she presents to her public she has a certain mannish way to her that again is to my liking. She smokes — yes, did you not know? — with burly application, thrusting her face forwards and sideways and dragging on the fag with her lips stuck out, which makes her look as plebeian as any gaffer or grip. She sits with her elbows planted on her knees and holds things, a tea mug, a rolled-up script, in a tight, two-handed grasp, those big knuckles taut and shiny and more like knuckle-dusters than knuckles. Her voice, too, in certain registers, is huskier surely than it should be. I wonder if there is something particular to the movie life that coarsens actresses and hardens their sensibilities, as too much exercising overdevelops their muscles. Perhaps that is what makes them so disturbingly attractive to most of the male half of the audience, and probably to half of the female half as well, that impression they give of being a third gender, overmastering and impregnable.

But that face, ah, that face. I cannot describe it, which is to say I refuse to describe it. Who does not know it, anyway, its every plane and shade and pore? What young man's fevered dreams has it not gazed out of, or into, grave and grey-eyed, sweetly sad, omnivorously erotic? There is a delicate sprinkle of freckles to either side of the bridge of her nose; they are russet, old gold, dark chocolate; for the screen she hides them under extra-thick applications of slap, but should not, for they are terribly affecting, as we actors say, in their delicate appeal. She is poised and thoroughly self-possessed, as you would imagine, yet I detect, deep down in her, at the very base of her being, a beat of primordial terror, a quivering along the nerves so rapid and faint it hardly registers, the vibration of that fear that everyone in our trade is prone to — and everyone outside it, too, for all I know — the simple, blank, insupportable fear of being found out.

I liked her from the moment when shambling Toby Taggart took her by the elbow — talk about a contrast! — and steered her to where I was loitering, studiedly inspecting my fingernails, and introduced her to me, her superannuated leading man. As she approached I did not miss the faint frown, half dismay and half appalled amusement, that puckered the flawless patch of pale skin between her eyebrows when she beheld me, nor the infinitesimal grim squaring of the shoulders that she could not keep herself from doing. I was not offended. The script calls for some strenuous grapplings between her and me, which cannot be an appetising prospect for one so lovely, so delicate, so flagrantly young. I do not recall what I said, or stammered, when Toby had introduced us; she, I think, complained of the cold. Toby, mishearing her, surely, gave a big, slow, desperate-seeming laugh, a noise like that of a heavy item of furniture being trundled across an uncarpeted wooden floor. We were all by now in a state of faint hysteria.

Shaking hands always gives me the shivers, the unwarranted clammy intimacy of it and that awful sense of having something pumped out of one, plus the impossibility of knowing just when to disengage and take back one's poor, shrinking paw; Dawn Devonport must have had lessons, however, and that veinous hand of hers had hardly touched mine before it was briskly withdrawn — no, not briskly, but in a swiftly sliding caress that slowed for a quarter of a second just as it was letting go, as trapeze artists let go of each other's fingertips in that languorous and seemingly wistful way when they part in mid-air. She gave me, too, the same sideways-glancing smile that she had given Toby, and stepped back, and a moment later we were all trooping into a high-ceilinged, many-windowed room on the ground floor, stumbling behind the star, the star of stars, like a chain gang in our invisible shackles and treading on each other's heels.

The room was entirely done in white, even the floorboards had been gone over with a daubing of what looked like pipe-clay, and there was nothing in it except a couple of dozen cheap-looking, hoop-backed wooden chairs ranged against the four walls, leaving a large bare space in the middle that had a worryingly punitive look to it, as if it were there that the dunces among us, the ones who forgot their lines or tripped over the props, would be made to stand, singled out in our confusion and shame. Three tall, rattly sash windows looked out on the river. Toby Taggart, thinking to put us at our ease, waved a broad square hand and told us we could sit wherever we wished, and as we bumped into each other, all heading in a herd for what looked like the most inconspicuous corner, something that had been there when we were milling outside in the hall, some hint of magical possibilities that we had all felt for a moment, was suddenly gone, and it was dispiritingly as if we were at the end and not the beginning of this fantastical dream-venture. How fragile is this absurd trade in which I have spent my life pretending to be other people, above all pretending not to be myself.

To start off, Toby said that he would call on the scriptwriter to fill us in on the background to our tale, as he put it. *Our tale:* so typical of Toby in his poshest mode — you do know his mother was Lady Somebody Somebody, I forget the name, very grand? What a contrast to his actor father, Taggart the Tearaway, which was the yellow press's delighted label for this larger-than-life, best-loved and worst actor of his generation. As you see, I have been making it my business to gather what facts I can about the principals in whose hothouse company I shall be working in these coming weeks and months.

Toby's mention of the writer set us all to craning like, well, like cranes, for most of us had not realised he was among us. We quickly isolated him, the mysterious Mr. Jaybee, lurking alone in a corner and, after we had all fixed on him, looking as alarmed as Miss Muffet on her tuffet when the spider came along. In fact, as I discovered, I had misheard again, and he is not Jaybee but JB, for this is how Axel Vander's biographer is known to those who have any claim to intimacy with him. Yes, the perpetrator of our script is the same one who wrote the life-story, a thing I had not been aware of until now. He is a somewhat shifty and self-effacing fellow of about my vintage; I had the impression he is ill at ease at finding himself here — probably he considers himself many cuts above mere screenwork. So this is the chap who writes like Walter Pater in a delirium! He hummed and hawed for a bit, while Toby waited on him with a smile of pained benevolence, and at last somehow the teller of our tale got going. He had very little to share with us that was not in the script, but rehearsed a long rigmarole of how he had embarked on his biography of Axel Vander after a fortuitous encounter in Antwerp — birthplace of the real, the ur-Vander, as you will recall if you have been paying attention — with the scholar who claimed to have unmasked the old fraud, the fake Vander, that is. This part itself makes quite a tale. The scholar, an emeritus professor of Post-Punk Studies from the University of Nebraska by the name of Fargo DeWinter — "No, sir, you are right, the fair town of Fargo ain't in Nebraska, as so many folk seem to think" — through diligence and application had found and brought to light a number of anti-Semitic articles written by Vander during the war for the collaborationist paper *Vlaamsche Gazet.* DeWinter confessed to being more amused than shocked by the enormities that Vander was said to have got away with, not merely foul writings in a now defunct newspaper but, if we are to believe it, the murder, or mercy-killing, which no doubt is what the scoundrel himself would have claimed it was, of an ailing and inconvenient spouse. The latter piece of mischief had remained hidden until JB put Billie

163

Stryker on to Vander's noisome scent and the whole truth came out — not, as JB observed with his sickly smile, that the truth is ever whole or, if it is, that it is likely to come out. These revelations were made too late to harm the egregious Vander, who by then was late himself, but they as good as destroyed his posthumous reputation.

We worked until midday. I felt giddy and there was a buzzing in my head. The white surfaces everywhere, and the gale outside that made the windows boom in their frames, and the river surging and the cold sunlight glittering on the roiling water, all gave me the sense of taking part in a nautical romp, a piece of amateur theatricals, say, put on aboard a sailing ship, with the crew for cast, the tars got up in shore rig and the cabin boy in flounces. Sandwiches and bottled water had been provided in an upstairs room. I took my paper plate and paper cup into the haven of the bay of one of the big windows and let the light of outdoors bathe my jangled nerves. The higher elevation here afforded a broader, more steeply angled view of the river, and despite the dizziness I kept my gaze fixed on this precipitous waterscape and away from the others milling about the trestle table at my back, where the makeshift lunch was laid out. It will seem absurd, but I always feel shy among a crowd of actors, especially at the start of a production, shy and vaguely menaced, I am not sure how or by what. A cast of actors is in some way more unruly than any other gathering, impatiently awaiting something, a command, a direction, that will give them purpose, will show them their marks, and make them calm. This tendency of mine to hold aloof is I suspect the reason for my reputation as an egoist — an egoist, among actors! — and a cause, in my years of success, for resentment against me. But I was always just as uncertain as the rest of them, gabbling over my lines in my head and shivering from stage-fright. I wonder people could not see that, if not the audience then at least my fellow players, the more perceptive among them.

The question recurred: Why was I there? How was it I had landed this plum part without applying for it, without even an audition? Had I felt one or two of the younger ones among the cast smirking in my direction with a mixture of resentment and mockery? Another reason to turn my back on the lot of them. But, Lord, I did feel the weight of my years. I always suffered worse stage-fright offstage than on.

I sensed her presence before I glanced to my right to find her standing beside me, facing out, as I was, also with a paper cup clutched in her cupped hands. All women for me have an aura but the Dawn Devonports, scarce as they are, fairly flare. *The Invention of the Past,* in its movie version, has a dozen characters, but really there are only two parts worth speaking of, me as Vander and she as his Cora, and already, as is the way of these things — she is probably no more immune than I am to the envy of others — a bond of sorts had begun to forge itself between us, and we found ourselves quite easy together there, or as easy as two actors standing in each other's light could hope to be.

I have known many leading ladies but I had never been thus close up to a real film star before, and I had the odd impression of Dawn Devonport as a scaled-down replica of her public self, expertly fashioned and perfectly animate yet lacking some essential spark — duller, slightly dowdier, or just human, I suppose, just ordinarily human — and I did not know if I should feel disappointed, I mean disenchanted. I cannot remember any more of what we talked about on this second encounter than I can of what was said when we were introduced in the hall downstairs. There was something about her, about the combination in her of frailty and faint mannishness, that was a sharp reminder of my daughter. I do not believe I have seen a single film in which Dawn Devonport stars, but it does not matter: her face, with that teasing pout, those depthless, dawn-grey eyes, was as familiar as the face of the moon, and as distant, too. So how, standing there under that tall, light-filled window, would I not be reminded of my lost girl?

Every aurate woman I have loved in my life, and I use the word loved in its widest sense, has left her impression on me, as the old gods of creation are said to have left their thumbprints on the temples of the men that they fashioned out of mud and turned into us. Just so do I retain a particular trace of each one of my women — for I think of them all as mine still — stamped indelibly on the underside of my memory. I will glimpse in the street a head of wheat-coloured hair retreating among the hurrying crowd, or a slender hand lifted and waving farewell in a certain way; I will hear a phrase of laughter from the far side of a hotel lobby, or just a word spoken with a recognised, warm inflection, and on the instant this or that she will be there, vividly, fleetingly, and my heart like an old dog will scramble up and give a wistful woof. It is not that all the attributes of all these women are lost to me save one, only the one that remains most strongly is most characteristic: is, it would seem, an essence. Mrs. Gray, though, despite the years that have elapsed since I last saw her, has stayed with me in her entirety, or as much of an entirety as one may have of a creature not oneself. Somehow I have gathered up all the disparate parts of her, as it is said we shall do with our own remains at the Last Trump, and assembled them into a working model sufficiently complete and life-like for memory's purposes. It is for this reason that I do not see her in the street, do not find her summoned up in the turn of a stranger's head, or hear her voice from the midst of an indifferent crowd: being so amply present to me, she does not need to send out fragmentary signals. Or perhaps, in her case, my memory works in a special way. Perhaps it is not memory at all that thinks it holds her fast inside me, but some other faculty altogether.

Even in those days themselves she was not always my she. When I was in their house and the family was there she was Mr. Gray's wife, or Billy's mother, or, worse, Kitty's. If

I called for Billy and had to come in and sit down at the kitchen table to wait for him — he really was a tardy soul — Mrs. Gray would let her not quite focused gaze slide over me, smiling in a remote fashion, and take up some vague chore as though the sight of me had reminded her of it. She moved more slowly than usual at those times, with an unwonted, telltale dreaminess that the others, had they really been others and not her family, would surely have taken suspicious note of. She would pick up something, anything, a teacup, a dishcloth, a butter-smeared knife, and look at it as if it had presented itself to her of its own volition, demanding her attention. After a moment, though, she would set the object down again, with an intensified air of abstractedness. I can see her there at the kitchen table, the thing put back where it had been yet not quite relinquished, her hand still resting lightly on it as if to retain the exact feel of it, the exact texture, while with the fingers of her other hand she twisted and twisted that unruly spring of hair behind her ear.

And I, what did I do on those occasions, how did I comport myself? I know it will seem fanciful, or just plain tendentious, when I say I believe that it was in those fraught intervals in the Grays' kitchen that, without knowing it, I took my first, groping steps out on to the boards; nothing like an early clandestine love to teach one the rudiments of the actor's trade. I knew what was required of me, knew the part I had to play. It was imperative above all to appear innocent to the point of idiocy. With what skill, therefore, did I adopt the protective cover of doltish adolescence and exaggerate the natural awkwardness of a fifteen-year-old, stumbling and mumbling, pretending not to know where to look or what to do with my hands, trotting out inappropriate observations and knocking over the salt cellar or slopping the milk in the milk jug. I even managed, when addressed directly, to make myself blush, not guiltily, of course, but as if out of an agony of shyness. How proud I was of the polish of my performance. Though I am sure I over-acted wildly, I believe neither Billy nor his father noticed that I was acting at all. Kitty, as usual, was the one who worried me, for every so often, in the midst of one of my little pantomimes, I would catch her eyeing me with what seemed a knowing and sardonic glint.

Mrs. Gray for all her worked-at air of hazy detachment was, I have no doubt, permanently on tenterhooks, fearful that sooner or later I was bound to go too far and take a pratfall and send us both sprawling in the disarray of our perfidy at the feet of her astonished loved ones. And I, I am ashamed to say, teased her heartlessly. It amused me to let the mask drop now and then, just for a second. I would wink at her sultrily when I judged the others were not looking, or in passing would softly bump against some part of her as if by accident. I found endearingly erotic the way in which if, say, I touched her leg under the breakfast table she would try to cover up her start of fright, reminding me of the flustered, helpless attempts at modesty she used to make in our earliest days together when I would bundle her into the back seat of the station wagon and claw at her clothes in my haste to get at this or that high or hollow of her bared flesh as it shrank from me and at the same time enticed me onwards. What a pressure she must have been under at those times, in her own kitchen, what a panic-fright she must have felt. And how callous I was, how careless, to put her through such trials. Yet there was a side to her, the wanton side, that cannot but have thrilled, however fearfully, to these prods that I so cavalierly gave to the blandly domestic surface of her day.

I am thinking of the occasion of Kitty's party. How did I come to be there, who invited me? Not Kitty herself, I know, nor Billy, and certainly not Mrs. Gray. Curious, these holes one encounters when one presses over-insistently upon the moth-eaten fabric of the past. Anyway, for whatever reason, I was there. The little monster was celebrating her birthday, I do not remember which one — she always seemed ageless to me. It was an occasion of wild misrule. The guests were all girls, a score of undersized hoydens who romped unchecked in a pack through the house, elbowing each other and grabbing at each other's clothes and screaming. One of them, a whey-faced creature, neckless and fat, displayed an alarmingly adhesive interest in me, and kept popping up at my elbow with a congested, insinuating smile; Kitty must have been talking about me. There were party games all of which ended in violent scuffles, with hair pulled and blows exchanged. Billy and I, whom Mrs. Gray, before taking refuge in the kitchen, had charged with keeping order, waded into these mêlées shouting and slapping, like a bo'sun and his mate struggling to quell a riot among a gang of drunken sailors on shore leave in a dockside tavern of an unlicensed Saturday night.

172

At one particularly boisterous passage of these revels I, too, retreated into the kitchen, tousled and unnerved. Kitty's fat friend, called Marge, if I recall — she probably grew up a sylph and broke men's hearts with the arching of an eyebrow — tried to follow me, but I gave her a Gorgon's transfixing glare and she hung back dolefully and let me shut the kitchen door in her face. I had not come in search of Mrs. Gray but there she was, in her apron, with her sleeves rolled and her arms floury, bending to lift a tray of fairy cakes from the oven. Fairy cakes! I was creeping up on her, intent on embracing her about the hips, when, still bending, she turned her head and saw me. I began to say something, but she was looking beyond me now, to the door through which I had just entered, and her face had taken on an expression of alarm and warning. Billy had come in unheard behind me. At once I straightened and let my hands fall to my sides, unsure, though, that I had been quick enough, and that he had not seen me there, advancing at a crouch, ape arms outspread and fingers hooked, towards his mother's tautly proffered hindquarters. But luckily Billy was not an observant boy, and he swept us both with an indifferent glance and went to the table and took up a slice of plum-cake and began to stuff it into his mouth with slovenly dispatch. All the same, how my heart wobbled from the gleeful terror of such a close thing.

Mrs. Gray, making herself ignore me, came and set the tray of cakes on the table and stood back, pushing out her lower lip and sending a quick puff of breath upwards to blow a stray fall of hair from her forehead. Billy was still chewing cake, mumbling complaints of his sister and her riotous friends. His mother bade him absently not to speak with his mouth full — she was still admiring the cakes, each in its fluted paper cup and snug in its own shallow compartment in the tray and smelling warmly of vanilla — but he paid her no heed. Then she lifted a hand and laid it on his shoulder. This gesture, too, was absent-minded, but for that reason all the more shocking, to me. I was outraged, outraged to see the two of them together there, she with her hand resting so lightly on his shoulder, in the midst of all that homeliness, that shared, familiar world, while I stood by as if forgotten. Whatever liberties Mrs. Gray might grant me, I would never be as near to her as Billy was at that moment, as he always had been and always would be, at every moment. I could only get into her from the outside, but he, he had sprung from a seed and grown inside her, and even after he had shouldered his brute way out of her he was still flesh of her flesh, blood of her blood. Oh, I do not say these are the things I thought, exactly, but I had the gist of them, and suddenly, in that moment, I was sorely pained. There was no one and nothing that would not make me jealous; jealousy crouched inside me like a bristling, green-eyed cat, ready to spring at the slightest provocation, real or, more often, imagined.

She had Billy take up the remaining slices of plum-cake on its plate and a big bottle of lemonade and, bearing an imbricated array of banana sandwiches on a wooden tray, went after him out of the kitchen. Was there a swing door? Yes, there was: she stopped and held it ajar with her knee and cast back at me a grimful sort of glance that had in it both reproof and pardon, inviting me wordlessly to follow her. I gave her a sulky scowl and turned aside, and heard the spring make its comical, rubbery sound — *boing-g-g!* — as she let go the door and it swung shut, releasing as it did so a final creak and then a heavy after-sigh.

Left alone, I lingered moodily by the table, glaring at the tin tray of cooling fairy cakes. All was still. Even the hoydens had gone quiet, temporarily silenced, it must be, by banana sandwiches and glasses of lemon pop. Winter sunlight — no, no, it was summer, for heaven's sake keep up! — summer sunlight, calm, and heavy as honey, was shining in the window beside the fridge, which was silent, too. Mrs. Gray had left a kettle of water on the stove, grumbling to itself over a low flame. It was one of those conical-shaped whistling kettles that were so popular then and that one hardly ever sees nowadays, when everyone has given in to the electric kettle. The whistle was not on it, though, and from the stubby spout a broad slow column of steam was rising, dense with the sunlight in it and lazily undulant, and curling on itself in an elegant scroll at its topmost reach. When I made to approach the stove something of my own dense aura must have gone before me and this charmed cobra of steam leaned delicately away, as if in vague alarm; I paused, and it righted itself, and when I moved again it moved, too, as before. So we stood wavering there, this friendly wraith and I, held in tremulous equilibrium by the heavy air of summer, and all unexpectedly and for no reason I could think of, a slow burst of happiness enveloped me, a happiness without weight or object, like the simple sunlight itself in the window.

When I did return to the party, however, this bright and blissful glow was clouded on the instant by the unexpected arrival of Mr. Gray. He had left his assistant in charge of the shop — a Miss Flushing; I shall get round to her presently, if I have the heart for it — and had come home bringing Kitty's birthday present. Tall, thin, angular, he stood in the kitchen amidst a pool of little girls, like one of those poles that stick up crookedly out of the lagoon at Venice. He had a remarkably small and disproportionate head, which gave one the illusion that one was always farther off from him than was in fact the case. He wore a bedraggled, pale-brown linen jacket and brown corduroy bags and suede shoes scuffed about the toecaps. The bow-ties that he favoured were an affectation even in those archaic days, and represented the only mark of colour or character that I could discern in the otherwise washed-out aspect that he presented to the world. Spurning what must have been a shopful of styles and makes of frame, he chose to wear cheap, steel-rimmed spectacles, which he would remove slowly, holding them delicately at one hinge between a thumb and two fingers, as if they were pince-nez, and closing his eyes he would slowly massage with the first two fingers and thumb of his other hand the knotted flesh at the bridge of his nose, sighing the while to himself. Mr. Gray's soft sighs sounded at once imprecatory and resigned, like the prayers offered up by a minister who has long ago given in to religious doubts. He had about him permanently an air of troubled inadequacy, seeming incompetent to deal with the practicalities of everyday life. This dim distressfulness had the effect of rallying ministrators around him. People always seemed to be pressing forwards anxiously to aid him, to smooth his way, to make straight his path, to lift an invisible burden from his sloping shoulders. Even Kitty and her friends as they gathered about him now had a hushed and helping aspect. Mrs. Gray, too, was solicitous, as she handed to him over the heads of the children his after-work half-inch of whiskey in a cut-glass tumbler, perhaps the very tumbler that I used to drink from with Billy, upstairs, and from which afterwards I would guiltily wipe my fingerprints with a less than clean hankie. How tired was the smile of thanks he gave to her, how weary seemed the hand with which he put the drink down on the table behind him, untasted.

And maybe, indeed, he was ill. Do I not

recall hushed talk of doctors and hospitals after the Grays' flight from our midst? At the time, sunk in bitter sorrow, I thought it must be just the town as usual spinning a story to cover over for decency's sake a scandal the initial revelation of which had delighted so many. But maybe I was wrong, maybe all along he was suffering from some chronic ailment that was brought to crisis by the discovery of what his wife and I had been up to. That is an unsettling thought, or should be, anyway.

Kitty's birthday gift was a microscope — she was supposed to have a scientific bent — yet another cost-price item, I spitefully surmise, from Gray's the Optician. A sumptuous instrument it was, though, matt-black and solid where it stood on its single, semicircular foot, the barrel silky and cold to the touch, the little winding-nut so smooth in action, the lens so small yet giving on to so magnified a version of the world. I coveted it, of course. I was particularly taken by the box it came in, and in which it would live when not in use. It was made of pale polished wood hardly heavier than balsa, dovetailed at the corners — what a tiny blade such fine work must have called for! — and had a lid, with a thumbnail-shaped notch in it, that slid open lengthways along two waxed grooves in the sides. It was fitted within with a wonderfully delicate set of tiny trestles, carved from wafer-thin plywood, on which the instrument lay snugly on its back, like a doted-on black baby asleep in its custom-made crib. Kitty was delighted, and with a beadily possessive light in her eye took it off into a corner to gloat over it, while her friends, suddenly forgotten, stood about in leporine uncertainty.

Now I was torn between envying Kitty and keeping a jealous watch on Mrs. Gray as she attended to her husband, home wan and weary from the day's breadwinning. His arrival had affected the atmosphere, the wild party spirit had drained from the air, and the guests, sobered and subdued and disregarded still by their undersized hostess, were getting ready in their bedraggled way to go home. Mr. Gray, folding his long frame as if it were a delicate piece of geometrical equipment, a calipers, say, or a big wooden compass, sat down in the old armchair beside the stove. This chair, *his* chair, covered with a worn, pilled fabric that resembled mouse-fur, seemed wearier even than its occupant, sagging badly in the seat as it was and leaning drunkenly at one corner where a castor was missing. Mrs. Gray brought the whiskey glass from the table and once again pressed it on her husband, more tenderly this time, and again he thanked her with his invalid's dolorous smile. Then she stood back, her hands clasped under her bosom, and contemplated him with a worriedly helpless air. This was how it always seemed to be between them, he at the end of some vital resource that only the greatest effort would replenish, and she anxiously eager to aid him but at a loss to know how.

Where is Billy? I have lost track of Billy. How — I ask it again — how did he not see what was going on between his mother and me? How did they all not see? Yet the answer is simple. They saw what they expected to see and did not see what they did not expect. Anyway, why do I exclaim so? I am sure that I for my part was no more perspicacious than they were. That kind of myopia is endemic.

The attitude that Mr. Gray displayed towards me was curious — that is to say, it was strange, for certainly it betrayed no trace of interest. His eye would fall on me, would roll over me, rather, like an oiled ball-bearing, registering nothing, or so I believed. He never seemed quite to recognise me. Perhaps, with his poor eyesight, he imagined it was a different person he was seeing each time I appeared in the house, a succession of Billy's friends all inexplicably similar in appearance. Or perhaps he was afraid I was someone he was supposed to know perfectly well, a family relation, a cousin of the children's, say, who came on frequent visits and whose exact identity he was at this late stage too embarrassed to enquire into. For all I know he may have thought I was a second son, Billy's brother, whom he had unaccountably forgotten about and now must accept without comment. I do not think I was singled out particularly for his lack of attention. As far as I could see he looked upon the world in general with the same slightly puzzled, slightly worried, fogged-over gaze, his bowtie askew and his long, bony, twig-like fingers moving over the surface of things in feeble, fruitless interrogation.

We had an assignation that evening, the evening of Kitty's party, Mrs. Gray and I. Assignation: that is a word I like, suggestive as it is of the velvet cloak and tricorn hat, the fluttering fan, the bosom heaving under tautened satin; I fear our circumspect outings had little of such flash and dash. How did she manage to slip away, with so many chores to be done in the aftermath of the party? — in those days women cleared up and washed the dishes without expectation of help or thought of protest. In fact, it galls me that I do not know how she managed any of our desperate liaison, or how she got away with it for as long as she did. Our luck held remarkably, given the dangers we ran. I was not the only one who tweaked the love god's nose. Mrs. Gray herself took foolhardy risks. As it happened, that was the very evening we ventured together for a stroll on the boardworks. It was her idea. I had been expecting, indeed warmly anticipating, that we would do on this occasion what we always did when we managed to be alone together, but when she arrived at our meeting place on the road above the hazel wood she had me get into the station wagon and drove off at once, and would not answer when I asked where we were going. I asked again, more plaintively, more whiningly, and still getting no response I lapsed into a sulk. I should confess that sulking was my chief weapon against her, nasty little tyke that I was, and I employed it with the skill and niceness of judgement that only a boy as heartless as I would have been capable of. She would resist me for as long as she was able, as I fumed in silence with my arms clamped across my chest and my chin jammed on my collar-bone and my lower lip stuck out a good inch, but always it was she who gave in, in the end. This time she held out until, rattling along by the river, we had passed the entrance to the tennis club. "You're so selfish," she burst out then, but laughing, as if it were an undeserved compliment. "Honest to God, you have no idea."

At this of course I became at once indignant. How could she say such a thing of me, who for her sake risked the ire of Church, State and my mother? Did I not treat her as the sovereign of my heart, did I not indulge her every whim? So wrought was I that anger and self-righteousness formed a hot lump in my throat, and even if I had been willing to I would not have been able to speak.

It was June, midsummer, the time of endless evenings and white nights. Who can imagine what it was like to be a boy and loved in such of the world's weather? What I was still too young to recognise, or acknowledge, was that even at its glorious height the year was already poised to wane. Had I given time and time's vanishings their due it would perhaps have accounted for the prick of indefinite sorrow in my heart. But I was young, and there was no end in sight, no end to anything, and the sadness of summer was no more than a faint bloom, of a delicate cobweb shade, on the cheek of love's ripe and gleaming apple.

"Let's go for a walk," Mrs. Gray said.

Well, why not? The simplest, the most innocent thing in the world, you would think. But consider. Our little town was a panopticon patrolled by warders whose vigilance never flagged. True, there should not have been much to remark in the sight of a respectably married woman strolling along the quayside in the broad light of a summer evening in the company of a boy who was her son's best friend — not much, that is, for an observer of an averagely unspeculative and unsuspicious disposition, but the town and everyone in it had an unregenerately filthy mind that never ceased computing, and by putting one and one together was always sure to come up with an illicit two, clasped and panting in each other's guilty arms.

That outwardly blameless promenade along the boardworks — the local name for this construction — constituted, I believe, the most audacious and rashest risk we ever took, aside from the final risk, had we but known it as such, that led precipitately to our ruin. We had come to the harbour, and Mrs. Gray parked the station wagon on the clinkered verge beside the railway line — the railway ran along the boardworks, a single track, a thing for which our town was noted, and is to this day, for all I know — and we got out, I sulking still and Mrs. Gray humming to herself in a pretence of not noticing my surly glare. With one hand she reached quickly behind and plucked the seat of her dress free at the back in that way that every time she did it provoked in me an inward gasp of agonised desire. The air over the sea was still, and the water, high and motionless, had a thin floating of oil from the moored coal-boats, that gave it the look of a sheet of red-hot steel suddenly gone cool, aswirl with iridescent shades of silver-pink and emerald and a lovely lucent brittle blue, shimmery as the sheen on a peacock feather. We were not by any means the only promenaders. There were quite a few couples out, ambling dreamily arm in arm in the late soft glow of the evening's immemorial sunlight. Perhaps, after all, no one so much as noticed us, or paid us the slightest heed. A guilty heart sees glancing eyes and knowing grins on every side.

Now, I am sure this is too absurd to have been the case, but on that occasion I recall Mrs. Gray, in her short-sleeved summer dress, wearing a pair of pretty gloves made of a reddish-blue netlike material — I can *see* it — transparent and brittle, with ruffles at the wrist of a darker, purplish shade, and, more absurd still, a matching hat, small and round and flat as a saucer, set slightly off-centre on the crown of her head. Where do I get such fancies from? All she lacks, in this outlandishly demi-mondaine vision of her, is a parasol to twirl, and a pearl-handled lorgnette to peer through. And why not a bustle, into the bargain? Anyway, there we were, young Marcel in unlikely company with bare-armed Odette, pacing side by side along the boardworks, our heels knocking hollowly on the planking and I silently recalling, with arch compassion for a former unformed self, how not so long ago I used to lurk under here with my urchin pals when the tide was out and squint through the gaps between the sleepers in hope of seeing up the skirts of girls walking by above us. Although I would not have thought of touching her in the glare of this public place I could feel across the space between us the thrilling crackle of Mrs. Gray's dismay at her own daring; dismay, but determination, too, to brazen it out. She would not look at anyone we met, and went along as erect and studiedly empty-eyed as a ship's figurehead, her bosom thrust forwards and her head held aloft. I was at a loss as to what she thought she was up to, parading like this before the town, but there was a side to her that was still and always would be a romping girl.

I wonder now if secretly and without fully realising it she, too, yearned to be found out, if that was what this provocative display was for. Perhaps our liaison was all too much for her, as oftentimes it was for me, and she wished to be forced to have done with it. Need I say, such a possibility would not have entered my head at the time. When it came to girls I was as insecure and self-doubting as any average boy, yet that Mrs. Gray should love me I took entirely for granted, as if it were a thing ordained within the natural order of things. Mothers were put on earth to love sons, and although I was not her son Mrs. Gray was a mother, so how would she deny me anything, even the innermost secrets of her flesh? That was how I thought, and the thought dictated all my actions, and inactions. She was simply there, and not for a moment to be doubted.

We stopped by the stern of one of the coal boats to look across to the barrage bank, as it was called, a shapeless hulk of concrete stuck in the middle of the harbour, its original function long forgotten, even to itself, probably. Below the surface, under the slope of the boat's dirty rump, big grey-ish fish made desultory weavings, and farther down in the shallow brown water I could dimly see crabs at their stealthy, sideways scuttlings among the stones and sunken beer bottles, the tin cans and tyre-less pram wheels. Mrs. Gray turned aside. "Come on, we'd better go," she said, sound-ing weary now and in a gloom suddenly. What had happened that her mood had turned so swiftly? In all of the time we were together I never knew what was going on in her head, not in any real or empathetic way, and hardly bothered to try to find out. She talked about things, of course, all sorts of things, all the time, but mostly I took it that she was talking to herself, telling herself her own wandering, various and disconnected story. This did not bother me. Her ram-blings and ruminations and the odd breath-less flight of wonderment I regarded as no more than the preliminaries I had to put up with before getting her into the back seat of that pachydermous old station wagon or on to the lumpy mattress on Cotter's littered floor.

When we had got into the car she did not start the engine at once but sat watching through the windscreen the couples still passing to and fro in the deepening twilight. I do not see those net gloves now, or that silly hat. Surely I invented them, out of an impulse of frivolity; the Lady Memory has her moments of playfulness. Mrs. Gray sat with her back pressed against the seat, her arms extended and her hands clamped beside each other on the top of the steering wheel. Have I spoken of her arms? They were plump though delicately shaped, with a little whorled notch under each elbow and curving in a nicely swept arc to the wrist, reminding me happily of those Indian clubs we used to exercise with in the school yard on Saturday mornings. They were lightly freckled on the backs, and the undersides were fish-scale blue and wonderfully cool and silky to the touch, with delicate striations of violet veins along which I liked to slide the tip of my tongue, following them all the way to where they abruptly sank from sight in the dampish hollow of her elbow, one of the numerous ways I had of making her shiver and twitch and moan for mercy, for she was delightfully ticklish.

I laid an urging hand on her thigh, being eager to depart, but she took no notice. "Isn't it peculiar," she said, in a tone of dreamy wonderment, still gazing through the windscreen, "how permanent people

190

seem? As if they'll always be here, the same ones, walking up and down."

I thought for some reason of that swaying column of steam from the kettle in the kitchen, and of Mr. Gray setting down his untouched glass of whiskey on the table in his infinitely weary way. Then I wondered if there might still be time and enough left of the long day's light for Mrs. Gray to drive me to Cotter's place and let me lie down on top of her and assuage for a little while my so fierce, tender and inveterate need of her and her inexhaustibly desirable flesh.

Dawn Devonport, I have learned, has also suffered a bereavement, far more recent than mine. A little over a month ago her father died, of an unheralded heart attack, at the age of fifty-something. She told me of this last evening, at the end of the day's filming, as we walked together in the open air behind the studio where we are working this week. She had come out to smoke the fifth of the six cigarettes that she claims are her daily ration — why six, I wonder. She says she does not like to let the cast and crew see her smoking, though obviously I am an exception, being already a stand-in, as I suspect, for the father who so recently absconded from her life. We were both suffering somewhat in the aftermath of a scene of brutal passion we had spent the afternoon doing and redoing — nine long takes before Toby Taggart grudgingly consented to be satisfied; did I say film-acting was easy? —

and the chill air of late autumn, smelling of smoke and tinged with bronze behind far trees, was a balm for our throbbing brows. To be made to feign love-making before the camera was fraught enough, but to have had to follow the act with a mock blow of my fist between her small, bared and shockingly defenceless breasts — Axel Vander, at least as JB has written him, is decidedly not a nice man — had left me dry-mouthed and shaking. As we paced the strip of unconvinced grass under the high, windowless, gunmetal-grey back wall of the studio she spoke of her father in brief rapid bursts, drawing hard on her cigarette and expelling puffs of smoke like cartoon speech-bubbles in which exclamations of sorrow and anger and incredulity had yet to be inscribed. Dad was a taxi driver, a jolly fellow, it seems, never sick a day in his life until his arteries, all clogged up after forty years of forty a day — she looked at the cigarette in her fingers and gave a sour laugh — had shut off the valves one October morning and let the engine cough and die.

It turns out that it was Dad, dear old Dad, who lumbered her with the name Dawn Devonport. He dreamed it up for her when she was a ten-year-old hoofer and landed the part of First Fairy in a West End panto.

Why she stuck with the name I do not know. An excess of filial devotion, perhaps. The abrupt manner in which the old cabbie sped off while she stood at the kerb, desperately signalling, had left her puzzled and cross, as if before anything else his death had been a dereliction of duty. She, too, it seems, like Lydia and me, feels she has not so much lost as been eluded by a loved one. I could see she has not learned yet how to mourn — but does one ever learn that hard lesson? — and when we stepped away from the set on our way outside and in the sudden gloom beyond the lights she stumbled on one of those malignant fat black cables that turn a studio floor into a snake-pit and she grasped my wrist for support, I felt all along the bones of her strong, mannish hands the tremors of her inner distress.

Speaking of distress, I was tempted to tell her the singular thing that Billie Stryker has told me, which is that Axel Vander, the very he, was in Italy, and not only in Italy but in Liguria, and not only in Liguria but in the vicinity of Portovenere, on or about, as a policeman would say, giving evidence in the witness box, on or about the date of my daughter's death. I do not know what to think about this. Really, I would prefer not to think about it at all.

It is a strange business, movie-making, stranger than I expected it would be, and yet in an odd way familiar, too. Others had warned me of the necessarily disjointed, fragmentary nature of the process, but what surprises me is the effect that this has on my sense of myself. I feel that not only my actor self but my self self is made into a thing of fragments and disjointure, not only in the brief intervals when I am before the camera but even when I have stepped out of my role — my *part* — and reassumed my real, my supposedly real, identity. Not that I ever imagined myself either a product or a preserver of the unities: I have lived enough and reflected enough to acknowledge the incoherence and manifold nature of what used to be considered the individual self. Any day of the week I leave my house and in the street the very air becomes a forest of bristling blades that slice me imperceptibly into multiple versions of the singularity that indoors I presented myself as being and, indeed, was taken for. This experience before the camera, though, this sense of being not one but many — *my name is Legion!* — has an added dimension, for the many are not units, but segments, rather. So, being in a film is strange, and at the same time not strange at all; it is an intensification, a

195

diversification, of the known, a concentration upon the ramifying self; and all this is interesting, and confusing, and thrilling and unsettling.

I tried last evening to speak about all this to Dawn Devonport, but she only laughed. She agreed it is disorienting at first — "You lose track of everything" — but assured me that in time I shall get used to it. I think she did not fully grasp what I meant. As I have said, I feel I know already the otherwhere that I have found myself in, and all that is different is the intensity of the experience, the particularity of it. Dawn Devonport dropped her half-smoked cigarette in the grass and trod on it with the heel of her sensible black leather shoe — she was in costume as Cora, the nun-like young woman who gives herself to Axel Vander as a Christian martyr would give herself to an old but ravenous lion — and glanced at me sidelong with the shadow of a smile that seemed at once kindly and slyly mocking. "We have to live, you know," she said. "This is not life — my dad could have told you that." What can she have meant? There is a touch of the sibyl to Dawn Devonport. But then, does not every woman, to my enchanted eye, possess something of the prophetess?

She stopped at one point in our pacing

and turned and asked if I had told Billie Stryker about my daughter. I said that I had; that, indeed, I had surprised myself by blurting it all out the first day when Billie came to the house and sat with me so taciturnly in my crow's-nest in the attic. She smiled, and gave her head a deprecating shake. "That Toby," she said. I asked her what she meant. We walked on. Her costume was thin and she had only a light cardigan thrown over her shoulders, and I worried that she would be cold, and offered her my jacket, which she declined. It was well known, she said, that Toby's tactic when he was about to work with an actor new to him was to send in Billie Stryker to do a preliminary recce and come back with some choice bit of intimate information, preferably of a shameful or tragic nature, to be studied and stored away carefully and brought out again when and if needed, like an X-ray plate. Billie had a knack, she said, of luring people into confessing things without their being aware of what they were confessing to; it was a knack that Toby Taggart valued highly and made frequent use of. I recalled Marcy Meriwether announcing Billie Stryker the scout, and her hoarse laughter coming along the line to me all the way from sunny Carver City, and I felt slow-witted and foolish, not for the first or, I imagine, the last time, in this blended, garishly lit dream that Dawn Devonport and the rest of us are sleepwalking through together. So that is what Billie Stryker is, not so much a scout as a plain snoop. Surprisingly — at least it surprises me — I do not seem to mind that I was duped.

Speaking of dreams, I had one of my wilder ones last night; it has just come back to me this moment. It seems to demand being recounted in all its questionable detail; certain dreams have that quality. This one would require a rhapsode to do it justice. I shall try my best. I was in a house on a riverbank. It was an old house, tall and rickety, with an impossibly steep-pitched roof and crooked chimneys — a sort of gingerbread cottage out of a fairy tale, quaint yet sinister, or sinister because quaint, as is the way in fairy tales. I had been lodging there, on some sort of working holiday, I think, along with a group of other people, family, or friends, or both, although none of them was to be seen, and now we were leaving. I was upstairs, packing, in a small room with a big window open wide and looking out to a view of the river below. The sunshine outside was peculiar, a thin, pervasive, lemony element, like a very fine liquid, and it was impossible to tell from it what time of day it might be, morning, midday or eve. I did know that we were running late — a train or something would be leaving soon — and I was anxious, and clumsy in my haste to fit all my things, of which there were impossibly many, into the two or three hopelessly small suitcases standing open on the narrow bed. There must have been a chronic drought in the region, for the river, which I could see would not be wide or deep even in times of flood, was a shallow bed of sticky, light-grey mud. Busy though I was with the packing I was also on the look-out for something, although I did not know what, and I kept leaning far back, while going on with the packing, to scan the view outside the window. Glancing out now I realised that what I had taken for the trunk of a dead tree lying athwart the riverbed and slimed all over with glistening mud was in fact a living creature, a thing like a crocodile only not quite, or more than, a crocodile; I could see its great jaws moving and its ancient eyelids opening and closing slowly with what seemed a great effort. Probably it had been washed down in a flood that had preceded the drought and become lodged there in that morass, helpless and dying. Was this the thing I had been watching for? I felt anguish and annoyance in equal measure, anguish for the afflicted creature and annoyance that I would have to deal with it somehow, help to rescue it, or direct that it be put out of its misery. Yet it did not seem to be in pain, or even in much distress; indeed, it seemed quite calm and resigned — indifferent, almost. Maybe it had not been washed up here, maybe it was some mud-dwelling creature which the churnings of the recent flood as it passed by had exposed to view and which when the waters came back would sink again into its old, lightless, submerged world. I went down, my feet, in what felt like a deep-sea diver's leaden boots, thumping clumsily on the narrow stairs, and emerged into that strange, aqueous sunlight. At the riverbank I found that the thing had extricated itself from the mud and had turned into a darkly lovely young woman — even in the dream this transformation seemed hackneyed and altogether too easy, a thing that intensified my annoyance and anxious impatience: those suitcases were still not filled and here I was being diverted from my task by a piece of trumpery masquerading as magic. There she was, however, this girl from the deep, seated on a real log on a bank of springy green turf, wearing a haughty and petulant expression, her clasped hands resting on one knee and her shining, long dark hair falling over her shoulders and down her very straight back. It seemed I should know her or at least know who she was. She was got up elaborately in the style of a gypsy, or a chieftainess of old, all bangles and beads and swathes of heavy, shimmering cloth in dramatic hues of emerald and golden oatmeal and rich burgundy. She was waiting impatiently and in some irritation for me to do something for her, to perform some service the need of which she resented. As happens in dreams, I both knew and did not know the nature of this task, and did not at all like the prospect of performing it, whatever it was. Have I mentioned that in the dream I was very young, hardly more than a lad, though burdened beyond my years with cares and responsibilities, the packing, for instance, left unfinished in that high room the square open window of which I could look up at now, and where the timeless, pallid sunlight was streaming in? The shutters thrown back against the wall on either side were made of what looked like rush matting, a feature I noticed particularly and one that was of an inexplicable significance. I was aware of being in danger of falling in love on the spot, instantly, with this girl, this imperious princess, but I knew that if I did I would be destroyed, or at least put through great pains, and besides, there was so much I had to do, much too much, to allow of so frivolous a surrender. Now the dream began to lose focus and grew hazy, or does so at least in my recollection of it. The location had suddenly moved inside the house, into a cramped room with tiny square windows with deep and shadowed embrasures. Another girl had materialised, the princess's friend, or companion, older than both of us, brisk and businesslike and somehow coercive, whose coercions the princess resisted, and so did I, and who in the end lost patience with us and thrust her fists into the very deep pockets of her very long coat and went off in very high dudgeon. Left alone with the dark-haired beauty, I tried to kiss her, in a perfunctory way — I was still worrying about those half-stuffed suitcases upstairs, agape like the mouths of chicks in a nest and overflowing untidily — but she rebuffed me in a matchingly offhand fashion. Who can she have been, whom did she represent? Dawn Devonport is the obvious candidate, yet I think not. Billie Stryker, oneirically slimmed down and beautified?

Hardly. My Lydia, daughter of the desert of old? Hmm. But wait — I know. She was Cora, Axel Vander's girl, of course; not Dawn Devonport's portrayal of her, which if I am honest I consider superficial so far, but as I see her in my imagination, strange and estranged, difficult, proud and lost. The end of the dream, as I retain it, was a wavering, a vaguening, as the enchanting girl — I have called her a princess but only for convenience, for she was certainly a commoner, though of an uncommon kind — departed from me along the barren river's bank, not striding but as if sustained on air, moving away soundlessly and yet at the same time somehow returning to me. This phenomenon continued for some time, this impossible, simultaneous coming and going, departing and returning, until my sleeping mind could bear it all no longer and everything went slack and slowly sank, into the unregistering darkness.

Why, I asked Dawn Devonport — we are still pacing that insulted strip of grass behind the studio — why does Toby Taggart employ Billie Stryker to nose out the secret weaknesses and sorrows of his players? I knew the answer, of course, so why did I ask? "To have what he thinks will be power over us," she said, and laughed. "He imagines he is Svengali — don't they all?"

It will seem odd, perhaps, but I did not think badly of Toby for this, no more than I did of Billie Stryker. He is a professional, as am I; in other words we are cannibals, the pair of us, and would eat our young for the sake of a scene. I cannot help but like him. He is large and ill-assembled, built on the lines of a buffalo, with absurdly tiny feet and skinny legs and a broad chest and broader shoulders and a shaggy mop of mahogany-coloured curls from under which shine out those glossy sad brown eyes of his, pleading love and forbearance. His name is Tobias — yes, I asked him — it is a family tradition on his mother's side, from her father the duke back through the centuries to an originary Tobias the Terrible who fought at Hastings and is said to have cradled the mortally wounded King Harold in his armoured arm. This last is the kind of dusty heirloom that Toby loves to bring out proudly from the vault of the family's past for us to admire. He is a sentimentalist and a patriot of the old school and cannot understand my disregard for the deeds of doughty ancestors. I explained to him that I have no ancestors to speak of, only a motley line of petty tradesmen and near-peasants who never swung an axe in battle or comforted a king with an arrow in his eye. I would say that Toby is an anachronism in the movie world if I thought there was anyone in it who is not — look at me, for heaven's sake. How he agonises on the set. Are we all happy in our parts? Is he being true to the spirit of JB's wonderful script? Is the studio's money being well spent? Will audiences understand what we are attempting? There he stands, always to the right and a little behind the cameraman, amid a clutter of wiring and those mysterious long black boxes with reinforced metal corners that are strewn at random about the floor, in his big brown jumper and ragged jeans, nibbling at his nails like a squirrel at a nut, as if he were trying to get at the elusive essence of himself, and worrying, worrying. The crew adore him and are fiercely protective, flexing their biceps and glowering at anyone seeming to offer the slightest slight. There is something saintly about him. No, not saintly, not quite. I know, I know what it is he reminds me of: one of those prelates the Church militant used to produce, muscular but soft, big-hearted, privy to the world's cesspit of sin yet ever undaunted, not for a moment doubting that this chaotic phantasmagoria into which he must sink himself each day will in the end be redeemed and turned into a paradisal vision of light and grace and resplendently cavorting souls.

I can hardly believe it — we are already in the final week of filming. They move so fast, the movies.

How pleased and proud Mrs. Gray would be if she could see me on the set, her boy made good. She was something of an aficionado — aficionada? — of the cinema, though she called it the pictures. On almost every Friday night the Gray family would get dressed up and proceed, parents in front and the children two paces behind, to the Alhambra Kino, a barn-like converted music-hall that stood on a blind corner halfway along the Main Street. Here they sat four abreast in the one-and-sixpennies, the best seats in the house, to view the latest offerings from Parametro, from Warner-Goldwyn-Fox, from Gauling or Eamont Studios. What shall we say of the lost picture palaces of our youth? The Alhambra, despite the spits on the wooden floor and the fug of fag smoke in the dirty air, was for me a place of deep erotic suggestion. I admired especially the magnificent scarlet curtain, with its softly curved fluting and delicate gold frills, which put me in mind, inevitably, of the Kayser Bondor lady in her pleated frock and lacy petticoat. It did not rise, this curtain, as it would surely have done in music-hall times, but parted in the middle and drew back on either side with a hushed, silken swish, while the houselights slowly dimmed and the louts down in the fourpenny seats set to whistling like cockatoos and made a jungle drumming on the floorboards with their cleated heels.

On a couple of successive Friday nights that spring, and inadvisedly, as I would too late discover — the thing turned out nothing less than a torture — I wheedled a florin out of my mother and went to the Alhambra myself, not to see the film but to spy on the Grays. Now, this required some nice timing and careful placement. For instance, if I was to avoid being spotted, it was imperative for me not to go in before the lights went down at the start of the show, and to slip out before they went up again at the close so as not to be trapped by the National Anthem. I could picture Mrs. Gray's alarmed and furious glare, or Billy's slow grin of surprise, could see Kitty jumping up in her seat to point me out with delighted malevolence, while her father fumbled under the seat in search of his umbrella. And what about the interval between the ads and the main feature, when the lamps were turned on to show us the magical apparition of the ice-cream girl posed in a spot in front of the curtain with her little tray hitched under her starched bosom? Just how far down in a cinema seat was it possible to slide? I arrived too late the first time, so that the place was nearly full and the only seat I could find was six rows behind the Grays, from where I had a maddeningly intermittent view of the back of what I took for Mrs. Gray's head but which turned out to be, inexplicably, the bald pate of a fat old fellow with a large and shinily ripe boil on the back of his neck. The next time was better; that is, I had a better view but experienced even worse frustration and torment. And not much of a better view, either. I got a seat two rows in front of the Grays but over at the far end of the aisle, so that to glimpse Mrs. Gray at all I had to keep twisting my head sideways and back, as if my shirt collar were too tight, or as if I were suffering from some affliction that made me twitch and turn every thirty seconds or so.

How terrible it was to witness Mrs. Gray caught up in such innocent enjoyment —

the innocence more than the enjoyment was what was terrible, to me. She sat there, canted backwards a little, her face lifted in dreamy ecstasy to the screen and her lips parted in a smile that kept trying to achieve itself but never quite succeeded, lost as she was in blissful forgetfulness, of self, of surroundings and, most piercingly, of *me.* The twitchy light from the screen sliding over her face made it seem that she was being slapped, repeatedly, lasciviously, with a grey silk glove. The way in which I was seeing her, snatching a moving series of images by repeatedly turning my head quickly to the side, was a clumsy version of the process going on inside the clackety projector up in its little room behind us. Despite my covert manoeuvres, had she spotted me come in? Did she know I was there and had decided to ignore me and not let me spoil her fun? If so she gave no sign of it, and afterwards I was too ashamed to ask, for how could I admit to such despicable peeping-tommery? For her husband at her side, for Billy, for his sister, I had no eyes at all — let them see me, I did not care now — fixed as I was on her, on her, on *her,* until my neighbour but one, a burly chap in a tight suit, with a shiny quiff and smelling strongly of hair-oil, leaned across his girlfriend and assured me in a confiding undertone that if I did not stop that jerking and lepping he would put my front teeth down my fucking throat for me.

My beloved's taste in film was broad, though there were exclusions. Musicals she did not like, having no ear for a tune, as she admitted. Nor did she care for the plangent, plunging love stories that were still so popular then, the women all shoulder-pads and lipstick and the men either craven or treacherous or both — "sloppy stuff," she would say with dismissive scorn, pursing her mouth and giving it a Betty Huttonish twist. Action was what she craved. She loved war pictures, with lots of explosions and German soldiers in square helmets being fired straight up into the air like mortar shells amid fountains of flying masonry. Westerns were her favourites, though, or Cowboys-and-Indians, as she would have it. She believed in it all, the noble-hearted gunslinger and the cowpuncher in his chaps, the ginghamed schoolmarm, the bedizened saloon girl who is no better than she should be but who could break a whiskey bottle over a bushwhacker's head without pausing in the midst of a sentimental ditty. Nor was it enough for her merely to see a picture: she had to replay the entire thing over again afterwards. I was her ideal auditor for these recountings of what in her version of them were impossibly convoluted plots, with multiple side turnings and back-trackings and a wild confusion of half-remembered names and wholly forgotten motives. I was happy to listen, or pretend to, so long as she consented to lie in my embrace in the back seat of the station wagon or on the mattress in Cotter's place, she going on with her retold tale, trying to sort out who dry-gulched whom or which bit of the bulge the Jerries failed to breach, while I poked at and played with her various warm and, by her, temporarily disregarded parts. She had a cinematic lexicon all of her own. In Westerns the hero was always the Chap and the heroine the Girl, no matter what age the actors were. If she forgot a character's name she would replace it with an attribute — "and then Beardy-face grabbed the gun and plugged Wall-eye" — sometimes achieving a weird poetical or picturesque resonance, as in Lonesome Kid, or Barroom Belle or, my favourite, the Dirty Doc.

I speculate now that all these detailed re-hashings were at least in part a ruse by which she secured some respite from my urgent requirement that she lie down and let me do to her what I never tired of doing.

She was Scheherazade and Penelope rolled into one, weaving and unweaving endlessly her tales from the movies. I had read somewhere, or had been told by someone in school — there was a boy, I think his name was Hynes, who knew the most amazing things — that after coition the human male will have regenerated his juices and be capable of full erection after just fifteen minutes. It was a proposition I was keen to test. I do not recall that I succeeded, but certainly I went at it with application. And yet for all that, always, at the back of my mind, there was the suspicion that my efforts, and redoubled efforts, were not as welcome to Mrs. Gray as they might be or as she repeatedly assured me they were. I have a notion that all men worry that all women do not really care for the physical manifestations of love, and only acquiesce to them so as to indulge us, their overgrown, needful, insatiate infants. Hence the unwavering hold over us of the myth of the nymphomaniac, that fabulous creature more elusive than the unicorn or the unicorn's lady, which, once found, would allay our deepest fears. There were moments when, fastened to her breast or rootling about in her lap, I would chance to glance up and catch her smiling down on me with a fond benevolence that was nothing less, and nothing more, than maternal. At times, too, she was as impatient with me as any mother would be of her endlessly importuning child — "Get *off* me!" she would grunt, and tumble me aside and sit up scowling crossly, looking for her clothes. Always I could get her to lie down again, though, simply by touching the tip of my tongue to the chocolate-brown mole between her shoulder-blades or walking two fingers up the soft, fishbelly-white inner side of her arm. Then she would shiver, and turn to me with something that was more than a sigh and less than a moan, her eyes closed and her eyelids fluttering, and offer me helplessly her open hot slack mouth to kiss. She was never so desirable to me as in such moments of reluctant surrender. Those eyelids in particular I loved, carven shells of veined, translucent marble, always cool, always deliciously damp when I touched my lips to them. The milky backs of her knees too were peculiarly cherishable. I even prized the shiny mother-of-pearl stretch-marks on her belly.

Did I appreciate these things then as I appreciate them now, or am I only luxuriating in them in retrospect? Could a boy of fifteen have been possessed of my old roué's discriminating and hungry eye? Mrs. Gray taught me many lessons, the first and most precious of which was to forgive another human being for being human. I was a boy and therefore had in my mind's eye the platonically perfect girl, a creature bland as a manikin that did not sweat or go to the lavatory, that was docile, adoring and fabulously compliant. Mrs. Gray was as unlike this fantasy as could be. She only had to do her laugh, a high whinny in the sinuses with a deep diaphragm note underneath, to send that lifeless dummy flying in tatters from my head. It was not a smooth substitution, the actual woman for the imagined ideal. In the early days I found Mrs. Gray's fleshliness itself disconcerting, at certain moments, in certain postures. Remember, up to then my knowledge of the female form had been confined to the Kayser Bondor lady's legs and the bud-like breasts that Hettie Hickey had let me fondle in the Alhambra's smoky darkness years before. Though Mrs. Gray was not all that much more imposing in stature than Hettie, at times she seemed to me, in our early days, at least, a giantess looming over me, a figure of unassailable erotic power.

Yet she was thoroughly, inescapably, at times dismayingly, human, with all a human creature's frailties and failings. One day we were tussling on the floor in Cotter's place — she was dressed and had been attempting to leave but I had got hold of her and made her plump back down on the mattress with my hand under her behind — when she inadvertently released into my palm an abrupt soft fart. Its single note was followed by a terrible silence, such as there would be after a pistol shot or the first rumble of an earthquake. It was, of course, for me a great shock. I was still at an age when although I knew that in matters peristaltic the sexes are identical I could blithely deny to myself that it was so. A fart, however, was incontrovertible. In the aftermath of this one Mrs. Gray drew away from me quickly with a heave of the shoulders. "Now look," she said angrily, "now look what you made me do, yanking at me like that as if I was a tinker's trollop or something." The injustice of this left me speechless. When she turned back, though, and saw my look of outrage, she gave a spluttering laugh and pushed me hard in the chest and demanded to know, still laughing, if I was not thoroughly ashamed of myself. As so often, it was her laughter that saved the moment, and in time, far from being repelled by the thought of that fundamental report she had let go, I felt privileged, as though she had invited me to be with her in a place where no one before me had ever been permitted.

The fact is, she spoiled most other females for me. Girls like Hettie Hickey were nothing to me now, their meagre breasts and boyish hips, their knock-knees, their plaits and pony-tails — all this I discounted, I who had known the opulence of a grown-up woman, the feel of her full flesh straining inside the strictures of her clothing, the hot fatness of her lips when they went pulpy from passion, the cool moist touch of her slightly pitted cheek when she laid it against my belly. As well as fleshliness she possessed, too, a quality of lightness, of grace, that not the daintiest slip of a girl could match. Her colours, for me, were grey, naturally, but a particular lilac-grey, and umber, and rose, and another tint, hard to name — dark tea? bruised honeysuckle? — to be glimpsed in her most secret places, along the fringes of her nether lips and in the aureole of the pursed little star occluded within the crevice of her bum.

And she was, for me, unique. I did not know where in the human scale to place her. Not really a woman, like my mother, and certainly not like the girls of my acquaintance, she was, as I think I have already said, of a gender all to herself. At the same time, of course, she was womanhood in its essence, the very standard by which, consciously or otherwise, I measured all the women who came after her in my life; all, that is, save one. And what would Cass have made of her? How would it have been if Mrs. Gray and not Lydia had been my daughter's mother? The question fills me with alarm and consternation, yet since it is posed I must entertain it. Remarkable how the idlest piece of speculation can seem to invert everything in and for an instant. It is as if the world had turned around somehow in a half-circle and shown itself to me from an unfamiliar angle, and I am plunged at once into what feels like happy grief. My two lost loves — is that why I — ? Oh, Cass —

That was Billie Stryker just now calling on the telephone, telling me Dawn Devonport tried to kill herself. And failed, it seems.

II

When my daughter was a little girl she suffered from insomnia, especially in the weeks around midsummer, and sometimes, in desperation, mine and hers, late in those white nights I would bundle her in a blanket into the car and take her for drives northwards along the back roads by the coast, for we were still living by the sea then. She enjoyed these jaunts; even if they did not make her sleep, they induced in her a drowsy calm; she said it felt funny to be in the car in her pyjamas, as if she were asleep after all and travelling in a dream. Years later, when she was a young woman, she and I spent a Sunday afternoon retracing our old route up that coastline. We did not acknowledge to each other the sentimental implications of the journey, and I made no mention of the past — one had to be careful of what one said to Cass — but when we got out on that winding road I think she

221

no less than I was remembering those nocturnal drives and the dreamlike sensation of gliding through the greyish darkness, with the dunes beside us and the sea beyond them a line of shining mercury under a horizon so high it seemed it must be a mirage.

There is a place, quite far north, I do not know what it is called, where the road narrows and runs for some way beside cliffs. They are not very high cliffs, but they are high enough and sheer enough to be dangerous, and there are yellow warning notices at intervals all the way along. That Sunday, Cass made me stop the car and get out and walk with her on the clifftop. I was unwilling, having always been afraid of heights, but it would not have done to refuse my daughter so simple a request. It was late spring, or early summer, and the day was brilliant under a scoured sky, with a warm blast of wind coming in off the sea and the sting of iodine in the salt-laden air. I took scant interest in the sparkling scene, however. The look of the swaying waters far below and of the waves gnashing at the rocks was making me nauseous, though I kept up as brave a front as I could manage. Sea birds at eye-level and no more than a few yards away from us hung almost motionless on the updraughts, their wings trembling, their screeches sounding like derisive taunts. After some way the narrow path grew narrower still and made an abrupt descent. Now there was a steep bank of clay and loose stones on one side and nothing on the other save sky and the growling sea. I felt giddier than ever, and went along in a dreadful funk, leaning in towards the bank on my left and away from the windy blue abyss to the right. We should have gone in file, the way was so narrow and the going so treacherous, but Cass insisted on walking beside me, on the very edge of the path, with her arm locked in mine. I marvelled at her lack of fear, and was even starting to feel resentful of her insouciance, for by now my own fright was such that I was sweating and I had begun to tremble. Gradually it became apparent, however, that Cass, too, was terrified, perhaps more terrified than I was, hearing the wooing wind crooning to her and feeling the emptiness plucking at her coat and the long fall that was only the tiniest sidestep away opening its arms to her so invitingly. She was a lifelong dabbler in death, was my Cass — no, she was more, she was a connoisseur. Striding along that cliff-edge was for her, I am sure, a sip of the deepest, most darksome, brew, the richest vintage. As she held on tight to my arm I could feel the fear thrumming in her, the thrill of terror twitching along her nerves, and I realised that, perhaps because of her fear, I was no longer afraid, and so we went on briskly, father and daughter, and which of the two of us was sustaining the other it was impossible to say.

If she had jumped that day, would she have taken me with her? That would have been a thing, the pair of us plummeting down, feet first, arm in arm, through the bright, blue air.

The private hospital to which they rushed the comatose Dawn Devonport — by helicopter, no less — stands in handsome grounds, amid a broad sea of closely barbered, unreal-looking grass. A creamy-white and many-windowed cube, it looks like nothing so much as an old-style ocean-going luxury liner viewed head-on, complete with big flag whipping importantly in the breeze and air-conditioning vents that might be smoke-stacks. Since childhood I have secretly entertained the idea of hospitals as places of romantic enchantment, an idea which no number of drear visits and more than a few brief but unpleasant stays have managed to disabuse me of entirely. I trace this fancy to an autumn afternoon when I was five or six and my father took me on the bar of his bicycle to the Fort Mountain outside our town, where we sat in the bracken on a steep slope eating bread-and-butter sandwiches and drinking milk from a lemonade bottle that had been corked with a screw of greaseproof paper. The TB hospital loomed high up behind us, cream-coloured also, and also many-windowed, on the unseen terraces of which I imagined neat rows of pale girls and neurasthenic young men, too refined and fastidious to live, reclining on extended deckchairs under bright-red blankets, drowsing and fitfully dreaming. Even the smell of a hospital suggests to me an exotically pristine world where specialists in white coats and sterile masks move silently among narrow beds overhung with phials feeding priceless ichor drip by drip into the veins of fallen moguls and, yes, afflicted film stars.

It was pills Dawn Devonport took, a whole bottle of them. Pills are, I note, the preferred choice among our profession, I wonder why. There is a question as to the seriousness of her intention. But an entire bottle, that is impressive. What did I feel? Dread, confusion, a certain numbness, a certain annoyance, too. It was as if I had been strolling unconcernedly along an unfamiliar, pleasant street when suddenly a door had been flung open and I had been seized by the scruff and hauled unceremoniously not into a strange place but a place that I knew all too well and had thought I would never be made to enter again; an awful place.

When I first walked into the hospital room — crept would be a better word — and saw this hitherto so vivid young woman lying there still and gaunt my heart gave a gulp, for I thought that what they had told me must be mistaken and that she had succeeded in what she had set out to do and that this was her corpse, laid out ready for the embalmers. Then she gave me an even greater start by opening her eyes and smiling — yes, she smiled, with what at first seemed to me pleasure and genuine warmth! I did not know whether to take this for a good sign or a bad. Had she lost her reason to desperation and despair, to be lying there in a hospital bed smiling like that? Looking closer I saw, however, that it was less a smile than a grimace of embarrassment. And in fact that was the first thing she said, struggling to sit up, that she felt embarrassed and disgraced, and she put out a trembling hand for me to take. Her skin was hot, as if she were running a fever. I set up her pillows for her and she lay back on them with a groan of anger against herself. I noted the plastic name-tag around her wrist, and read the name on it. How tiny she looked, tiny and hollowed out, propped there weightless-seeming as a fledgling fallen from the nest, her enormous eyes starting from her head and her hair lank and drawn back and her sharp bones pressing into the shoulders of the washed-out, drab-green hospital gown. Those big hands of hers appeared bigger than ever, the fingers stubbier. There were flakes of dried grey stuff at the corners of her mouth. What turbulent depths had she leaned out over, what windy abyss had called to her?

"I know," she said ruefully. "I look like my mother did on her deathbed."

I had not been at all sure that I should come. Did I know her well enough to be here? In such circumstances, where cheated death lingers rancorously, there is a code of etiquette more ironbound than any that applies outside, in the realm of the living. Yet how could I not have come? Had we not achieved an intimacy, not only in front of the camera but away from it, too, that went far beyond mere acting? Had we not shared our losses, she and I? She knew about Cass, I knew about her father. Yet there was the question whether precisely this knowledge would hover between us like a troublesome, doubled ghost, and strike us mute.

What did I say to her? Cannot think: mumbled some trite condolence, no doubt. What would I have said to my daughter if she had somehow survived those slimed, rust-coloured rocks at the foot of that headland at Portovenere?

I drew a plastic chair to the bedside and sat down, leaning forwards with my fore-arms on my knees and my hands clasped; I must have looked a father-confessor to the life. One thing I was certain of: if Dawn Devonport mentioned Cass I would get up from that chair without a word and walk out. Around us the many noises of the hospital were joined together in a medleyed hum, and the air in the overheated room had the texture of warm damp cotton. Through the window on the far side of the bed I could see the mountains, distant and faint, and, closer in, an extensive building site with cranes and mechanical diggers and many foreshortened workmen in helmets and yellow safety-jackets clambering about in the rubble. It does not know how heart-less it is, the workaday world.

Dawn Devonport had withdrawn the hand that she had briefly given me and it lay now limp at her side, pallid as the sheet on which it rested. The name on the plastic identity bracelet was not hers, I mean the name that was printed there was not Dawn Devonport. She saw me looking and smiled again, grimly. "That's me," she said in a Cockney voice, "my real name, Stella Stebbings. Bit of a tongue-twister, ain't it?"

At noon a maid had discovered her in the bedroom of her hotel suite at Ostentation Towers, the curtains drawn and she sprawled halfway out of a disordered bed with foam on her lips and the empty pill bottle clasped in her fist. I could see the scene, blocked out in classic fashion, under, of course, in my vision of it, the suggestion of a proscenium arch, or in this case, I suppose, within the rectangle of a sombrely glowing screen. She did not know why she had done it, she said, reaching out her hand again and fixing it on my clasped fists, as it was broad enough to do — they must be her father's hands she has. She supposed, she said, that she had acted on impulse, yet how could that be, she wanted to know, when it had taken such an effort to swallow all those pills? They were a very mild dose, otherwise she would certainly be dead, the doctor had assured her of it. He was an Indian, the doctor, mild-mannered and with such a sweet smile. He had seen her as Pauline Powers in the remake of *Bitter Harvest*. That had been one of her father's favourite pictures, the original version, though, with Flame Domingo playing Pauline. It was her father who had encouraged her to be a film actress. He had been so proud to see his daughter's name in lights, the very name he had dreamed up for her when she was a fleet-footed prodigy in cellophane wings and a tutu. The shell of her hand tightened over both of mine, and I unclasped my fingers and turned up one of my hands and felt her palm hot against mine, and as if this touch between us were scalding she snatched her hand away again and sat forwards, making a tent of her knees, and looked out of the window, a moist sheen on her forehead and her hair hooked behind her ears and that penumbral down on her skin all aglow and her eyes lit with a fevered gleam. Sitting there like that, so erect and stark with her profile etched against the light, she had the look of a primitive figure carved from ivory. I imagined tracing the line of her jaw with a fingertip, imagined placing my lips against the side of her smooth, shadowed throat. She was Cora, Vander's girl, and I was Vander: she the damaged beauty, I the beast. We had been acting their savage love

230

for weeks now: How could we not in some way be them? She began to weep, the big glistening tears making grey splashes on the sheet. I pressed her hand. She should go away, I told her, in a voice thick with an emotion I was too moved to try to identify — she should have Toby Taggart call a week-long, a month-long halt to the filming and get away from everything altogether. She was not listening. The far-off mountains were blue, like motionless pale smoke. *My lost girl,* Vander calls her in the script. My lost girl.

Careful.

In the end we had not much to say to each other — should I have given her a stern talking-to, should I have urged her to cheer up and look on the bright side of things? — and after a short while I left, saying I would come again tomorrow. She was still far away in herself or in those far blue hills and I think she hardly noticed my going.

In the corridor I encountered Toby Taggart, loitering uneasily, fidgeting and biting his nails and looking more than ever like a wounded ruminant. "Of course," he burst out straight off, "you'll think I'm only worried about the shoot." Then he looked abashed and set to nibbling again violently at a thumbnail. I could see he was putting

231

off going in to see his fallen star. I told him of how when she had woken up she had smiled at me. He took this with a look of large surprise and, I thought, a trace of reprehension, though whether it was Dawn Devonport's hardly appropriate smile or my telling him about it that he deplored I could not say. To distract myself in my shaken state — I had a fizzing sensation all over, as if a strong electric current were passing along my nerves — I was thinking what a vast and complicated contraption a hospital is. An endless stream of people kept walking past us, to and fro, nurses in white shoes with squeaky rubber soles, doctors with dangling stethoscopes, dressing-gowned patients cautiously inching along and keeping close to the walls, and those indeterminate busy folk in green smocks, either surgeons or orderlies, I can never tell which. Toby was watching me but when I caught his eye he looked aside quickly. I imagine he was thinking of Cass, who had succeeded where Dawn Devonport had failed. Was he thinking, too, guiltily, of how he had sent Billie Stryker to lure her story out of me? He has never let on that he knows about Cass, has never once so much as mentioned her name in my presence. He is a wily fellow, despite the impression he likes to give of being a shambler and dim.

There was a long rectangular window beside us affording a broad view of roofs and sky and those ubiquitous mountains. In the middle distance, among the chimney pots, the November sunlight had picked out something shiny, a sliver of window-glass or a steel cowling, and the thing kept glinting and winking at me with what seemed, in the circumstances, a callous levity. Just to be saying something, I asked Toby what he would do now about the film. He shrugged and looked vexed. He said he had not yet told the studio what had happened. There was a great deal of footage already in the can, he would work on that, but of course there was the ending still to be shot. We both nodded, both pursed our lips, both frowned. In the ending as it is written Vander's girl Cora drowns herself. "What do you think?" Toby asked cautiously and still without looking at me. "Should we change it?"

An ancient fellow in a wheelchair was bowled past, white-haired, soldierly, one eye bandaged and the other furiously staring. The wheels of the wheelchair made a smoothly pleasant, viscous whispering on the rubber floor tiles.

My daughter, I said, used to make jokes

about killing herself.

Toby nodded absently, as if he were only half listening. "It's a shame," he said. I do not know if he was speaking of Cass or of Dawn Devonport. Both, perhaps. I agreed that, yes, it was a shame. He only nodded again. I imagine he was still brooding on that ending. It was a tricky problem for him. Yes, suicide, even if only the attempt of it, does make for awkwardness.

When I got home I went into the living room, to the telephone extension there, and, pausing only to make sure that Lydia was nowhere in earshot, called Billie Stryker and asked if she would come and meet me, straight away. Billie at first sounded unwilling. There was a racket going on behind her; she said it was the television set, but I suspect it was that unspeakable husband of hers, berating her — I am sure I recognised the combination of menace and whine that is his characteristic tone. At one point she put her hand over the receiver and shouted angrily at someone, which must have been him. Have I mentioned him before? A frightful fellow — Billie retains even yet a sallow trace of the black eye she had when I first met her. There were more raised voices and again she had to cover the receiver, but in the end, in a hurried whisper, she said that she would come, and hung up.

I tiptoed out to the hall again, listening still for Lydia, and took my hat and coat and gloves and slipped out of the house again as nimble and soft of step as a cat-burglar. In my heart I have always fancied myself a bit of a cad.

It occurs to me that of all the women I have known in my life I know Lydia the least. This is a thought to stop me in my tracks. Can it be the case? Can I have lived all these years with an enigma? — an enigma of my making? Perhaps it is only that, having been for so long in such close proximity to her, I feel I should know her to an extent that is not to be achieved, not by us, that is, not by human beings. Or is it just that I can no longer see her properly, in a proper perspective? Or that we have walked so far together that she has become merged with me, as the shadow of a man walking towards a street light gradually merges with him until it is no longer to be seen? I do not know what she thinks. I used to think I knew, but no more. And how should I? I do not know what anyone thinks; I hardly know what I think myself. Yes, that is it, perhaps, that she has become a part of me, a part of what is the greatest of all my enigmas, namely, myself. We do not fight, any more. We used to have seismic fights, violent, hours-long eruptions that would leave us both shaking, I ashen-faced and Lydia mute and outraged, the tears of fury and frustration spilling down her cheeks like runnels of transparent lava. Cass's death conferred, I think, a false weight, a false seriousness upon us and our life together. It was as if our daughter by her going had left us some grand task which was beyond our powers but which we kept on aspiring to fulfil, and the constant effort goaded us repeatedly into rage and conflict. The task I suppose was no more and no less than that of continuing to mourn her, without stint or complaint, as fiercely as we had in the first days after she was gone, as we had for weeks, for months, for years, even. To do otherwise, to weaken, to lay down the burden for the merest moment, would be to lose her with a finality that would have seemed more final than death itself. And thus we went on, scratching and tearing at each other, so the tears would not cease nor our ardour grow cool, until we had exhausted ourselves, or got too old, and called an unwilling truce that nowadays is disturbed by no more than an occasional, brief and half-hearted exchange of small-arms

236

fire. So that, I suppose, is why I think I do not know her, have ceased to know her. Quarrelling, for us, was intimacy.

I had arranged to meet Billie Stryker by the canal. How I love the archaic sunlight of these late-autumn afternoons. Low on the horizon there were scrapings of cloud like bits of crinkled gold leaf and the sky higher up was a layering of bands of clay-white, peach, pale green, all this reflected as a vaguely mottled mauve wash on the motionless and brimming surface of the canal. I still had that agitated sensation, that electrical seething in the blood, that had started up in me at Dawn Devonport's bedside. I had not felt like this for a very long time. It was the kind of feeling I remembered from when I was young and everything was new and the future limitless, a state of fearful and exalted waiting like that into which, all those years ago, Mrs. Gray had stepped, crooning distractedly under her breath and twisting that recalcitrant curl behind her ear. What was it today that had tapped me on the shoulder with its tuning fork? Was it the past, again, or the future?

Billie Stryker was in her accustomed rig-out of jeans and worn running shoes, the lace of one undone and straggling, and a short, shiny black leather jacket over a too-small white vest that was moulded like a second skin around her bosom and over the two puffy pillows of flesh into which her stomach above her belt was bisected by a deep, median wrinkle. Her hair, since I had seen her a couple of days before, had been dyed orange and violently cropped, by her own hand, I judged, and bristled in stubby clumps as if her skull were studded all over with tufted darts. She seems to derive a vengeful satisfaction from cultivating her unloveliness, pampering and primping it as another would her beauty. It is sad how she mistreats herself; I should have thought her horrible husband could be depended on to do that for her effectively enough. Over these past weeks of plodding and repetitious make-believe I have come to appreciate her for her stolid practicality, her doggedness and disenchanted resolve.

That husband. I find him a peculiarly un-appetising specimen. He is tall and thin, with many concavities, as if slices had been taken off him at flanks, stomach, chest; he has a pin-head and a mouthful of rotting teeth; his grin is more like a snarl. When he looks about him, the things his eye falls on seem to quail under his tainting glance. Early on he took to hanging about the set, so that Toby Taggart, soft-hearted as ever, felt compelled to find odd jobs for him. I would have had him seen off the premises, with threats, if necessary. I do not know what he does for a living otherwise — Billie is evasive on this as on so much else — but he gives an impression of constant busyness, of significant doings about to begin, of grand projects that at a word from him will get under way. I am sceptical. I think he lives on his wits, or on Billie's, which are bound to be sharper. He gets himself up like a workman, in bleached-out dungarees and collarless shirts and boots with rubber soles an inch thick; also he keeps himself very dusty, even his hair, and when he sits down he does so at a weary sprawl, an ankle crossed on a narrow knee and an arm hooked over the back of his chair, as if he had finished a punishingly long stint of work and had stopped now briefly for a well-earned break. I confess I am a little afraid of him. He surely hit poor Billie and I can easily see him swinging a fist at me. Why does she stay with him? Futile question. Why does anyone do anything.

I said to Billie now that I wanted her to track down Mrs. Gray for me. I said I did not doubt she would succeed. Nor do I. A pair of swans approached upon the water, a pen and her mate, surely, for are they not a monogamous species? We stopped to watch them as they came. Swans in their outland-ish and grubby gorgeousness always seem to me to be keeping up a nonchalant front behind which really they are cowering in a torment of self-consciousness and doubt. These two were skilled dissemblers, and gave us a speculative stare, saw our hands were empty of crusts, and sailed onwards with a show of cool disdain.

Billie, tactful as ever, did not enquire as to why I should be suddenly so eager to trace this woman from my past. It is hard to guess what Billie's opinion is on any matter. To talk to her is like dropping stones into a deep well; the response that comes back is long-delayed and muted. She has the wari-ness of a person much put-upon and men-aced — that husband again — and before speaking seems to turn over every word carefully and examine it from all sides, test-ing its potential to displease and provoke. But she must have wondered. I told her Mrs. Gray would be old by now or possibly no longer living. I said only that she had been my best friend's mother and that I had not seen her or heard anything of her for nigh-on half a century. What I did not say, what I emphatically did not say, was why I

240

wished to find her again. And why did I? — why do I? Nostalgia? Whim? Because I am getting old and the past has begun to seem more vivid than the present? No, something more urgent is driving me, though I do not know what it is. I imagine Billie told herself that my age allowed of quixotic self-indulgence, and that if I was prepared to pay her good money to trace some old biddy from my young days she would be a fool herself to question my foolishness. Did she guess my doings with Mrs. Gray involved what I had heard her at other times refer to scornfully as hanky-panky? Perhaps she did, and was embarrassed for me, fond old codger that I must appear in her eyes, and that I appear, indeed, in my own. What would she have thought if she knew what thoughts I was thinking about that stricken girl lying in her hospital bed as we spoke? Hanky-panky, indeed.

We walked on. Moorhens now, a hissing stand of reeds, and still those little gold clouds.

Our daughter's death was made so much the worse for her mother and me by being, to us, a mystery, complete and sealed; to us, though not, I hope, to her. I do not say we were surprised. How could we have been surprised, given the chaotic state of Cass's inner life? In the months before she died, when she was abroad, an image of her had been appearing to me, a sort of ghost-in-waiting, in daytime dreams that were not dreams. *You knew what she was going to do!* Lydia had cried at me when Cass was dead. *You knew and never said!* Did I know, and should I have been able to foresee what she intended, haunted by her living presence as I was? Was it that, in those ghostly visitations, she was sending me somehow a warning signal from the future? Was Lydia right, could I have done something to save her? These questions prey upon me, yet I fear not as heavily as surely they should; ten years of unrelenting interrogation would wear down even the stubbornest devotee of an absconded spirit. And I am tired, so tired.

What was I saying?

Cass's presence in Liguria

Cass's presence in Liguria was the first link in the mysterious chain that dragged her to her death on those bleak rocks at Portovenere. What or who was in Liguria for her? In search of an answer, a clue to an answer, I used to pore for hours over her papers, creased and blotted wads of foolscap sheets scratched all over in her minuscule hand — I have them somewhere still — that she left behind her in the room in that foul

242

little hotel in Portovenere that I shall never forget, at the top of the cobbled street from where we could see the ugly tower of the church of San Pietro, the very height she had flung herself from. I wanted to believe that what looked like the frantic scribblings of a mind at its last extremity were really an elaborately encoded message meant for me, and for me alone. And there were places indeed where she seemed to be addressing me directly. In the end, however, wish as I might, I had to accept that it was not me she was speaking to but someone other, my surrogate, perhaps, shadowy and elusive. For there was another presence detectable in those pages, or better say a palpable absence, the shade of a shade, whom she addressed only and always under the name of Svidrigailov.

Flung herself. Why do I say she *flung* herself from that place? Perhaps she let herself drop as lightly as a feather. Perhaps she seemed to herself to be drifting down to death.

"She was pregnant, my daughter, when she died," I said.

Billie took this without comment, and only frowned, protruding a pink and shiny lower lip. These frowns of hers give her the look of a vexed cherub.

243

The sky was fading and a chilly dusk was coming on, and I suggested we should stop at a pub to have a drink. This was unusual, for me — I could not remember the last time I had been inside a public house. We went to a place on a corner by one of the canal bridges. Brown walls, stained carpet, a huge television set above the bar with the sound turned down and sportsmen in garish jerseys sprinting and shoving and signalling in relentless dumbshow. There were the usual afternoon men with their pints and racing papers, two or three spivvish young fellows in suits, and the inevitable pair of gaffers sitting opposite each other at a tiny table, smeared whiskey glasses at hand, and sunk in an immemorial silence. Billie looked about with sour disdain. She has a certain hauteur, I have noticed it before. She is, I think, something of a puritan, and secretly considers herself a cut above the rest of us, an undercover agent who knows all our secrets and is privy to our tawdriest sins. She has been a researcher for too long. Her tipple, it turned out, is a splash of gin drowned in a big glass of orange crush and further neutralised by a hefty shovelful of groaning ice cubes. I began to tell her, nursing a thimbleful of tepid port, which I am sure she thought a sissy's drink, how Billy

Gray and I in time discovered that we preferred gin to his father's whiskey. It was as well, since the bottle we had been winkling out of the cocktail cabinet had over the weeks become so watered down that the whiskey was almost colourless. Gin, quicksilver and demure, now seemed to us altogether more sophisticated and dangerous than whiskey's rough gold. In the immediate aftermath of my first frolic in the laundry room with Mrs. Gray, I had been in deep dread of encountering Billy, thinking he was the one, more than my mother, more than his sister, even, who would detect straight off the scarlet sign of guilt that must be blazoned on my brow. But of course he noticed nothing. Yet when he came and leaned down to pour another inch of gin into my glass and I saw the pale patch on the crown of his head the size of a sixpence where his hair whorled, a sense of uncanniness swept over me so that I almost shivered, and I shrank back from him, and held my breath for fear of catching his smell and recognising in it a trace of his mother's. I tried not to look into the brown depths of those eyes, or dwell on those unnervingly moist pink lips. I felt that suddenly I did not know him, or, worse, that through knowing his mother, in all senses of the word, ancient and modern, I knew him also and all too intimately. So I sat there on his sofa in front of the flickering telly and gulped my gin and squirmed in secret and exquisite shame.

I told Billie Stryker that I would be going away for a time. To this also she offered no response. She really is an incommunicative young woman. Is there something I am missing? There usually is. I said that when I went I would be taking Dawn Devonport with me. I said I was counting on her to break the news of this to Toby Taggart. Neither of his leads would be available for work for a week, at least. At this, Billie smiled. She likes a bit of trouble, does Billie, a bit of strife. I imagine it makes her feel less isolated in her own domestic disorders. She asked where it was I was going. Italy, I told her. Ah, Italy, she said, as if it were her second home.

A trip to Italy, as it happens, was prominent on the list of things that Mrs. Gray had longed for and felt she should have by right. Her dream was to set out from one of those fancy Riviera towns, Nice or Cannes or somesuch, and motor along the coast all the way down to Rome to see the Vatican, and have an audience with the Pope, and sit on the Spanish Steps, and throw coins in the Trevi Fountain. She also desired a mink coat to wear to Mass on Sundays, a smart new car to replace the battered old station wagon — "that jalopy!" — and a red-brick house with a bay window on the Avenue de Picardy in the posher end of town. Her social ambitions were high. She wished her husband were something more than a lowly optician — he had wanted to be a proper doctor but his family had been unable, or unwilling, to pay the college fees — and she was determined that Billy and his sister would *do well.* Doing well was her aim in everything, giving the neighbours one in the eye, making the town — "this dump!" — sit up and take notice. She liked to daydream aloud, as we lay in each other's arms on the floor of our tumbledown love nest in the woods. What an imagination she had! And while she was elaborating these fantasies of bowling along that azure coast in an open sports car swathed in furs with her husband the famous brain surgeon at her side, I would divert myself by pinching her breasts to make the nipples go fat and hard — and these, mark you, were the paps that had given my friend Billy suck! — or running my lips along that pinkly inflamed, serrated track the elastic of her half-slip had imprinted on her tender tummy. She dreamed of a life of romance, and what she got was me, a boy with blackheads and bad teeth and, as she often laughingly lamented, only one thing on his mind.

She never seemed so young as when she was weaving these happy fantasies of success and moneyed opulence. It is strange to think that I was less than half as young as she while she was not much more than half the age that I am now. The mechanism of my memory has difficulty grappling with these disparities, yet at the time, after the initial shock of that rainy afternoon in the laundry room, I began to take it all blandly for granted, her age, my youth, the unlikeliness of our love, everything. To me, at fifteen, the most implausible thing had only to take place more than once to become the norm. The real puzzle is what she thought and felt. I cannot recall her ever acknowledging, aloud, the disproportion and incongruity of our — I still do not know quite what to call it; our love affair, I suppose I must say, though it rings falsely to my ear. People in the stories in the magazines that Mrs. Gray read, or characters in the films that she went to see on Friday nights, they had affairs; for me, as for her, what we did together was far more simple, far more elemental, far more — if I may employ such a word in this context — childish, than the adulterous doings of adults. Perhaps that is what she accomplished for herself through me, a return to childhood, not the childhood of dolls and hair ribbons, however, but of swollen excitements, of sweaty fumblings and happy dirt. For my goodness but she could be on occasion a naughty girl.

There was a river in our wood, a secret, brown, meandering stream that seemed to have got diverted into this bosky glade on the way to somewhere far more important. In those days I had a deep regard for water, a reverence, even, and would still if it were not so grimly associated in my mind with Cass's death. Water is one of those things that are everywhere present — air, the sky, light and darkness, these are others — that nonetheless strike me as uncanny. Mrs. Gray and I were very fond of our little river, stream, brook, freshet, whatever to call it. At a particular spot it made a loop around a clump of alder trees, I think they were alders. The water was deep there and moved so slowly it might not have been moving at all were it not for the small telltale eddies that formed on the surface, formed and dissolved and formed again. There were trout sometimes, speckled wraiths barely to be made out near the bottom, poised in stillness against the current yet so quick when they took fright that they would give a quiver and seem to vanish on the spot. We spent happy hours together there, my love and I, in the balmiest days of that summer, in the cool shadows under those stunted and excitable trees. Mrs. Gray liked to wade in the water, the depths of which were the same glossy shade of brown as her eyes. Venturing out gingerly from the bank, watching for sharp stones on the bottom, with that self-forgetting smile and her skirts lifted to her hips, she was Rembrandt's Saskia, sunk to the shins in her own world of umber and gold. One day it was so hot that she took her dress off altogether, pulled it over her head and threw it back for me to catch. She had been wearing nothing underneath, and advanced now naked out into the middle of the stream and stood there, up to her waist, her arms outstretched on either side, happily patting the surface of the water with her palms and humming — did I mention that she was an inveterate hummer, even though she had not a note of music in her head? The sun through the alder leaves scattered her about with flickering gold coins — my Danaë! — and the hollows of her shoulders and the undersides of her breasts glimmered with reflected, swaying lights. Impelled by the madness of the moment — what if some rambler from the town had chanced upon the scene? — I waded in after her, in my khaki shorts and shirt. She watched me coming towards her, my elbows sawing and neck thrust out, and gave me that look from under her eyelashes that I liked to imagine she reserved for me alone, her chin tucked in and her lips compressed in a thin upturned impish arc, and I dived, down into the brown water, my shorts suddenly a sodden weight and my shirt clutching with breathtaking coldness at my chest, and managed to flip over on to my back — at that age, my God, I was as agile as one of those speckled trout! — and reached my hands around her bottom and pulled her to me and got my face between her thighs that at first resisted and then went shudderingly slack, and pressed my fish-mouth to her nether lips that were chill and oysterish on the outside and hot within, and a cold shock of water went up my nose and gave me an instant ache between my eyes, and I had to let go of her and flounder to the surface, flailing and gasping, but triumphant, too — oh, yes, every advantage I got of her represented a nasty, miniature victory for my self-esteem and sense of lordship over her. Once out of the water we scampered back to Cotter's place, I with her dress in my arms and she naked still, a birch-pale dryad flickering ahead of me through the sunlight and shadows of the wood. I can still feel, as I felt when presently we threw ourselves panting on to our makeshift bed, the rough texture of her goosefleshed arms, and can smell, too, the excitingly stale tang of river-water on her skin, and taste the lingering, brackish chill between her thighs.

Ah, days of play, days of — dare I say it? — days of innocence.

"Did she tell you why she did it?" Billie asked.

She was perched before me on a high wooden stool with her tubular thighs in those tight jeans splayed and her glass held in both hands between her knees. I was confused for a moment, my mind having been off doing bold things with Mrs. Gray, and thought she was referring to Cass. No, I said, no, of course not, I had no inkling why she did it, how could I? She gave me one of her balefully deprecating looks — she has a way of making her eyes seem to bulge that is distinctly unnerving — and I realised it was Dawn Devonport she meant. To cover up for my mistake I looked away, frowning, and fiddled with my glass of port. I said, sounding rather prim to my own ears, that I was sure it had been a mistake and that Dawn Devonport had not meant to do it. Billie, seeming to lose interest, only gave a grunt and glanced idly about the bar. I studied her puffy profile, and as I did so I had briefly a vertiginous sensation, as if I had been brought up short at the very lip of a high sheer cliff. It is a feeling I have sometimes when I look, I mean really look, at other people, which I do not often do, which no one does, often, I expect. It is linked in a mysterious way with the feeling that used to come over me occasionally on stage, the feeling of falling somehow into the character I was playing, literally falling, as one might trip and pitch forwards on one's face, and losing all sense of my other, unacting, self.

The statisticians tell us there is no such thing as coincidence, and I must accept they know what they are talking about. If I were to believe that a certain confluence of events was a special and unique phenomenon outside the ordinary flow of happenstance I would have to accept, as I do not, that there is a transcendent process at work above, or behind, or within, commonplace reality. And yet I ask myself, why not? Why should I not allow of a secret and sly arranger of seemingly chance events? Axel Vander was in Portovenere when my daughter died. This fact, and I take it as a fact, stands before me huge and immovable, like a tree, with all its roots hidden deep in darkness. Why was she there, and why was he?

Svidrigailov.

I intended to go, I said now, to Portovenere, and that although I intended taking Dawn Devonport with me, she did not know it yet. I think that was the first time ever I heard Billie Stryker laugh out loud.

In former times the only access to those little towns was from the sea, for the hinterland along that coast is formed largely of a chain of mountains the flanks of which plunge at a sharp angle into the bay. Now there is a narrow railway track cut through the rock that runs under many tunnels and affords abrupt, dizzying vistas of steep landscapes and inlets where the sea gleams dully like stippled steel. In winter the light has a bruised quality, and there is salt in the air and the smell of sea-wrack and of diesel fumes from the fishing boats that crowd the tiny harbours. The car that I had hired turned out to be a surly and recalcitrant beast and gave me much trouble and more than one fright on the road as we travelled eastwards from Genoa. Or perhaps the fault was mine, for I was in a state of some agitation — I am not a good traveller, being nervous of foreign parts and a poor linguist

255

besides. As we drove I thought of Mrs. Gray and how she would have envied us, down here on this blue coast. At Chiavari we abandoned the car and took the train. I had difficulty with the bags. The train was smelly and the seats were hard. As we chugged along eastwards a rain storm swept down from the mountains and lashed at the carriage windows. Dawn Devonport watched the downpour and spoke out of the depths of the upturned big collar of her coat. "So much," she said, "for the sunny south."

From the moment when we stepped on to foreign soil she had been recognised everywhere, despite the headscarf and the enormous sunglasses that she wore; or perhaps it was because of them, they being the unmistakable disguise of a troubled star on the run. This prominence was something I had not anticipated, and although I was a largely disregarded presence at her side or, more often, in her wake, I still felt unnervingly exposed, a chameleon that has lost its adaptive powers. We were due that day at Lerici, where I had booked hotel rooms for us, but she had insisted on seeing the Cinque Terre first, and so here we were, uncertainly astray on this cheerless winter afternoon.

Dawn Devonport was not as she had

been. She was prone to flashes of irritation, and fussed constantly with things, her handbag, her sunglasses, the buttons of her coat, and I had a vivid and unsettling glimpse of what she would be when she was old. She was smoking heavily, too. And she had a new smell, faint yet definite behind the masking smells of perfume and face powder, a flat dry odour as of something that had first gone rank and then become parched and shrivelled. Physically she had taken on a new and starker aspect, which she wore with an air of dull forbearance, like a patient who has been suffering for so long that being in pain has become another mode of living. She had grown thinner, which would have seemed hardly possible, and her arms and her exquisite ankles looked frail and alarmingly breakable.

I had expected her to resist coming away with me, but in the end, to my surprise and, I confess, faint unease, she needed no persuading. I simply presented her with an itinerary, which she listened to, frowning a little, turning her head to one side as if she had become hard of hearing. She was sitting up in her hospital bed, in her faded green gown. When I finished speaking she looked away, towards the blue mountains, and sighed, which, in the absence of any other, I decided to take as a sign of acquiescence. The resistance, need I say, came from Toby Taggart and Marcy Meriwether. Oh, the noise they made, Toby's bass rumblings and Marcy shrieking like a parrot down the transatlantic line! All this I ignored, and next day we simply took to the air, Dawn Devonport and I, and flew away.

It was odd, being with her. It was like being with someone who was not entirely present, not entirely conscious. When I was a very little boy I had a doll, I do not know how I came by it; certainly my mother would not have given me a girl's toy to play with. I kept it in the attic, hidden under old clothes at the back of a wooden chest. I called it Meg. The attic, where one day years later I was to glimpse the shade of my dead father loitering irresolutely, was easy of access by way of a narrow set of wooden stairs running up along the wall from the landing. My mother stored onions up there, spread out on the floor; I think it was onions, I seem to remember the smell, or maybe it was apples. The doll, that must once have had abundant hair, was bald now, except for a scant blonde fringe at the back of the skull stuck in a clot of glittery yellow gum. It was jointed at the shoulders and the hips, but its elbows and knees were rigid, the limbs moulded in a bowed shape so that it seemed to be locked in a desperate embrace with something, its twin, perhaps, that was no longer there. When it was laid on its back it would close its eyes, the lids giving a faint sharp click. I doted on this doll, with a dark and troubling intensity. I spent many a torrid hour dressing it in scraps of rag and then lovingly undressing it again. I performed mock operations on it, too, pretending to remove its tonsils, or, more excitingly, its appendix. These procedures were hotly pleasurable, I did not know why. There was something about the doll's lightness, its hollowness — it had a loose bit inside it that rattled around like a dried pea — that made me feel protective and at the same time appealed to a nascent streak of erotic cruelty in me. That was how it was with Dawn Devonport, now. She reminded me of Meg, she of the boneless, brittle limbs and clicking eyelids. Like her, Dawn Devonport, too, seemed hollow and to weigh practically nothing, and to be in my power while yet I was in hers, somehow, alarmingly.

We got down from the train at random at one of the five towns, I cannot remember which. She walked off rapidly along the platform with her head down and her handbag clutched to her side, like one of those thin intense young women of the nineteen-twenties, in her narrow coat with the big collar, in her seamed stockings, her slender shoes. Meanwhile, I was left yet again to struggle behind her lugging our three suitcases, two large ones hers, one small one mine. The rain had stopped but the sky still sagged and was the colour of wetted jute. We ate a late lunch in a deserted restaurant on the harbour. It stood at the head of a slipway where dark waves jostled like so many big metal boxes being tossed about vigorously. Dawn Devonport sat crouched over an untouched plate of seafood with her shoulders hunched, working fretfully at a cigarette that might have been a slip of wood she was whittling with her teeth. I spoke to her, asking her random things — these silences of hers I found unnerving — but she rarely bothered to answer. Already this venture I had embarked on with her seemed more improbable even than the extravaganza of light and shadow that her suicide attempt and our subsequent flight had so severely disrupted and, for all I knew, might have brought to an unfinished, unfinishable and ignominious end. What an ill-assorted pair we must have looked, the obscurely afflicted, stark-faced girl with her scarf and dark glasses, and the grizzled, ageing man sunk in glum unease, sitting there silent in that ill-lit low place above a winter sea, our suitcases leaning against each other in the glass vestibule, waiting for us like a trio of large, obedient and patiently uncomprehending hounds.

When Lydia heard of my plan to go off with Dawn Devonport, she had laughed and given me a disbelieving look, head back and one eyebrow arched, the selfsame look that Cass used to turn on me when I had said something she considered silly or mad. Was I serious, my wife asked. A girl, again, at my age? I replied stiffly that it was not like that, not like that at all, that the trip was intended to be purely therapeutic and was a charitable act on my part. Saying this, I sounded even to myself like one of Bernard Shaw's more pompous and tendentious leading asses. Lydia sighed and shook her head. How could I, she asked quietly, as if there were someone who might overhear, how could I take anyone, least of all Dawn Devonport, to that place, of all places in the world? To this I had no reply. It was as if she were accusing me of besmirching Cass's memory, and I was shocked, for this, you must believe me, was something I had not considered. I said she was welcome to come with us but that only seemed to make things worse, and there was a very long silence, the air vibrating between us, and slowly she lowered her head, her brow darkening ominously, and I felt like a very tiny toreador facing a frighteningly cold and calculating bull. Yet she packed my suitcase for me, just as she used to do in the days when I still went on tour. The task done, she headed off at a haughty slouch to the kitchen. At the door she stopped and turned to me. "You won't bring her back, you know," she said, "not like this." I knew she was not speaking of Dawn Devonport. Her curtain line delivered — not for nothing has she lived all these years with an actor — she went into her lair and shut the door behind her with a thud. Yet I had the conviction, greatly to my consternation, that she found the whole thing more than anything else absurd.

I had not told Dawn Devonport about Cass — that is, I had not told her that Portovenere was where my daughter died. I had proposed Liguria to her as if I had hit on it by chance, a place in the south where it would be quiet, a place of recuperation, uncrowded and tranquil at this time of year. I suppose it did not matter much to Dawn Devonport where she went, where she was taken. She came away with me in a stupor, as if she were a sleepy child whom I was leading by the arm.

Abruptly now, there in the restaurant, she spoke, making me jump. "I wish you'd call me Stella," she said in an angry undertone, through gritted teeth. "It's my name, you know. Stella Stebbings." Why was she so irritated all of a sudden? Had I been in a sunnier mood myself I might have taken it as a sign in her of a return to life and vigour. She ground out her cigarette in the plastic ashtray on the table. "You don't know the first thing about me, do you?" she said. I watched through the window the rollicking waves and, irritated, enquired in a tone of patient and faintly offended mildness what she considered the first thing about her to be. "My name," she snapped. "You could start by learning that. Stella Stebbings. Say it." I said it, turning my gaze from the sea and giving her a steady look. All this, the opening skirmishes of a quarrel with a woman, was lamentably familiar, like something known by heart that I had forgotten I knew and that now was coming balefully back, like a noisy play I had played in and that had flopped. She glared at me narrowly with what seemed a venomous contempt, then all at once leaned back in her chair and shrugged one shoulder, as indifferent now as a moment ago she had been furious.

"You see?" she said with weary disgust. "I don't know why I bothered trying to do away with myself in the first place. I'm hardly here at all, not even a proper name."

Our waiter, an absurdly handsome fellow with the usual aquiline profile and thick black hair slicked back from his forehead, was at the kitchen door at the rear, where the chef had put out his head — chefs in their smeared bibs always look to me like struck-off surgeons — and now they both came forwards, the chef shy and hesitant in the wake of his undauntably cocky colleague. I knew what they were about, having witnessed more or less the same ritual on countless occasions since we had stepped on to Italian soil. They arrived at our table — by now we were the only customers left in the place — and Mario the waiter with a flourish introduced Fabio the chef. Fabio was roly-poly and middle-aged, and had sandy hair, unusual in this land of swarth Lotharios. He was after an autograph, of course. I do not think I had ever before seen an Italian blushing. I waited with interest for Dawn Devonport's response — not a minute ago she had seemed ready to hit me with her handbag — but of course she is a professional to the tip of her little silver pen, which she produced now and scribbled on

the menu that red-faced Fabio had proffered, and handed it back to him with that
slow-motion smile she reserves for close-up
encounters with her fans. I managed to
glimpse the signature, with its two big,
looped, opulent Ds like recumbent eyelids.
She saw me seeing, and granted me a wry
small smile in acknowledgement. Stella
Stebbings, indeed. The chef rolled away
happily, the precious menu pressed to his
soiled front, while smirking Mario struck an
attitude and enquired of the diva if she
would care perhaps for *caffè,* while point-
edly ignoring me. I suppose they all think I
am her manager, or her agent; I doubt they
take me for anything more.

Since it seems that nothing in creation is
ever destroyed, only disassembled and
dispersed, might not the same be true of
individual consciousness? Where when we
die does it go to, all that we have been?
When I think of those whom I have loved
and lost I am as one wandering among eye-
less statues in a garden at nightfall. The air
about me is murmurous with absences. I
am thinking of Mrs. Gray's moist brown
eyes flecked with tiny splinters of gold.
When we made love they would turn from
amber through umber to a turbid shade of
bronze. "If we had music," she used to say

at Cotter's place, "if we had music we could dance." She sang, herself, all the time, all out of tune, "The Merry Widow Waltz," "The Man Who Broke the Bank at Monte Carlo," "Roses Are Blooming in Picardy," and something about a skylark, skylark, that she did not know the words of and could only hum, tunelessly off-key. These things that were between us, these and a myriad others, a myriad myriad, these remain of her, but what will become of them when I am gone, I who am their repository and sole preserver?

"I saw something, when I was dead," Dawn Devonport said. She had her elbows on the table and was leaning forwards again at a crouch, dabbling with a fingertip among the cold ashes in the ashtray. She was frowning, and did not look at me. Outside the window the afternoon had turned to the colour of ash. "I was technically dead for nearly a minute, so they told me — did you know that?" she said. "And I saw something. I suppose I imagined it, though I don't know how I could be dead and imagine something."

Perhaps, I said, it was before she was dead, or afterwards, that she had undergone this experience.

She nodded, still frowning, not listening.

266

"It wasn't like a dream," she said. "It wasn't like anything. Does that make sense, something that wasn't like anything? But that was what it was — I saw something like nothing." She examined the ashy tip of her finger and then looked at me with curious dispassion. "I'm frightened," she said, quite calm and matter-of-fact. "I wasn't before but now I am. That's strange, isn't it?"

As we made our exit the waiter and the chef were at the door, bowing and grinning. Fabio the chef winked at me with a cheery, almost a fraternal, disdain.

It was late when we arrived at Lerici, suffering still from the sour wine at lunch and then the bad air and the clamour of the train. It had begun to snow, and the sea beyond the low wall of the promenade was a darkling tumult. I tried to make out the lights of Portovenere across the bay but could not for those great flocks of whiteness hosting haphazard in the brumous air. The lamp-lit town straggled ahead of us up a hillside towards the brute bulk of the *castello*. In the snow-muffled silence the winding, narrow streets had a closed and sombre aspect. There was the sense of everything holding its breath in amazement before the spectacle of this relentless, ghostly falling.

267

The Hotel le Logge was wedged between a little grocery shop and a squat, stuccoed church. The shop was still open, despite the lateness of the hour, a startling, brightly lit windowless box with crowded shelves stacked all the way to the ceiling and at the front a big slanted counter on which were displayed a profusion of damply glistening vegetables and polished fruits. There were crates of mushrooms, cream and tan, and shameless tomatoes, ranks of tufted leeks as thick as my wrist, zucchini the colour of burnished palm leaves, open burlap bags of apples, oranges, Amalfitan lemons. Stepping from the taxi, we stopped and looked with incomprehension and a kind of dismay upon this crowding and unseasonal abundance.

The hotel was old and shabby and, inside, appeared to be of an all-over shade of brown — the carpet had the look of monkey-fur. Along with the usual whiff of drains — it came in wafts, at a fixed interval, as if rising out of ancient, rotting lungs — there was another smell, drily wistful, the smell, it might be, of last summer's sunshine trapped in corners and in crevices and gone to must. As we entered there was much bowing and beaming before the brisk and imperious advance of Dawn Devonport — public attention always bucks her up, as which of us, in our business, does it not? The high fur collar of her coat made her already thinned face seem thinner and smaller still; the headscarf she had folded in and tucked close to her skull in the style of what's-her-name in *Sunset Boulevard.* How she managed to make her way through the lobby's crepuscular gloom with those sunglasses on I do not know — they are unsettlingly suggestive of an insect's evilly gleaming, prismatic eyes — but she crossed to the desk ahead of me at a rapid, crisply clicking pace and plonked her handbag down beside the nippled brass bell and took up a sideways pose, presenting her magnificent profile to the already undone fellow behind the counter in his jacket of rusty jet and his frayed white shirt. I wonder if these seemingly effortless effects that she pulls off have to be calculated anew each time, or are they finished and perfected by now, a part of her repertoire, her armoury? You must understand, I felt permanently as abject before the spectacle of her splendour as did the poor chap behind the desk — this absurdity, O heart, O troubled heart.

Then the rattly lift, the vermiform corridors, the crunch of the key in the lock and a stale sigh of air released out of the shadowed room. The muttering porter with his stooped back went ahead and placed the bags just so at the foot of the big square bed that had a hollow in the middle of it and looked as if generations of porters, this one's predecessors, had been born in it. How accusingly a suitcase once set down can seem to look at one. I could hear Dawn Devonport next door making many mysterious small noises, clinks and knocks and softly suggestive rustlings as she unpacked her bags. Then there came that moment of mild panic when the clothes had been hung, the shoes stowed, the shaving things set out on the bathroom's marble shelf, where someone's forgotten cigarette had left a burned stain, a black smear with amber edges. Down in the street a car swished past, and the flare of its head-lamps poked a pencil-ray of yellow light through a chink in the curtains that probed the room from one side to the other before being swiftly withdrawn. Upstairs a lavatory gulped and swallowed, and in response the drain in the bathroom here, getting into the spirit, made a deep-throated sound that might have been a gurgle of lewd laughter.

Downstairs, a humming quiet reigned. I paced on soundless feet over the carpet's coarse pelt. The restaurant was closed;

270

dimly through the glass I saw the many chairs standing on their tables, as if they had leaped up there in fright of something on the floor. The fellow at the desk mentioned the possibility of room service, though sounding doubtful. Fosco, he was called, so I was told by a tag on his lapel, Ercole Fosco. This name seemed a portent, though I could not say of what. Ercole Fosco. He was the night manager. I liked the look of him. Middle-aged, greying at the temples, heavy-jowled and somewhat sallow in complexion — Albert Einstein in his pre-iconic middle years. His soft brown eyes reminded me a little of Mrs. Gray's. His manner was touched with melancholy, though it was reassuring, too; he reminded me of one of those unmarried uncles who used to appear with gifts at Christmas time when I was a child. I dawdled at the desk, trying to find something to talk to him about, but could think of nothing. He smiled apologetically and made a little fist — what small hands he had — and put it to his mouth and coughed into it, those soft eyes sagging at the outer corners. I could see I was making him nervous, and wondered why. I thought him perhaps not a native of these parts, for he had a northern look — Turin, perhaps, capital of magic, or

271

Milan, or Bergamo, or even somewhere farther off, beyond the Alps. He asked, on a weary note, mechanically, if my room was to my satisfaction. I told him it was. "And the *signora,* she is satisfied?" I said yes, yes, the *signora* also was satisfied. We were both very satisfied, very happy. He made a little bow of acknowledgement, bobbing to one side so that it seemed he was not so much bowing as shrugging. I wondered idly if my manner and movements seemed as foreign to him as his seemed to me.

I went and stood inside the front door and looked out through the glass. It was deeply dark out there, in the gap between two street-lights, and the snow appeared almost black, falling rapidly straight down in big wet flakes, in a softly murmurous silence. Perhaps the ferries to Portovenere would not be plying at this time of year, in this weather — that was a subject I could have talked about to Ercole the night manager — perhaps I would have to go by road, back through La Spezia and out by the coast. It was a long way, and on the road there were many twists and bends above ragged cliffs. What a thing it would be for Lydia to hear of, her husband dashed to pieces against rocks on the way to where her daughter had died in similar fashion, in other circumstances.

When I moved, somehow my reflection in the glass did not move with me. Then my eyes adjusted and I saw that it was not my reflection I was seeing, but that there was someone out there, facing me. Where had he appeared from, how had he come to be there? It was as if he had materialised on the instant. He was not wearing an overcoat, and had no hat, or umbrella. I could not quite make out his features. I stood back and pulled the door open for him, it made a sucking sound, and the night bounded in like an animal, agile and eager, with cold air trapped in its fur. The man entered. There was snow on his shoulders, and he stamped his feet on the carpet, first one, then the other, three times each. He gave me a keen, a measuring, look. He was a young man, with a high, domed forehead. Or perhaps, I thought on second glance, perhaps he was not young, for his neatly trimmed beard was grizzled and there were fine wrinkles at the outer corners of his eyes. He wore spectacles with thin frames and oval-shaped lenses, which lent him a vaguely scholarly appearance. We stood there for a moment, facing each other — confronting each other, I was going to say — just as we had a moment

273

ago but with no glass between us now. His expression was one of scepticism tempered with humour. "Cold," he said, fitting his lips around the word in a wine-taster's pout. He spoke as if there were some small hindrance in his mouth, a seed or stone, that he must keep manoeuvring his tongue around. Had I already seen him somewhere? I seemed to know him, but how could I?

In the days when I was still working, in the theatre, I mean, for the duration of a run I did not dream. That is, I must have, since we are told the mind cannot be idle, even in sleep, but if I did dream I forgot what I dreamed about. Strutting and prating on stage five nights a week and twice on Saturdays must have fulfilled whatever the function is that dreaming otherwise performs for us. When I retired, though, my nights turned to riot, and more often than not I would wake of a morning in a sweaty tangle, panting and exhausted, having endured long and torturous passages through a chamber of horrors, or a tunnel of love, or sometimes both combined, tumbling helplessly headlong through all manner of grotesque calamities, and with no trousers on, as often as not, my shirttails flapping and my backside on show. Nowadays, ironically, one of my most frequent nightmares — those ungovernable steeds — carries me irresistibly back on stage and dumps me again at the footlights. I am playing in some grand drama or impossibly intricate comedy, and I dry in the middle of a lengthy speech. This did happen to me, famously, in real life, I mean waking life — I was playing Kleist's Amphitryon — and it brought my theatrical career to an abrupt and inglorious end. It was odd, that lapse, for I had a remarkable memory, in my prime, it may even have been what is called a photographic memory. My method of learning off lines was to fix the text itself, I mean the very pages, as a series of images in my head, to be read and recited from. The terror of this particular dream, though, is that on the pages I have memorised, the text, so black and sharp one moment, the next begins to decay and crumble before my mind's, my sleeping mind's, desperately squinting eye. At first I am not greatly worried, convinced that I will be able to recall sufficient portions of the speech to bluff my way through it, or that if worse comes to worst I can improvise the entire thing. However, the audience soon realises that something is going badly awry, while the rest of the actors on stage with me — there is a milling crowd of them — suddenly finding a corpse in their midst, begin to fidget and to throw big-eyed looks at each other. What is to be done? I try to get round the audience, to win it over, by adopting a cravenly ingratiating manner, smiling and lisping, shrugging my shoulders and mopping my brow, frowning at my feet, peering up into the flies, all the while inching sideways towards the blessed shelter of the wings. A horrible comedy attaches to all this, a comedy that is all the more distressing in that it has nothing to do with stage business. Indeed, this is the very essence of the nightmare, that all theatrical pretence has been stripped away, and with it all protection. The scraps of costume that cling to me have become transparent, or as good as, and I am there, bare and exposed, in front of me a packed and increasingly restive house and at my back a cast that would happily kill me if it could and make of me a real corpse. The first catcalls are rising as I start awake, and find myself huddled around myself piteously in the middle of a disordered, hot and sweat-soaked bed.

There was someone at the door. There was someone pounding at the door. I did not know where I was, and lay palpitant and motionless like a hunted criminal cowering in a ditch. I was on my side, one arm in a cramp under me and the other thrown up as if to shield myself from assault. At the window the gauze curtains were yellowly aglow, and behind them there was a rapid and general downward undulation, which I could not understand or identify, until I remembered the snow. Whoever was at the door had stopped hammering, and instead seemed to be pressed against it, making a low keening sound that buzzed against the wood. I got up from the bed. The room was cold and yet I was sweating, and had to step through a miasma of my own fetor. At the door I hesitated, a hand on the knob. I had not switched on a lamp and the only illumination in the room was provided by the sulphurous glow of the street-light through the curtains behind me. I opened the door. At first I thought that someone in the hall had hurled an item of flimsy clothing at me, for the impression I had was the chill, shivery slither of something silken, with no one, it seemed, inside it. Then Dawn Devonport's fingers were scrabbling at my wrist, and all at once she materialised within her nightdress, trembling and panting and redolent of night and terror.

She could not say what was the matter. Indeed, she could hardly speak. Was it a dream, I asked, an actor's nightmare, perhaps, like the one her pounding at the door had woken me from? No — she had not been asleep. She had felt some vast thing in the room with her, a knowing, malignant and invisible presence. I led her to the bed and switched on the lamp on the table beside it. She sat with her head bowed and her hair hanging down and her hands resting lax on her thighs with the palms turned up. Her nightdress was made of pearl-grey satin, so fine and thin that I could have counted the links of her spine. I took off my jacket and draped it over her shoulders, and it was only then I noticed that I was still fully dressed — I must have come in and crawled on to the bed and fallen asleep straight off. What was I to do, now, with this shivering creature, who in her night attire seemed more naked than she would have been without it, so that I hardly dared to lay a hand on her? She said I did not have to do anything, only let her stay for a minute, until whatever it was had passed. She did not look up when she spoke, but sat as before, abject and trembling, with her head hanging and her hands turned helplessly up and the exposed pale back of her neck gleaming in the light of the bedside lamp.

How strange a thing it is, the immediate

and intimate proximity of another. Or is it only I who think it strange? Perhaps for others others are not other at all, or at any rate not as they are for me. For me, there are two modes of otherness only, that of the loved one or of the stranger, and the former is hardly other, but more an extension of myself. For this state of affairs I believe I have Mrs. Gray to thank, or blame. She took me into her arms so early on that there was not time for me to learn the laws of proper perspective. She being so close, the rest inevitably were pushed disproportionately farther off. Here I pause a moment to consider. Is this really the case, or am I indulging in that sophistry which from earliest days has bedevilled me? But how can I know if I am? I feel it to be so, that Mrs. Gray was the original and, to an extent, abiding arbiter in my relations with other people, and no effort of thought, however extended or intense, will convince me otherwise. Even if I were to coerce myself into a contrary opinion by the force of thinking, feeling would still feel itself in the right, and be an ever-present, disgruntled rump, ready to assert its claim at every smallest opportunity. Such are the speculations a man will indulge in when in the snowy small hours of the morning many miles from hearth and home he finds himself unexpectedly entertaining in his hotel room a famous and notoriously beautiful film star wearing nothing but her nightie.

I got her to lie down on my unfragrantly sweaty bed — she was so limp I had to put a hand behind her ankles and help her to lift her chilly feet from the floor — and spread the blanket over her. She still had my jacket around her shoulders. It was apparent that she was even yet not entirely awake, and I was reminded of Lydia when she goes flying through the house on her frantic nocturnal quests for our lost daughter; is this the only role there is to be for me now, a comforter of driven and afflicted women? I drew a rush-bottomed chair to the bed and sat down to consider my position, here with this young woman whom I hardly knew, sleepless and harried, on this wintry shore. Yet there was something starting up, too, at the base of my spine, a hot trickle of secret excitement. When I was a boy, after Meg the doll but long before the advent of Mrs. Gray, I used to entertain a recurring fantasy in which I was required to attend to certain cosmetic requirements of a grown-up woman. The woman was never specific but generic, woman in the abstract, I suppose, the celebrated *Ewig-Weibliche*. It was all very innocent, in action, at least, for I was not called upon to do more than administer to this imaginary idol a thorough hair-wash, say, or buff her fingernails, or, in exceptional circumstances, apply her lipstick — this last no easy feat, by the way, as I was to find out later on when I got Mrs. Gray to let me have a go at her gorgeously pulpy, unfixable mouth with one of those sticks of crimson wax that always look to me like a brass cartridge case in which is embedded a surreally soft and glistening scarlet bullet. What I felt now, here in this dingy hotel room, was something of the same mildly tumescent pleasure that I used to enjoy all those years ago when I imagined assisting my phantom lady at her toilet.

"Tell me," my unlooked-for visitor asked now, in an urgent whisper, breathlessly, opening wide those slightly hazed grey eyes of hers, "tell me what happened to your daughter."

She was lying on her back with her hands folded on her breast and her head turned sideways towards me and her cheek crushing the lapel of my jacket underneath her. She has a way, I have come to know it by now, of speaking out suddenly like this, suddenly and softly, when least expected, and it is the suddenness that confers on what she

281

says an oracular quality, so that her words, no matter how mundane or inconsequential they might be, generate an archaic throb. I presume this is a trick she has learned from her years before the camera. A film set does have, it is true, something of the airless intensity of the shrine of a sibyl. There, in that cave of hot light, with the mike at the end of its boom dangling over our heads and the crew fixed on us from the shadows like a circle of hushed suppliants, we might be forgiven for imagining that the lines we recite are the utterances, transmitted through us, of the riddling god himself.

I told her that I did not know what had happened to my daughter, except that she had died. I told her how Cass used to hear voices, and said perhaps they had driven her to it, the voices, as often is the case, so I understand, with those whose minds are damaged and who are led to damage themselves. I was remarkably calm, I might even say detached, as if the circumstances — the anonymous hotel room, the lateness of the hour, this young woman's unwavering, grave regard — had at a stroke, and so simply, released or at any rate paroled me from the toils of the ten-year-long pact of restraint and reticence that I had made with Cass's spirit. Anything might be spoken here, it seemed, any thought might be summoned up and freely expressed. Dawn Devonport waited, her great eyes fixed on me unblinking. There had been, I told her, someone with my daughter. "And so," she said, "you have come back here, to find out who it was."

I frowned at that, and looked away from her. How yellow was the lamplight, how thickly beyond it the shadows thronged. In the window behind the web of curtain the heavy wet flakes fell down, fell down.

Her name for him, I said measuredly, whoever he was, was Svidrigailov. She reached a hand from under the blanket and laid it lightly, briefly, on one of mine, more in restraint, it seemed, than encouragement. Her touch was cool and curiously impersonal; she might have been a nurse testing my temperature, taking my pulse. "She was pregnant, you see," I said.

Had I told her that already? I could not recall.

That was, to my faint surprise, the end of our exchange, for like a child satisfied with only the opening of a goodnight story Dawn Devonport sighed and turned her face away and slept, or pretended to. I waited, not moving for fear of making the chair creak and causing her to have to wake up again.

In the quiet I fancied I could hear the snow falling outside, a faint susurrus that yet bespoke unstinting labour and muffled suffering steadfastly endured. How the world works on, uncomplaining, no matter what, doing what it has to do. I was, I realised, at peace. My mind seemed bathed in a pool of limpid darkness that acted on me like a balm. Not since the far-off days of Father Priest and the confessional had I felt so lightened and — what? — shorn? I looked at the phone on the bedside table and it occurred to me to call Lydia, but it was too late at night, and anyway I did not know what it might be that I would say to her.

I stood up cautiously and eased my jacket from under the sleeping young woman and put the chair away and took up my key and left the room. As I was closing the door, I glanced back at the bed under its low canopy of lamplight, but there was no movement to be seen, and no sound save that of Dawn Devonport steadily breathing. Was she, too, at peace for the moment, for a moment?

The corridor had its hush. I shied from the lift — its narrow double doors of dented stainless steel gave off a sinister shine — and took the stairs instead. They delivered me to an area of the lobby that I did not

284

know, with a lavish palm in a pot and a cigarette-dispensing machine, as big as an upright sarcophagus, with a darkly opalescent shimmer down its side, and for a moment I lost my bearings entirely and experienced a flicker of panic. I turned this way and that, swivelling on a heel, and at last located the reception desk, off beyond that dusty splurge of palm fronds. Ercole the night manager was there, or at least his head was, in profile, for that was all of him I could see, resting so it seemed on the counter, behind a plate of boiled sweets. I thought of Salome's grisly prize on a platter. Those sweets, by the way, are a convention left over from the days of the old currency, when they were offered in place of pocketfuls of negligible change. The things I retain, memory's worthless coin.

I approached the desk. It was high, and Ercole was seated sideways behind it on a low stool, reading one of those old-style comic-books with curiously washed-out photographs instead of drawings. He glanced up at me with a mixture of deference and faint irritation, his droopy eyes looking more disconsolate than ever. I asked if it would be possible for me to have a drink, and he sighed and said of course, of course, if I would please to go to the bar he would come immediately. However, as I was walking away he spoke my name and I stopped and turned. He had put away his comic and risen from the stool, and was leaning forwards slightly, in a confidential attitude, supporting himself on fists set down before him on the desk, one to each side. I went back slowly and — devoutly, I was about to say. Signora Devonport, he asked, was everything all right with her? He spoke softly, with a breathy catch, as if in the aftermath of some ritual of sorrow and lamentation. Those melting eyes seemed to feel my face all over, like the fingertips of a blind seer. I said yes, that everything was well. He smiled, gently disbelieving, as I saw. I did not know what he meant by this question, I did not know what he intended by it. Was it a caution? Had Dawn Devonport been heard banging on my door, had she been spied entering my room in distress? I am always uncertain about hotel rules. In the old days, if a lady were to come at night clandestinely to a gentleman's room, the house detective would have been up like a shot and collared them both, or the lady at least, whom he would have assumed was no lady at all, and driven her out into the snow. After a searching pause Ercole nodded, regretfully, I thought, as if I had disappointed him in some way. So many lies and petty evasions he must deal with, night after night. I tried to think of something to add in mitigation of whatever wrong I was guilty of in his sad brown eyes, but in vain, and instead I turned away. For all that, however, I felt I had been delivered, I do not know how, a benediction of some kind, my forehead crossed with chrism and my spirit salved.

The bar, when I found it, was unexpectedly new and sleek, with dark mirrors and black marble tables and low lamps that seemed to shed not light but a sort of radiant shadow, and gave the place a deceptive cast. I picked my way through this dim, glassy maze and settled myself on a tall stool at the bar. Behind the bar was another mirror, with shelves of bottles in front of it that were lit from below in an eerie fashion. I could barely see myself, reflected in fragments behind the bottles, where I seemed to be ducking and hiding even from myself. I waited for Ercole to come, and drummed my fingers. It was late, after a long day, yet I felt not at all tired or in need of sleep — on the contrary, I was almost painfully alert, the very follicles of my hair simmering. What could be the cause of this state of strange elation, strange expectation? Behind me someone coughed softly and, as it seemed, interrogatively. I turned quickly on the stool and peered into the gloom. A person was seated before a small table close by, calmly regarding me. Why had I not noticed him when I came in? I must have walked straight past that very table. He was leaning back in a low black leather armchair with his legs extended before him and crossed at the ankles and his fingers steepled in front of his chin. At first I did not know him. Then a chance dart of light from the illuminated shelves behind me slid across the lenses of his spectacles and I recognised the man I had met earlier at the front door of the hotel, the man with the snow on his shoulders. *"Buenas noches,"* he said, and made a tiny bow, inclining his head an inch. There was a bottle on the table before him, and a glass — no, two glasses. Had he been expecting someone? Me, apparently, for now he gestured towards the bottle with his steepled fingers and asked if I would care to join him. Well, why not, in this endless night of strange encounters, fateful crossings?

He indicated the armchair opposite him, and I sat down. He was definitely younger than I, as I saw now, yes, a lot younger. I also noticed that the bottle was still full — had he indeed been waiting for me? How had he known I would come? He leaned forwards and, unhurriedly, with deliberation, filled our two glasses almost to the brims. He handed me mine. The heavy red wine looked black on the surface, with purple bubbles jostling around the edge. "It is an Argentinian vintage, I am afraid," he said. He smiled. "Like me."

We raised our glasses in a wordless toast and drank. Wormwood, bitter gall, the taste of ink and luscious rot. We both leaned back, he opening his arms in a curious, flowing, arching movement and shooting his cuffs, and I thought of a priest in the days of the old dispensation turning from the faithful and setting down the chalice and lifting his shoulders and his arms in just that way, under the chasuble's heavy yoke. He introduced himself. His name was Fedrigo Sorrán. He wrote it down for me, in a page of a little black notebook. I thought of far plains, the roaming herds, a hidalgo on a horse.

Ercole came and looked at us, and nodded, and smiled, as if all this had been arranged, and went away again, padding softly on flat feet.

What did we talk about at first, the man from the south and I? He told me he liked the night, preferring it to daytime. "So

289

quiet," he said, smoothing the air before him with a flattened palm. *Sho gwyett*. He said he thought he recognised my name — could that be? I told him I used to be an actor, but that I doubted he would ever have heard of me. "Ah, then, you are perhaps a friend of" — he prodded a finger towards the ceiling and arched his eyebrows and rounded his eyes — "the divine Señorita Devonport."

We drank some more of the bitter wine. And what, I asked, did he do? He considered my question for a moment, smiling faintly, and joined his fingers together again and touched the tips of them lightly to his lips. "I am, let us say," he said, "in mining." This formulation seemed to amuse him. He directed towards the floor a mock-significant glance. "Underground," he whispered.

My mind must have wandered then, sent astray by the wine and the lack of sleep, or perhaps in fact I did sleep, a little, in some way. He had begun by speaking of mines and metals, of gold and diamonds and all precious elements buried deep in the earth, but now, without my knowing how, he had ranged out into the depths of space, and was telling me of quasars and pulsars, of red giants and brown dwarfs and black holes, of heat death and the Hubble constant, of quarks and quirks and multiple infinities. And of dark matter. The universe, according to him, contains a missing mass we cannot see or feel or measure. There is much, much more of it than there is of anything else, and the visible universe, the one that we know, is sparse and puny in comparison. I thought of it, this vast invisible sea of weightless and transparent stuff, present everywhere, undetected, through which we move, unsuspecting swimmers, and which moves through us, a silent, secret essence.

Now he was speaking of the ancient light of galaxies that travels for a million — a billion — a trillion! — miles to reach us. "Even here," he said, "at this table, the light that is the image of my eyes takes time, a tiny time, infinitesimal, yet time, to reach your eyes, and so it is that everywhere we look, everywhere, we are looking into the past."

We had finished the bottle, he was pouring out the dregs. He tipped the rim of his glass against mine and made a ringing note. "You must take care of your star, in this place," he said in the softest of whispers, smiling, and leaning so far forwards in the chair that I could see myself reflected, doubly reflected, in the lenses of his spectacles. "The gods watch over us, and are jealous."

291

It was a hot summer, that summer of Mrs. Gray. Records were broken, new ones were set. There was a drought that lasted for months, water was rationed and stand-pipes were set up at street corners where vexatious mothers had to queue with buckets and saucepans, complaining, their sleeves pugnaciously rolled. Cattle died in the fields, or went mad. Gorse fires burst out spontaneously; entire hillsides were left blackened and smouldering and for hours afterwards the air in the town was acrid with smoke that made a scratch in the throat and gave everyone a headache. Tar in the roadways and in the cracks between paving stones melted and stuck to the soles of our sandals, and the tyres of our bicycles sank into it, and one boy fell off his bike that way and broke his neck. Farmers warned plaintively of a disastrous harvest, and in the churches special prayers for rain were offered.

For my part I recall those months as no more than bright and soft. I have an image, as in one of those sedulously crafted landscape paintings that were so popular in these parts in those days, of a big sky adrift with cotton clouds, and far gold fields with pudding-shaped haystacks, and a single distant spire, thin as a tack, and at the horizon the merest brushstroke of cobalt blue to suggest a glimpse of sea. Impossibly, I even remember rain — Mrs. Gray and I loved to lie quiet in each other's arms on the floor in Cotter's place and listen to it sizzling through the leaves, while an impassioned blackbird somewhere close by whistled its heart out. How safe we felt then, how far removed from everything that would threaten us. The parched world around us might shrivel up and turn to tinder, we would be slaked by love.

I thought our idyll would never end. Or, rather, I would not entertain the thought of an end to it. Being young, I was sceptical of the future, and saw it as a matter of potential only, a state of things that might or might not arise and probably never would. Of course, there were markers to be observed, of an immediate kind. For instance, the

293

summer certainly would come to a close, the holidays would be over, and I would be expected to start calling for Billy again in the mornings on the way to school — how would I carry that off? Would I be able to maintain the insouciant front that I did before the summer, when Mrs. Gray and I were still merely strolling hand in hand up the lower slopes of what was soon to become Mount Hymettus itself, complete with golden honey-combs and cliffs of lovely blue-grey marble and naked nymphs in dells? The truth is, despite all youth's daring and defiance, there hovered directly above my head a little cloud of foreboding. It was no more than a cloud, weightless, indefinite in shape, yet dark, outside its malignantly radiant silver lining. For the most part I managed to ignore it or pretend it was not there. What was a cloud, in comparison with love's blazing sun?

It baffled me that people around us did not guess our secret; almost, at times, I found myself growing indignant at their lack of insight, their lack of imagination — in a word, at their underestimation of us. My mother, Billy, Mr. Gray, these were not formidable enough figures to inspire much fear — though Kitty's face I often seemed to glimpse in that menacing cloud over my head, grinning out at me gloatingly like the Cheshire Cat — but what about the town's busybodies, the moral guardians, the powder-blue Legionnaires of Mary? Why were they so slack in their bounden duty to nose out Mrs. Gray and me as we indulged ourselves shamelessly in endlessly inventive acts of concupiscence and lust? Heaven knows we took risks, at which Heaven itself must have been aghast. In this regard, of the two of us Mrs. Gray was by far the more reckless, as I must already have said. It was a thing I could not account for, could not understand. I was about to say she had no fear, but it was not the case, for I had seen her on more than one occasion trembling in terror, I assumed at the prospect of being caught with me; at other times, though, she acted as if she had never known a moment of misgiving, parading with me brazenly that day on the boardworks, for example, or running naked in broad daylight through the wood, where the very trees seemed to throw up their arms and draw back, shocked and scandalised at the sight of her. Inexperienced in these matters though I was, I felt I could say with confidence that such behaviour was not commonplace among the matrons of our town.

I ask myself, again, if she were deliberately

daring the world to find us out. One day she summoned me to meet her after she had been to an appointment with the doctor — "women's trouble," she would say brusquely, and make a face — and when she arrived in the station wagon at our meeting place on the road above the hazel wood she insisted I make love to her there and then, on the spot. "Come on," she said, almost angrily, her rump waggling at me as she clambered into the back seat of the station wagon, "do it to me, come on." I have to admit I was shocked by her shamelessness, and for once I was even a little unwilling — the spectacle of such raw desire threatened to have a deflating effect on me — but she put an arm that seemed as hard as a man's around my neck and drew me fiercely down to her, and I could feel her heart already hammering and her belly shaking, and of course I did to her what she demanded. It was over in a minute and then she was all dismissive briskness, pushing me away and pulling at her clothes and using her pants to wipe herself. We had left a glistening smear on the leather seat between us. She had parked hardly ten yards off the road, and although there was little traffic in those days, any motorist who happened to slow down going past could have seen us, her upraised nyloned legs and my bare white backside plunging and rearing between them. Now we climbed back into the front seat, exclaiming at the hotness of the leather where the sun had been shining on it, and she lit a cigarette and sat half turned away from me with her elbow out of the open window and a fist under her chin, saying nothing. I waited meekly for her mood to pass, frowning at my hands.

What had happened, I wondered, that she was so wrought? Had I done something to anger her? For most of the time I was unshakeably confident of her love, with all of youth's callous assurance, yet it would have taken no more than a harsh word or a disparaging glance from her to convince me on the spot that all was as good as over. It was peculiarly exciting, to be certain of her affections and yet always in fear of forfeiting them; to be in some sort of control of this passionate woman and yet also at her mercy. Such lessons she was teaching me about the human heart. That day, though, as always, it was not long before the gloom lifted. She stirred herself and flicked the unsmoked half of her cigarette out of the window — she might have been the cause of burning down the hazel wood and our love nest along with it — and then leaned forwards and drew her skirt back and peered into her lap. She saw my startled and disbelieving look — could she be ready to start up again, already? — and gave a throaty chuckle. "Don't worry," she said, "I'm only searching for the button that you tore off my suspender." The button was not to be found, however, and in the end she had to borrow a threepenny piece from me to use in its place. It was an expedient I was familiar with, for I had seen my mother more than once do the same thing. My mother used Pond's Cold Cream, too, as Mrs. Gray did now. She took a little fat pot of the stuff from her handbag and unscrewed the cap with a quick turn of the wrist, as if deftly wringing the neck of some small creature, and, holding the pot and the cap both in a slack left hand, shimmied forwards on the seat, straining upwards to see herself in the driving mirror, and with a fingertip applied the ice-white salve to her forehead and cheeks and chin. I do not know if there is such a thing as wholly disinterested love, but if there is I came closest to it at moments such as this, when she was engaged in some ritual she had performed so often she was no longer really conscious of it, and her eyes struggled to focus and her features relaxed into a look of lovely vacancy except in the space between her eyebrows where the skin drew itself tight in a tiny frown of concentration.

I think that must have been the day she told me she would be going away — the family was to take its annual holiday at the seaside. At first I found it hard to grasp what she was saying. This is something I recall with fascination now, the way in which my mind, before the batterings of experience had sufficiently softened it up and made it porous, would refuse to accommodate the things it found unpalatable. In those days there was nothing I could not believe or disbelieve, accept or reject, if it suited me and fitted with my view of how matters must be. She could not go away; it was simply not possible for us to be parted, not possible at all. It could not be the case that I would be left alone while she went off for two weeks — two weeks! — to disport herself half naked on a beach, and play games of tennis and clock golf, and enjoy candle-lit dinners with her dopey husband before waddling upstairs tipsily and falling on her back laughing on to a hotel bed — no no no! Contemplating this appalling, this not-to-be-entertained prospect, I had the sense of horror-struck incredulity that comes in the instant after the knife-blade

299

has sliced into the ball of the thumb or the acid has splashed into the eye, when everything is suspended while pain the playful demon takes a deep and determined breath preparatory to getting down to the serious work at hand. What would I do without her all that time — what would I do? She was gazing at me in amused dismay, shocked at my shock. She pointed out that she was not going far, that Rossmore was only ten miles away by train — she would be practically down the road, she said, hardly away at all. I shook my head. I may even have clasped my hands before her in supplication. A sob of anguish was forming inside me like a big soft warm unlayable egg. She did not seem capable of grasping the essential fact that I could not think of being separated from her, that I could not imagine her being in a place where I was not. Something would happen to me, I declared, I would fall ill, I might even die. At this she laughed but quickly checked herself. I was not to be silly, she said in her married-woman's voice, I would not get sick, I would not die. Then I would run away from home, I said, narrowing my eyes at her, I would pack my things in my schoolbag and come to Rossmore and live on the beach for the two weeks while she was there, and every time she and the other

Grays stepped out of doors there I would be, dragging myself and my sorrow about the hotel grounds, and the tennis courts, and the golf range, her hollow-eyed, heartsick boy.

"Now listen to me," she said, turning sideways and draping an arm on the steering wheel and lowering her head to glare at me sternly, "I have to go on this holiday — do you understand? I have to."

I shook my head again, shook it and shook it until my cheeks rattled. She was becoming alarmed by my vehemence, I saw with satisfaction, and in her alarm I saw, too, a tiny sharp gleam of hope. I must press on — I must press harder. The sun was beating through the windscreen, greying the glass, and the leather upholstery was giving off a strong animal odour to which no doubt Mrs. Gray and I were adding a post-coital tang. I had a shaky sensation, as if everything inside me had turned to crystal and was vibrating at a very fast and uniform pitch. I think if I had heard a car coming I would have leaped out and stood in the middle of the road with my hand up and made it stop, so that I might denounce Mrs. Gray to the driver — *Look, sir, upon this heartless jade!* — for in my distress I was working up a steaming head of fury, and I

301

would have welcomed a witness to the sore injustice I was being made to suffer. Who can do outrage and injury better than a boy in love? I said I would not let her go to Rossmore, and that was final. I said I would tell Billy what his mother and I had been up to, and he would tell his father, and Mr. Gray would throw her out on the street, and then she would have no choice but to run away with me to England. I could see from the way her lips were twitching that she was finding it hard not to smile, and this drove me to a new extreme of fury. If she went away she would be sorry, I said narrowly. When she came back I would not be here, she would never see me again, and then how would she feel? — yes, I would go, I would leave this place altogether, I told her, and then she would know what it felt like to be abandoned and alone.

At last, after all these efforts, I ran out of energy, and turned away from her and folded my arms and glowered into the ragged hedgerow beside which we were parked. Silence erected itself between us like a barrier of glass. Then Mrs. Gray stirred, and sighed, and said she would have to go home, that everyone would be wondering where she was, why she was so late. Oh, everyone would, would they? I said, with what was intended to be biting sarcasm. She laid a hand lightly on my arm. I would not unbend. "Poor Alex," she said cajolingly, and it struck me how seldom she spoke my name, which served to bring on yet a further access of anger and bitter resentment.

She started up the engine, mashing the gears as always, and reversed the station wagon and turned it in a storm of dust and flying gravel. Only then did we notice the three small boys standing with their bikes on the opposite side of the road, watching us. Mrs. Gray spoke a word under her breath, and took her foot off the clutch too quickly and the engine gave a grunt and a heave and died. The dust continued to swirl lazily around us. The boys were homunculoid, grimy-faced, and had scabby knees and hacked-at hair — tinker children, probably, from the camp over by the town dump. They went on looking at us without expression, and there we sat, helplessly absorbing their blank stares, until presently they turned away in what seemed bland disdain and mounted up and rode off down the road at a leisurely glide. Mrs. Gray laughed unsteadily. "Well, you needn't worry so," she said, "for if those fellows tell on us I won't be going anywhere, and nor will you, my bucko, unless it's to the reformatory."

■ ■ ■ ■

But she did go. Until the very last I did not believe she would have the resolve to part from me and leave me to suffer, yet the moment of her going came, and she went. Is it possible for a boy of fifteen to know love's torments, I mean really to know them? Surely one would have to be fully and bleakly aware of the inevitability of death to experience the true anguish of loss, and to me as I was then the notion that I would one day die was preposterous, hardly to be entertained at all, the stuff of a bad and barely remembered dream. But if it was not actual pain I was experiencing, then what was it? In form it was, or felt most like, a sort of pained, general dithering, so that I seemed to have grown old suddenly, old and fussed and infirm. In the week and more that I had to endure before her departure there continued and intensified in me the sense of agitation, of inner vibrating, that had started that day at the side of the road in the station wagon when she first made her announcement of the holiday. It might have been a form of ague, an interior St. Vitus's Dance. Outwardly I must have been much as usual, for no one, not even my mother, appeared to notice anything amiss with me. Inside, however, all was fever and confusion. I felt as one must feel who has been sentenced to death, torn between disbelief and stark dread. Had it never occurred to me that I would have to suffer some kind of separation from her sooner or later, even if only a temporary one? No, it had not. For me, lolling complacently in the lap of Mrs. Gray's opulent, all-embracing love, there was only the present, with no future in view, certainly not a future in which she did not figure. Now the sentence had been passed, the last meal had been eaten, and I was in the tumbril, I could hear its wheels harshing on the cobbles and could see clear the scaffold erected in the dead centre of the square, with its attendant hangwoman awaiting me, in her black hood.

It was a Saturday morning when they went. Imagine if you will a small-town summer day: flawless blue sky, birds in the branches of the cherry trees, a not unpleasant, sweetish reek of slurry from the pig farms out in the purlieus, the knock and clatter and cry of children at play. And now see me, skulking hunched and harrowed through the innocent, sunlit streets, on the way to meet in all its pitiless magnitude the first great sorrow of my young life. I will say

305

this for suffering, that it lends a solemn weight to things and casts them in a starker, more revealing, light than any they have known hitherto. It expands the spirit, flays off a protective integument and leaves the inner self rawly exposed to the elements, the nerves all bared and singing like harpstrings in the wind. Approaching across the little square I kept my eyes averted from the house until the last minute, not wanting to see the dark-blue sun-blinds drawn in the windows, the note for the milkman screwed into the neck of an empty milk bottle, the front door locked impassively against me. Instead, I pictured in my mind, concentrating fiercely, as though by force of imagination I might make it be so, the battered station wagon, my accommodating, faithful old friend, standing at the kerb as always, and the front door of the house ajar and every window open, and in one of them a penitent Mrs. Gray leaning far out and smiling radiantly down at me with welcoming arms flung wide. But then I was there, and had to look, and no station wagon was to be seen, and the house was shut, and my love had gone away and left me standing here in a puddle of grief.

How did I get through the rest of that day? I drifted, outwardly listless yet all aquiver within. My world yesterday with Mrs. Gray in it had the lightness and glossy tension of a freshly inflated party balloon; now, today, with her gone, everything was suddenly slack, and tacky to the touch. Anguish, this constant, unremitting anguish, made me tired, terribly tired, yet I did not know how I might rest. I felt dry all over, dry and hot, as if I had been scorched, and my eyes ached and even my fingernails pained me. I was like one of those big sycamore leaves, resembling parched claws, that scuttled and scratched their way along the pavements, driven by the autumn gusts. What am I saying? It was not autumn, it was summer, there were no dead leaves on the ground. Yet that is what I see, the caducous leaves, and dust-eddies in the gutters, and my suffering self facing into a bitter wind portending the onset of winter.

Late in the afternoon, however, came the great revelation, followed by the greater resolution. In my wanderings I found myself outside Mr. Gray's glasses shop. I do not think I went there intentionally, although throughout the day I had lingered deliberately in this or that place with which for me my departed darling was associated, such as the tennis courts where I had once seen her play, and the boardworks where we had so fearlessly paraded ourselves and our love. The shop, like its proprietor, was unremarkable. There was a room at the front with a counter and a chair that customers could sit in to admire their new eyewear in a magnifying mirror in a circular silver frame set at a convenient angle on the counter. At the back was a consulting room, I knew, where the walls were fitted with stacks of shallow wooden drawers containing spectacle frames, and there was a machine with two big, round, startled-looking lenses, like the eyes of a robot, that Mr. Gray tested his patients' vision with. To supplement the optical business — remember how few people wore glasses in those days? — Mr. Gray sold pricey trinkets and items of cosmetics, and even retorts and test tubes, in various sizes, if I am not mistaken. Looking at these things displayed in the window, I was not in such an extreme of agony that I did not recall Kitty's birthday present that I still coveted and the thought of which now only added to my suffering and my sense of injury.

Business must have been slow that afternoon, for Miss Flushing, Mr. Gray's assistant, was standing in the shop doorway with the door open, enjoying the sunlight that had already begun to decline at a sharp angle over the rooftops but that was still strong and dense with heat. Was Miss Flushing smoking a cigarette? No, in those days women did not smoke in public, though bold Mrs. Gray sometimes did, sometimes even in the street. Miss Flushing was bigboned and blonde, high at bosom and waist, with prominent and very white teeth that were impressive though somewhat alarming to look at. She gave a sense of all-over fairness and pinkness, and there was always a faint, delicate shine, like that on the inner whorl of a seashell, along the edges of her nostrils and the rims of her slightly starting eyes. She favoured angora cardigans that she must have knitted herself, unless she had a mother who knitted them for her; she kept them tightly buttoned so that they emphasised the impossibly sharp points of her perfectly conical breasts. She was extremely short-sighted, and wore spectacles with lenses as thick as the bottoms of bottles. Is it not remarkable that Mr. Gray, myopic himself, should have hired an assistant whose vision was even worse than his own? Unless she was meant to be a sort of advertisement, an awful warning against the neglect of defective eyesight. She was a kindly if somewhat scattered person, although with slow or indecisive patients she could on occasion be distinctly short. My mother, a mistress of indecision, disliked and disapproved of her, and when once a year she took ten shillings from the petty cash and went to have her eyesight tested she would insist on being received and treated exclusively by Mr. Gray, who was, as she often said, smiling wistfully, a lovely man. The notion of my mother submitting herself to the professional attentions of Mr. Gray caused in me an unpleasant, even a queasy, sensation. Did they speak of Mrs. Gray? Did my mother enquire after her well-being? I imagined the subject coming up, being briefly, tentatively contemplated, then put away carefully like a pair of glasses into their silk-lined case, after which there would be a silence into which my mother would let drop a soft, faint cough.

I was not acquainted with Miss Flushing, except insofar as everyone in our hardly populous little town could be said to be acquainted, more or less, with everyone else. When I arrived in the street that evening and, seeing her in the doorway, lifted up my chin and knotted my brow into a frown and made to walk past as if I were hurrying on a vital errand elsewhere — it was imperative she should not imagine I was there for any reason to do with the Grays, particularly

Mrs. Gray — she suddenly spoke to me, to my surprise and even some fright, addressing me by name, which I did not know she knew. I confess that, in my boy's beady fashion and out of nothing other than a desire for a model against which to compare Mrs. Gray's full-fleshed charms, I had more than once in recent times speculated on how Miss Flushing would look if, somewhere like Cotter's place some lazy afternoon, she were to be persuaded to take off that fluffy cardigan and the pointy paraphernalia of lace and whalebone underneath it, and I suspect that now when she spoke my name I must have blushed — not, I suppose, that she would have noticed.

She said the Grays had gone away. I nodded, still frowning, still trying to pretend I was about important business from which she was keeping me. She was peering at me in her short-sighted way, which made her lift her full upper lip a little in the middle and wrinkle her nose. In those big lenses her pale, protuberant eyes were the size and shade of two shrunken gooseberries. "They've gone to Rossmore," she said, "for a fortnight. They went this morning." I seemed to catch in her tone a note of commiseration. Was she also in some way bereft? Was she, too, sorrowing, like me, and offer-

311

ing sympathy? The sun was striking down on some polished surface in the shop window and dazzling my already sorrow-dazed eyes. "Mr. Gray is going to come up to town every day on the train," Miss Flushing was saying, smiling out of what I was sure now was a fixed, bright misery. "He'll be working here and going down to them at night." *Them.* "It's not far, on the train," she added, and a wobble came into her voice. "Not far at all."

And then I saw it. Miss Flushing was commiserating not with me but with herself. The sorrow she could not keep from betraying was not on my part, it was on her own. Of course! For she was in love with Mr. Gray, at that moment I was suddenly certain of it. And he? — was he in love with her? Were they as Mrs. Gray and I were to each other? It would account for so many things — Mr. Gray's other kind of myopia, for instance, that prevented him from seeing what was going on under his nose between his wife and me, which perhaps was not myopia at all, I thought now, but the indifference of one whose affections had been transferred elsewhere. Yes, that was it, it had to be: he did not care if his wife spent her afternoons not shopping as she said she did or playing tennis with her housewife friends

— what housewife friends did she have, anyway? — but tumbling top over tail with me at Cotter's place, because meanwhile he was in the back room here with the shades pulled and the closed sign displayed, busy ridding flushed Miss Flushing of her ugly specs and clingy cardigan and underwired armour plating. Oh, indeed, I saw it all now, and was exultant, and the balloon of life's possibilities was on the instant full to bursting again and tugging at its tether. And I knew what I would do. Come Monday morning, when Mr. Gray was bound for town on the up line I would be on the down, speeding in a welter of steam and sparks towards my beloved, whose lovely limbs were sure to be by then already touched with a first alluring sunny flush. What of my mother, though, and what she would say? Well, what of her? It was the school holidays still, I would make some excuse to be gone for the day; she would not object, she credited my every lie and subterfuge, the poor, dim thing.

I pause. I am suddenly assailed by a memory of her, my mother, sitting on a beach on a windy bright day in the midst of the remains of a picnic, paper plates and crushed paper cups, bread crusts in a big tin biscuit-box, a banana skin rudely splayed, a bottle with the dregs of milky tea in it sunk at a drunken angle in the sand. She is sitting up straight with her bare mottled legs extended before her, and there is something on her head, a headscarf, or a shapeless cotton hat. Is she at her sewing? — for she wears that abstracted half-smile that she does when she is doing her embroidery. Where is my as yet undead father? I do not see him. He is down at the shallows, it must be, where he often was, paddling, his trousers rolled, his calves and his knobbed ankles on show, greyish-white, the colour of lard. And I, where am I, or what? — an eye suspended in mid-air, a hovering witness only, there and not there? Ah, Mother, how can the past be past and yet still be here, untarnished, gleaming, bright as that tin box? And did you never suspect what your son was up to, never once, throughout that broiling, tumid summer? Surely a mother would not be so blind to the passions of her only child. You said no word, dropped no hint, posed no pointed question. Yet what if you did suspect, what if you did know, and were too appalled, too terrified, to speak, to challenge, to forbid? This possibility troubles me, more, even, than the possibility that everyone knew, all along. So many people I have betrayed in my life, starting with her, the first casualty.

Would I really go to Rossmore? Countless times throughout that Saturday night and all of Sunday my resolution failed me, then rallied, only to falter and fail again. But go I did, surprising myself. The business of getting away turned out to be simplicity itself — I am sure there is a devil's apprentice whose special task it is to smooth the way for clandestine lovers. I told my mother, at the demon's dictation, that Billy Gray had invited me to come down and spend the day with him. Not only was she not suspicious, she was positively pleased, for the Grays were what she called a professional family and therefore a desirable connection for me to have and to cultivate. She gave me the train fare and something extra to buy an ice cream, made sandwiches for me to bring, ironed one of my two good shirts, and even insisted on whitening my plimsolls with pipe-clay. Her fussing infuriated me, of course, in my impatience to be away, but I kept my temper for fear of provoking capricious Fate, which so far had been smiling upon me with such unwonted tolerance.

Boarding the train, I had a twinge of misgiving that was something mysteriously to do with the smell of coal smoke and the bristly feel of the upholstery of the seats.

Was I recalling then, too, my mother at Rossmore? Was I ashamed of having lied to her that morning with such oily ease? It is remarkable how few such pricks of conscience I was prey to in those days — I saved them all up for later, for now — yet in that moment, as the train wheezed and clanked its way out of the station, was it that I was afforded a glimpse of the fiery plain and the burning lake of sorrows, did I hear the cries of doomed lovers rising from the pit? *This is a grave sin, my child,* Father Priest had said, and surely it was. Well, let damnation come, I did not care. I got up from the seat, accompanied by little jets of ancient dust squirting out of the upholstery, and let the heavy wooden window down on its thick leather strap, and summer with all its promise leaped into my arms.

I have always liked trains. The old ones were best, of course, their soot-black engines venting bursts of steam and chuffing links of stylised white smoke, and the carriages rattling and yawing and the wheels violently clanging — so much might and effort, yet producing such a gay and toy-like effect. And then the way the landscape seemed to rotate like a vast, slow wheel, or to keep opening like a fan, and the telegraph wires dipped and slid, and birds flew past the window backwards, slowly, effortfully, like so many discarded bits of black rag.

How broad and flat the silence is that spreads along a station platform in summer when the train pulls out. I was the only one who had got off. The fat-necked station master in his peaked cap and navy-blue coat spat on the line and ambled off, that hoop thing he had got from the driver — was it? or from the guard in the guard's van? — dangling on his shoulder. Parched grass on the far side of the track made ticking noises in the sun. A crow was perched on a post. I went through the little green gate up to the road. Dimly I saw, with a sort of inward undulation like that of a heavy black curtain stirring in a cold wind, how mad a thing it was to have come here like this; but still, no, I did not care, I would not care. I was too far gone to go back, and anyway there would not be an up train for hours. I took out of my pocket the packet of sandwiches my mother had made for me and hurled it across the track into the grass, as a pledge of my commitment, I suppose, of my determination not to be daunted. The crow on the post gave a put-upon squawk and unwrapped its wings of black crape and with a few lazy flaps flew down inexpectantly to investigate. All this had happened before

317

somewhere.

The Beach Hotel, where the Grays were staying, a long, low, one-storeyed establishment with a glassed-in veranda, was a hotel in name only, being hardly more than a boarding-house, though a distinct cut above the shabby place my mother kept. I flitted past, not daring even to glance in the direction of those many sky-reflecting panes. What if Billy or, more calamitously, Kitty, were to come out and see me there? How would I account for myself? I did not have the necessary props to support an alibi, not even swimming trunks or a towel. I went on down the road, and presently came to a gap between a café and a shop that led on to the beach. The morning was hot, and I thought of buying the ice cream my mother had given me the money for, but decided to wait, since I did not know how long this day might last. I was already regretting the sandwiches I had so profligately thrown away.

I went and sat on the beach, and made a funnel of my fist and let sand pour through it while I gazed dolefully out to sea. The water with the sun on it was a broad sheet of rapidly bobbing sharp metallic flakes, old-gold, silver, chrome. People were out walking their dogs, and there were a few swimmers in the sea already, splashing and squealing. I was sure that all eyes were on me, that I was the centre of attention. What if that old boy with the bulldog, for instance, or that skinny woman with the sprig of lilac in the band of her straw hat, what if one of them were to become suspicious and challenge me — what defence of my idle presence would I be able to offer? And Mrs. Gray, what would she say when she saw me, what would she do? There were times when she was for me only another adult, just as preoccupied and unpredictable and prone to outbursts of unreasoning anger; just as unlike me, that is, as all the rest of the grown-up world.

I stayed squatting there miserably in the sand for what seemed at least an hour but which when I checked by the clock on the bell-tower of the Protestant church behind the beach turned out to have been not a full ten minutes. I got up and brushed myself down and set off to walk through the village, to see what might be seen, which was only the usual: holiday-makers in wide shorts and silly hats, shops with clusters of beach balls in the doorways and ice-cream machines that whirred and thumped, golfers on the golf course in sleeveless yellow pullovers and big shoes with frilled wings.

Sunlight glanced on passing windscreens and made sharp shadows in gateways. I stopped to watch a dog fight between three dogs but it was quickly over. As I was going by the galvanised-iron church I thought I spotted Kitty approaching on a bike and hid behind a hedge, my heart a hot lump struggling in my chest like a cat in a sack.

In those echoless caverns of empty time, being unobserved, unnoticed, I became increasingly detached from myself, increasingly disembodied. At moments I seemed to have become a phantom, and felt that I might walk up to people and pass straight through them and they would not even register a breath. At midday I bought a bun and a bar of chocolate and ate them sitting on a bench outside Myler's grocery shop. Boredom and the beating sun were making me feel slightly sick. In desperation I began to devise stratagems so that I could call at the Beach Hotel and ask for Mrs. Gray. I had got on the Rossmore train by mistake and was stranded here and needed to borrow the fare home; there had been an attempted break-in at their house on the square and I had rushed down to tell them of it; Mr. Gray had thrown himself out of the carriage on the way up because Miss Flushing had threatened to jilt him, and they were still searching along the tracks for his mangled body — what did it matter? I was ready to say anything. But still I wandered, agitated and desolate, and the time went slower and slower.

I did encounter Billy. It was the most peculiar thing. I turned a corner and ran smack into him. He was coming from the public tennis courts, along with three or four other fellows, none of whom I knew. We faltered, Billy and I, then stopped, and stared. Stanley and Livingstone could not have been more startled. Billy was in tennis whites, a cream-coloured jumper with a blue band tied by the arms around his waist, and carried a racket — no, two rackets, I see them, both of them in shiny new wooden presses. He blushed, and I am sure I did, too, in the exquisite awkwardness of the moment. We both began to say something at the same time, and stopped. This was not supposed to have happened, we were not supposed to meet here like this — what did I mean by being here, anyway? And what was to be done? Billy was trying to hide those two rackets in their ostentatious presses, holding them down at his side with a show of negligence. The others had gone on a little way but now they paused, and looked back at us with not much curiosity.

Mark, I was not thinking of Mrs. Gray or my purpose in being there, that was not what was making for this discomfiting sensation, this hot mixture of embarrassment, dull dread and sharp annoyance. Then what was? Just the surprise, I suppose, the being caught off-guard. It was as if we had both become unfairly entangled in something shaming and could not think how to extricate ourselves; in a moment it seemed we would be snarling at each other, like two beasts halted snout to snout on a jungle path. Then everything suddenly relaxed, and Billy did his lopsided and faintly apologetic smile, ducking his head to one side — for a moment he was his mother — and with eyes downcast stepped past me, in a gingerly sinuous fashion, as if he were negotiating a barbed and bristling obstacle that had risen in his way. He spoke a word, too, that I did not catch, and went on to join his new seaside friends, who by now were grinning in ignorant enjoyment of what they had seen and had not understood. I could make out clearly the still reddened back of Billy's neck. One of them clapped him on the shoulder, as if he had come valiant and safe through some tricky trial, and then they went on together, laughing, and a second one of them put an arm around Billy's shoulders and glanced back at me with spiteful scorn. It all was done with so quickly that as I walked on it was as if it had not happened at all, and with a calm that surprised me I resumed my wanderings.

It was eerie how often that day I seemed to see — no, how often I *saw* Mrs. Gray appear out of the throngs of summer people. She was everywhere, a tantalising brightness flitting among so many featureless shades. It was exhausting, coping with these surges of joyful recognition that no sooner rose up in me than they were dashed down again. It was like being teased by a mischievous and cruel-hearted sprite playing hide-and-seek with me among the drifting crowd. The more often I spied her and immediately lost her again, the more maddened with longing for her I became, until I thought I should faint, or lose my reason, if the real she did not soon appear. Yet when she did, I had seen so many imaginary versions of her that I did not at first believe my eyes.

I had relinquished hope by then and was trudging up the road to the station on my way to take the last train home. So dispirited was I that I did not so much as cast a glance at the Beach Hotel as I passed by. She came towards me from the direction of the station with the sun at her back, a moving silhouette outlined in burning gold. She was wearing sandals, and her short-sleeved dress with the flower pattern — it was the dress I recognised first — and her hair was pinned back in a way that made her seem very young, a bare-legged girl slapping along in her sandals, swinging a shopping bag. At first she, too, I saw, could not believe the evidence of her eyes, and stopped on the path and stared in astonishment and dawning alarm. This was not at all the way I had imagined us meeting. What was I doing here, she demanded — was there something wrong? I did not know what to say. I had been right about the sunburn: there was a pink flush on her forehead and in the hollow of her throat, and a few freckles were sprinkled very fetchingly across the saddle of her nose.

She tilted her head and was regarding me with a sharp, sidewise stare, her eyes narrowed and her mouth set. The look of fright that had come into her face at the sight of me was turning now into a frown of suspicion and angry reproach. I could see her urgently calculating in her mind the dimensions of the problem that my sudden, shocking appearance here had presented her with. At any moment one of her children might walk out at the hotel gate not a hundred yards down the road and see the two of us there, and then what? In return I eyed her sulkily, kicking with my toe at a crack in the pavement. I was disappointed — more, I was disillusioned, bitterly so. Yes, I had given her a shock; yes, there was a danger we might be spotted and unable to account for ourselves; but what of her repeated affirmations of love for me, that love that was supposed to be careless of all convention? What of the heedless passion that had led her to lie down with me in her laundry room on an April afternoon, that had sent her prancing naked through the summer woods, and for the sake of which she was willing to park the station wagon at the side of a public road in broad daylight and scramble into the back seat and without preamble hike her skirt up to her waist and draw me peremptorily down upon her, her bucking boy? Her eyes now had taken on a harried look, and she kept glancing past me down the road towards the hotel and pressing the tip of her tongue back and forth along her lower lip. Something, I saw, would have to be done, and done quickly, to draw her attention away from herself and all she might lose and turn it back on me. I let my shoulders droop and lowered my gaze in chastened fashion — oh, yes, an actor in the making — and in a voice that had the merest hint of a sob in it I told her that I had come to Rossmore because I had not known what else to do, since I could not have borne to be away from her another day, another hour. She peered at me for a long moment, startled by the seeming intensity of my words, and then smiled, in that delighted, slow, blurry way of hers. "Aren't you a terrible fellow?" she murmured, her voice thickening, and she shook her head, and was mine again.

We went together back the way she had come, passing by the station, and having crossed the little humpbacked bridge we were at once in the countryside. Where had she been, I wanted to know, where had she come from? She laughed. She had been in town, all day. She showed me her bulging shopping bag. "They haven't a thing in that place," she said, jerking her head disdainfully backwards in the direction of the Beach Hotel, "only sausages and spuds, spuds and sausages, every damned day." So she had gone up this morning, and come back, now, on the train? Yes, and she had been idling, like me, wandering about the town for hours, wondering where I might be, when all the time I was here! She laughed again, to see my chagrined scowl. We were walking along by the side of the road. The sun was in our eyes, and the evening light had turned to tarnished gold. Long grasses leaned out from the ditch and slapped at us lazily and left their dust on our legs. A wispy white mist was forming ankle-deep over the fields, and cattle stood on invisible hoofs and watched us as we went past, their lower jaws moving sideways and up in that mechanical, bored way. Summer, and the silence of evening, and my love by my side.

If she had come on the train, I said, what about Mr. Gray — where was he? He was stuck in town, she said, and would catch the late mail train. *Stuck in town.* I thought of Miss Flushing's blonde waves and high-set waist and those two big damply glistening front teeth of hers. Should I say something, should I let fall a hint of what I thought I knew of Mr. Gray's guilty secret? Not yet. And when I eventually did tell her, some time afterwards, how she laughed — "Oh, God, I think I've wet myself!" — clapping her hands and shrieking. She knew her husband better than I did.

We stopped at a bend of the road, in the purple-brown shade of a stand of rustling trees, and I kissed her. Have I said she was taller than I was, by an inch or so? I was still a growing lad, after all; hard to think of that. Her sunburned skin was plushly hot against my lips, slightly swollen, delicately adhesive, more like a secret inner lining than an outer skin. Of all the kisses we exchanged, that is the one I recall most sharply, simply for the strangeness of it, I suppose, for it was strange to be standing up like that, under trees, at dusk on an otherwise unremarkable summer evening. Though we, too, were innocent, in our way, and that is strange, too. I see us as in one of those old rustic woodcuts, the youthful swain and his freckled Flora chastely embracing in a shady arbour under tangled honeysuckle and dew-sweet eglantine. All a fancy, you see, all a dream. When the kiss was done we each took a step back, cleared our throats, and turned together and walked on in decorous silence. We were holding hands, and I, the aspiring gallant, was carrying her shopping bag. What were we to do now? It was growing late, and I had missed the last train. What if someone who knew us were to come driving along and see us there, strolling hand in hand between those misty fields so late in the day, a beardless boy, a married woman, and yet a pair of lovers, plainly? I pictured it, the car swerving wildly and the driver's disbelieving look over the wheel, his mouth opening to exclaim. Mrs. Gray began to tell me how when she was small her father used to take her out on evenings such as this to gather mushrooms, but then broke off and became pensive. I tried to see her as a girl, picking her way barefoot through the mist-white meadows, with a basket on her arm, and the man, her father, going ahead of her, bespectacled, whiskered and waistcoated, like the fathers in fairy tales. For me she could have no past that was not a fable, for had I not invented her, conjured her out of nothing but the mad desires of my heart?

She said she would go back and fetch the station wagon and drive me home. But how would she manage it, I wanted to know, how would she get away? — for I had begun at last to weigh the perils of our predicament. Oh, she said, she would think of some story or other. Or had I, she enquired, a better plan to suggest? I did not like her sarcastic tone and did as I so often did and set to sulking. She laughed, and said I was a big baby, and drew me to her with both arms and gave me what was half a hug and half a shake. Then she pushed me away again, and brought out her lipstick and made herself a new mouth, pouting, and sucking in her lips until it looked as if she had no teeth and making faint smacking sounds. I was to wait by the railway bridge, she said, and she would come back and pick me up there. I should keep an eye out in case Mr. Gray's train arrived in the meantime. What, I asked, was I supposed to do if it did? "Hide behind the ditch," she said drily, "unless you want to explain to him how you happened to be hanging about here at this hour of the night."

She took the shopping bag from me and went off. I watched her dimmening figure waver away through the twilight, over the bridge, and disappear, slipping like a shadow through a gap between two worlds, hers and mine. Why in so many of my memories of her is she walking away from me? I had not asked her what she had bought in town. I had not cared to know, but now I pictured her as in one of those brightly coloured cheery advertisements of the day, freckled and tanned in her summer frock, attended by Billy and Kitty, the two of them gazing up at her with rosy cheeks propped on their fists, grinning and eager, their eyes bright as buttons, as she produces from the cornucopia of her bag all manner of comestible delights — biscuits and bonbons, cobs of corn, sliced pans in wax-paper wrappers, oranges the size of bowling balls, a squamous pineapple with its gay topknot — while in the background Mr. Gray, husband, father, only provider of all this abundance, looks up from his newspaper and smiles indulgently, modest, dependable, square-jawed Mr. Gray. Their world, never to be mine. The summer was ending.

I went and sat on a stile. Below me the rail lines shone in the day's last light, and in the station master's office a wireless set inserted its needle of buzzing sound into the silence. Night came on, diffusing the purple-grey gloam that passes for darkness at that time of year. Now a light went on in the waiting-room window, and moths wove drunken, zigzag patterns under a buzzing lamp at the end of the platform. Behind me in the fields a corncrake began insistently to shake its wooden rattle. There were bats out, too, I could sense them flickering here and there above me in the indigo air, their wings making a tiny sound like that of tissue paper being surreptitiously folded. Presently a huge, fat-faced moon the colour of honey hoisted itself up out of somewhere and goggled down at me, mirthful and knowing. And shooting stars! — when is the last time you saw a shooting star? By now Mrs. Gray had been gone a worryingly long time. Had something happened, had she been waylaid? Maybe she would not be able to come back for me at all. I was growing chilled, and hungry, too, and I thought mournfully of home, my mother in the kitchen, in her chair by the window, reading a detective story from the library, her glasses on the end of her nose, one ear-piece repaired with sticking-plaster, licking her thumb to turn the pages and blinking sleepily. But maybe she would not be reading, maybe she would be standing by the window, peering out worriedly into the dark, wondering why I was abroad so late, and where I could be, and what doing.

The arm of the railway signal below the bridge came down with a jerk and a clack, startling me, and the signal light had turned from red to green, and away off in the distance I could see the light of the approaching mail train. Mr. Gray would shortly arrive, would step down to the platform, with his briefcase, and a rolled newspaper under his arm, and stand a moment, peering about and blinking, as if he were not sure he was in the right place. What should I do? Should I try to divert him? But as Mrs. Gray had sensibly said, what excuse could I offer for being there, alone, so late at night, cold and shivering?

Then the station wagon appeared over the crest of the hill. One of its headlamps was permanently askew, so that the lights had a comically wall-eyed, groping glare. It drew up and stopped by the stile. The window on the driver's side was open and Mrs. Gray was smoking a cigarette. She glanced past me at the light of the approaching train that was as big now and as yellow as the moon. "Jeepers," she said, "just in time, eh?" I got in beside her. The leather seat felt cold and clammy. She reached out a hand and touched my cheek. "Poor you," she said, "your teeth are chattering." She gouged at the gears and in a burst of tyre-smoke we shot off into the night.

She said she was sorry she had been so long away. Kitty had not wanted to go to bed, and Billy had been out somewhere with his friends and she had felt she must wait for him to come back. His friends, I thought, oh, yes, his new friends that he had lost no time in making. She began to tell me about an old man staying at the hotel who haunted the beach all day spying on girls changing into their swimsuits. As she spoke she made large, hooping gestures with the cigarette, as if it were a stick of chalk and the air a blackboard, and laughed whinnyingly down her nose, seeming not to have a worry in the world, which annoyed me, of course. She still had her window open, and as we sped through the moonlit landscape the night kept snapping up at her elbow, and her hair shivered in the wind and the stuff of her dress at her shoulder rippled and slapped. I told her how I had met Billy, and his friends. I had been saving up that piece of news. She was silent for a long time, thinking. Then she shrugged, and said he had been out all day, that she had hardly seen him since morning. I was not interested in any of this. I asked if we might stop somewhere, by the side of the road, or up a lane. She looked at me sidelong and shook her head, pretending to be shocked. "Do you ever," she asked, "think of anything else?" But she did stop.

Later, when we got to town, she drew up at the far end of my street. The house, I saw, was dark. My mother must have gone to bed, after all — what should I think of that? Mrs. Gray said I had better go in, yet I lingered. Beyond the windscreen the moonlight was carving the street into a jumble of sharp-edged cubes and cones, and everything seemed covered in a thin, smooth coating of silver-grey dust. Another shooting star, and then another. Mrs. Gray was silent now. Was she thinking of her children?

Was she wondering what she would say to her husband when she returned, what explanation she would offer for her absence? Would he be waiting up for her, sitting in the dark on the glassed-in veranda, drumming his fingers, his spectacle lenses shining accusingly? At length she sighed and drew herself up in the seat with a weary wriggle, and patted me on the knee and said again that it was very late and that I should go in. She did not kiss me goodnight. I said I would come down to Rossmore another day, but she made a line of her lips and gave her head a quick small shake, keeping her eyes on the windscreen. I had not meant it, anyway. I knew I would not go there again and spend another day like the one that had just passed. She waited until I was halfway along the street before driving off. I stopped and turned and watched the twin jewels of the station wagon's rear lights dwindle and fade. I was recalling how she had looked when she saw me walking towards her up Station Road, how she had started in panic and dismay, and how after a second her eyes had taken on that narrow, calculating look. Was that how it would be again one day, one final day, her eyes cold and her face set against me, against all my begging and

335

bawling, against my bitterest tears? Was that how it would be, in the end?

But what, you will be asking, what happened, what *transpired,* as Mrs. Gray would have said, on that night in Lerici after my encounter in the snowbound hotel with the mysterious man from the pampas? For surely, you will say, surely something happened. After all, was it not the stuff of the sweaty fantasies of my boyhood to have all unbidden in my bed a creature such as Dawn Devonport, a star in need of succour, a goddess in want of tender tending? Was a time, after boyhood days were done, when in such circumstances I would have known exactly what to do and would not have hesitated for a second. Not that I was ever really a womaniser, even in the days of my hot youth and vigour, despite what certain people will say. An actress in distress, though, I could never resist. Tours especially saw brisk nocturnal activity, for the rooms were cold and the beds lonely in those

337

cheerless digs and fleabag hotels where our little troupes used to put up, establishments that were dispiritingly familiar for me, son of the boarding-house that I was. In the febrile aftermath of the night's show, often it would take no more than a wounding notice in an early edition to cause a girl still with dabs of greasepaint behind her earlobes to come tumbling in tears into my arms. I was known for my soft touch. Lydia was aware of these chance collisions, or at least she guessed at them, I know that. Did she stray, too, when I was off gallivanting? And if she did, what do I feel about it, now? I press upon the place that should smart and nothing returns. Yet I adored once, and was myself adored. Such a long time ago, all that, I might be speaking of a lost antiquity. Ah, Lydia.

Dawn Devonport, I have to tell you, is a snorer. I hope she will not mind my revealing this unflattering fact. It will not harm her, I am sure — we prefer our deities to display a human flaw or two. Anyway, I like to listen to a woman snore; I find it soothing. Lying there in the dark with that sonorous rhythm going on beside me I feel I am out on a calm sea at night, being borne along in a little skiff and gently rocked from side to side; a buried recollection of the amniotic voyage, perhaps. That night, when at last I slipped back into my room, the street-light outside was still shedding a soiled glow in the window and the snow was still steadily falling. Have you ever thought how odd a thing it is that all hotel rooms are bedrooms? Even in suites, even in the grandest of them, the other rooms are just anterooms to the inner sanctum where the bed stands in all its smug and canopied majesty, like nothing so much as a sacrificial altar. In mine, now, Dawn Devonport still lay sleeping. I contemplated my choices. What was it to be, a few uncomfortable hours — by now it was very late and first light could not be far off — huddled in my clothes on that rush-bottomed Van Gogh chair, or reclining with a crick in my neck on the equally uninviting sofa? I looked at the chair, I looked at the sofa. The former seemed to shrink under my gaze, while the latter was pressed against the wall opposite the bed with its back up and its padded arms braced to the floor, regarding me through the gloom with an air of smouldering suspicion. I note how more and more I feel my presence resented by supposedly inanimate objects. Perhaps it is the kindly world's way, by making me increasingly unwelcome among its furniture, of easing me towards the final door, the one through which I shall presently be seen out for the last time.

In the end I opted to risk the bed. I padded softly around the side of it, and out of habit took off my watch and set it down on the little glass-topped table there. The clink that it made, of metal on glass, brought suddenly back to me all those nighttime vigils spent beside Cass's sick-bed when she was little, the unquiet darkness and the staled air, and the child felled there and seeming not to sleep but to be away in some half-tormented trance. Slipping soundlessly out of my shoes, but still dressed, with even my jacket buttons demurely done, and without drawing back the covers, I lay down, very cautiously — though even so a few springs deep in the mattress twanged, in jubilant derision, so it sounded — and stretched out on my back beside the sleeping woman and folded my hands on my breast. She stirred and snuffled a bit but did not wake. If she had woken, and turned to see me there, what a fright she would have got, thinking that surely a corpse all neatly parcelled in its funeral suit had been laid out beside her while she slept. She was resting on her side, facing away from me. Against the backdrop of the dimly illumined window the high curve of her hip might have been the outline of a graceful hill seen at a distance in the darkness against a sallowly lit sky; I have always admired this view of the female form, at once monumental and homely. Her snores made a delicate rattling in the passages of her nostrils. Sleep is uncanny, I have always found it so, a nightly dress-rehearsal for being dead. I wondered what Dawn Devonport might be dreaming of, although I have the theory, based on no grounds whatever, that snoring precludes dreaming. For my part, I was in that state of late-night hallucinated wakefulness that makes the very notion of sleep seem preposterous, yet presently I felt myself to be suddenly stepping off a footpath and missing my step, and I came to with a jolt that made the bed recoil, and realised I had drifted into a sort of sleep, after all.

Dawn Devonport, too, had woken. She was as she had been before, lying on her side, and did not move, but she had stopped snoring and her stillness was that of one awake and intently attending. She was so still I thought she might be rigid with fear — it was entirely possible that she did not remember how she had come to be here, in someone else's bed, in the middle of the night, with that ghastly light in the window and the snow falling outside. Discreetly I cleared my throat. Should I slide from the bed and slip out of the room and take myself off downstairs again — Señor Sorrán might still be in the bar, broaching another bottle of Argentinian red — so that she might think I had been only the figment of a dream and thus reassured drift back into sleep? I was juggling these alternatives, none of them persuasive, when I felt the bed begin to tremble, or quake, in a way I could not at first account for. Then I understood the cause. Dawn Devonport was weeping, muffling violent sobs and making hardly a sound. I was shocked, and my hands on my breast clutched at each other in a spasm of fright. The sound of a woman sobbing to herself in the darkness is a terrible thing. What was I to do? How was I to console her — was I required to console her? Was anything at all to be asked of me? I was trying to recall the words of a silly little ditty that I used to sing with Cass when she was small, something about lying in bed on one's back and getting tears in one's ears — how Cass used to laugh — and in the extremity of the moment I think I, too, would have begun to weep had Dawn Devonport not reared up suddenly, giving the sheet and the blanket a mighty yank, and fairly flung herself from the bed with a wordless exclamation of what seemed anger and run from the room, leaving the door wide open behind her.

I switched on the lamp and sat up, blinking, and swung my legs over the side of the bed and set my stockinged feet on the floor. Weariness settled all at once on my bowed shoulders, like the weight of all that snow outside, or of the night itself, the great dome of darkness all above me. My feet were cold. I wriggled them into their shoes, and leaned forwards, but then just stayed leaning there, my arms hanging, incapable even of doing up the laces. There are moments, infrequent though marked, when it seems that by some tiny shift or lapse in time I have become misplaced, have outstripped or lagged behind myself. It is not that I think myself lost, or astray, or even that it is inappropriate to be where I am. It is just that somehow I am in a place, I mean a place in time — what an odd way language has of putting things — at which I have not arrived of my own volition. And for that moment I am helpless, so much so that I imagine I will not be able to move on to the next place, or go back to the place where I was before — that I will not be able to stir at all, but will have to remain there, sunk in perplexity, mured in this incomprehensible fermata.

But always, of course, the moment passes, as it passed now, and I got myself to my feet and shuffled in my unlaced shoes to the door Dawn Devonport had left open, and shut it, and returned and switched off the lamp, and lay down again, still in my clothes, with my tie still knotted, and passed at once into blessed oblivion, as if a panel had opened in the night's wall and I had been slid on a slab into the dark and shut away there.

We never did make the crossing to Portovenere, Dawn Devonport and I. Perhaps I had never intended that we should. We might have gone, there was nothing to stop us — unless it was everything, of course — for despite the winter storms the ferries were operating and the roads were open. She, it turned out, had known all along that it was in the little port across the bay that my daughter died — she had heard it from Billie Stryker, I imagine, or Toby Taggart, for it was no secret, after all. She did not ask why I had chosen not to tell her myself, why I had pretended to have picked our destination at random. I expect she thought I had a plan, a programme, a scheme of my own, one that she might as well go along with, for want of better. Perhaps she did not think anything at all, just let herself be taken away, as if she had no choice and were glad of it. "Keats died here," she said, "didn't he, drown or something?" We were walking on the front below the hotel in our overcoats and mufflers. No, I told her, that was Shelley. She paid no attention. "I'm like him, like Keats," she said, narrowing her eyes at the turbulent horizon. "I'm living a posthumous existence — isn't that what he said of himself somewhere?" She laughed briefly, seeming pleased with herself.

It was morning, and the disturbances and interrupted sleep of the night before had left me in a chafed and shaky state, and I felt as raw as a freshly peeled stick. Dawn Devonport on the other hand was preternaturally calm, not to say dazed. The hospital must have given her tranquillisers to take with her on the trip — her doctor, the nice Indian, had not wanted her to come at all — and she was remote and slightly bleared, and looked on everything around her with a sceptical expression, as if she were sure it had all been got up to deceive her. Every so often her attention would focus and she would peer at her watch, narrowing her eyes and frowning, as if something momentous that had been meant to happen were being inexplicably delayed. I told her of my encounter with Fedrigo Sorrán, although I was not sure that in my tired and travel-fevered state I had not dreamed him, or invented him, and indeed I still have doubts. In the hotel that morning there had been no sign of him, and I was convinced he was no longer staying there, if he had been there at all, in the first place. Of her coming to my room, of our chaste concumbence, of her tears and her subsequent abrupt and violent exit, we did not speak. Today we were like a pair of strangers who had met in a dockside bar the night before and gone on board together in tipsy good-fellowship, and now the vessel had sailed, and we were hungover, and the voyage was still all grimly ahead of us.

He had been on his way back from Leghorn, I told her, when his boat sank in a storm. She looked at me. "Shelley," I said. His friend Edward Williams was with him, and a boy whose name I could not recall. Their boat was named the *Ariel*. Some say the poet scuttled it himself. He was writing *The Triumph of Life*. She was no longer looking at me and I was not sure that she was listening. We stopped and stood and gazed across the bay. Portovenere was over there. We might indeed have been on the stern of a ship, steaming steadily away from what was meant to have been our destination. The sea was high and vehemently blue, and I could just make out a bustle of white water at the foot of that distant promontory.

"What was she doing there, your daughter?" Dawn Devonport asked. "Why there?"

Why indeed?

We walked on. Amazingly, impossibly, last night's snowfall was entirely gone, as if the stage designer had decided it had been ill-advised and had ordered it to be swept away and replaced with a few minimalist puddles of muddy slush. The sky was hard and pale as glass, and in the limpid sunlight the little town above us was sharply etched against the hillside, a confused arrangement of angled planes in shades of yellow ochre, gesso white, parched pink. Dawn Devonport, her hands plunged in the pockets of her calf-length, fur-trimmed coat, paced beside me over the flagstones with her head down. She was in full disguise, with those enormous sunglasses and a big fur hat. "I thought," she said, "when I did it, or tried to — when I took the pills, I mean — I thought I was going to a place I would know, a place where I'd be welcomed." She had some difficulty with the words, as if her tongue were thick and hard to manage. "I thought I was going home."

Yes, I said, or to America, like Svidrigailov, before he put the pistol to his head and pulled the trigger.

She said she was cold. We went to a café on the harbour front and she drank hot chocolate, crouched at the little round table and clutching the cup in both of those big hands of hers. An odd thing about those little cafés in the south is that they seem, to me, anyway, to have been something else originally, apothecary shops, or small offices, or even domestic living rooms, that had been gradually and as if unintentionally adapted to this new use. There is something about the counters, so high and narrow, and the way the tiny tables and the chairs are crammed in, that lends the place a makeshift, improvised look. The staff, too, bored and laconic, have a transitory air, as though they had been drafted in temporarily to fill a shortage and are irritably eager to get away and take up again whatever far more interesting pursuit it was they had been engaged in previously. And see all those flyers and playbills around the cash register, the postcards and signed photographs and scraps of messages stuck in the frame of the mirror behind the bar, that make the fat proprietor there — bald head with greasy grey strands draped over it, a scrunched-up moustache, a big gold ring on his fat little finger — look like a booking agent of some variety ensconced at his desk among the scraps and memorabilia of his trade.

You won't bring her back, you know, Lydia said, *not like this.* And of course she was right. Not like this, nor any other way.

Who, Dawn Devonport wanted to know, frowning and concentrating, who was Svidrigailov? That was, I told her again, patiently, the name my daughter gave to the person she had come here with, whose child she was carrying. Through the glass door of the café I could see, far out on the bay, a sleek white craft, low in the stern and high in the prow, shouldering its way over the purple swell and seeming as if it would take to the sky at any moment, a magic ship, breasting the air. Dawn Devonport was lighting a cigarette with a hand that trembled. I told her what Billie Stryker had told me, that Axel Vander had been here or hereabouts at the same time as my daughter. She only nodded; perhaps she knew it already, perhaps Billie Stryker had told her that, too. She took off her sunglasses and folded them and put them on the table beside her cup. "And now we're here, you and I," she said, "where the poet drowned himself."

We left the café and walked up through

349

the narrow streets of the town. In the hotel the lounge was deserted and we went in there. It was a cramped room with a high ceiling, very like the parlour in my mother's lodging-house, with its shadows and its silence and its vague but indispersible air of ill-content. I sat on a sort of sofa with a low back and a high-sprung seat; the upholstery smelt strongly of immemorial cigarette smoke. A grandfather clock, its toiling innards on show through an oval glass panel in its front, stood in a corner sentry-straight and ticked and tocked with ponderous deliberation, seeming to hesitate an instant before each tock and tick. The centre of the room was occupied by a high and somehow overbearing dining-table made of black wood, with stout carven legs, on which was spread a cloth of heavy brocade that hung low over the sides and was edged with tassels. On it the busy set designer had placed, of all things, and as if all so artlessly, an antique volume of the poems of Leopardi, with marbled edges and a tooled leather spine, in which I tried to read —

Dove vai? chi ti chiama
Lunge dai cari tuoi,
Belissima donzella?
Sola, peregrinando, il patrio tetto

350

Sì per tempo abbandoni? . . .

— but the poetry's gorgeous sonorities and sobbing cadences soon defeated me, and I put the book back where I had taken it from and returned to my seat creakingly, like a chided schoolboy. Dawn Devonport sat in a narrow armchair in a corner opposite the grandfather clock, leaning forwards tensely with her legs crossed, flipping rapidly and, as it seemed, contemptuously through the pages of a glossy magazine in her lap. She was smoking a cigarette, and after each puff, without turning her head, she would twist up her mouth as if to whistle and shoot out a thin jet of smoke sideways. I studied her. Often it seems to me the closer I come to a person the farther off I am. How is that? I wonder. I used to watch Mrs. Gray like that when we were in bed together, and would feel her grow distant even as she lay beside me, just as sometimes, disconcertingly, a word will detach itself from its object and float away, weightless and iridescent as a soap bubble.

Abruptly Dawn Devonport tossed the magazine on to the table — how flabbily the heavy pages flopped — and rose and said she would go to her room and lie down. She lingered a moment and looked at me strangely, with what seemed a strange surmise. "I suppose you think he was Svidrigailov," she said, "Axel Vander — you think he was him." She made herself shiver, wincing as if she had tasted something sour, and went out.

I sat on there alone for a long time. I was remembering — or I am remembering now, it does not matter which — Mrs. Gray talking to me one day about dying. Where were we? In Cotter's place? No, somewhere else. But where else was there that we could have been? Bizarrely, my memory places us in that upstairs living room where Billy and I used to drink his father's whiskey. Surely it is not possible, yet that is where I see us. But how would she have managed to smuggle me into the house, under what pretext, and for what purpose? — certainly not the accustomed one, given that we were in the living room, with our clothes on, and not down in the laundry room. I have a picture in my mind of the two of us sitting very properly in two armchairs set close to each other at an angle opposite the rectangular window with the metal frames. It was a Sunday morning, I believe, a late-summer Sunday morning, and I was wearing a tweed suit in which I was hot and itchy, and in which I felt ridiculous, more nearly naked than clothed, as I always did when I was made to put on my Sunday best. Where were the others, Billy and his sister and Mr. Gray? What can have been going on? I must have been there for a reason; Billy and I must have been going somewhere, on a school outing, maybe, and he was late as always and I was waiting for him. But would I have called for him, given that now I was devoting so much energy and ingenuity to avoiding him? Anyway, I was there, that is all there is to say. The sun was shining full upon the square outside and everything out there seemed made of vari-coloured glass, and a playful breeze was filling the lace curtain at the open window and making it billow inwards and upwards in ever-swelling languor. I always had a strong sense of estrangement on those Sunday mornings when I was young — the noose-like feel of my shirt collar, the birds at their excited business, those far church-bells — and there was always an air that seemed to waft from the south, yes, the south, with its lion-coloured dust and lemon glare. No doubt it was the future I was anticipating, the shimmering promise of it, for the future for me always had a southern aspect, which is strange to think of now, now that the future is arrived, up here in Ultima Thule, arrived

353

and steadily pouring through the pinhole of the present, into the past.

Mrs. Gray was dressed in a rather severe blue suit — a costume, she would have called it — and wore black shoes with high heels, seamed stockings, a pearl necklace. Her hair was done differently from usual, swept back in some way that even managed to subdue for the moment that wayward curl at her ear, and she smelt as my mother did, as I suppose everyone's mother did, on Sunday mornings in summer, of scent and cold cream and face powder, of sweat, a little, of flesh-warm nylon and faintly moth-bally wool, and of something vaguely ashen, too, that I was never able to identify. The jacket of her suit was fashionably high at the shoulders and tightly nipped at the waist — she must have been wearing a corset — and the calf-length skirt was narrow, with a slit at the back. I had not seen her dressed so formally before, so rigidly, all interestingly pinned and pent, and I sat surveying her with an impudent and, it might almost be, an uxorial sense of possession. It is a scene from one of those women's pictures of the day, of course, the kind that Mrs. Gray did not like, for I see it in black-and-white, or charcoal-and-silver, rather, she in the Older Woman role while I am played by, oh, some boy wonder with a cheeky grin and a quiff, as pert as you please in my neat tweed suit and starched white shirt and striped, clip-on tie.

At first I did not absorb what it was she was talking about, distracted as I was in studying the complicated system of seams — darts, I believe they are called — in the wonderfully full bosom of her dress, the brittle blue material of which had an excitingly metallic burnish, and made tiny crackling sounds with each breath she took. She had turned her head away and was looking pensively towards the window and the sunlit square, and was saying, with a finger to her cheek, how she wondered sometimes what it would be like not to be here — would it be like being under an anaesthetic, maybe, with no sense of anything, not even of time passing? — and how hard it was to imagine being somewhere else, and how harder still it was to think of not being anywhere at all. Slowly her words filtered their way into the inilluminable dimness of my self-regarding consciousness, until, with a sort of click, I understood, or thought I understood, exactly what she was saying, and suddenly I was all ears. Not to be here? To be somewhere else? What was all this, surely, but a roundabout way of letting me know that she was preparing to have done with me? Now, at other times, should the barest suspicion have entered my head that she was hinting at any such thing, I would straight away have set to whining and howling and drumming my fists, for I was a child still, remember, with all a child's conviction of the imperative need for an instant, tearful and clamorous response to even the mildest threat to my well-being. That day, however, and for whatever reason, I bided, warily, watchfully, and let her talk on until, perhaps sensing the vigilant quality of my attentiveness, she paused, and turned, and focused in that way she did, seeming to swivel and train on me an invisible telescope. "Do you ever think of it," she asked, "dying?" Before I could answer she laughed self-disparagingly and shook her head. "But of course you don't," she said. "Why would you?"

Now my interest switched on to another track. If she was really talking about death as death and not as a hint that she was leaving me, then she must be talking about Mr. Gray. The possibility that her husband was mortally ill had been taking an ever-strengthening hold on my imagination, with a consequent bolstering of my hopes of securing Mrs. Gray for myself on a long-term basis. If the old boy were to croak, there at last and gloriously would be my chance. I must not make a move precipitately, of course. We would have to wait, the two of us, until I was of age, and even then there would be obstacles, Kitty and my mother not the least of them, while Billy would hardly warm to the grotesque prospect of having for his stepfather a boy of his own age, and a sometime best friend, at that. In the interval, however, while we were anticipating my majority, what opportunities would offer themselves for me to fulfil my childhood dream of having not a bald and inarticulated doll to cuddle and care for and operate on, but a full-sized, warm-blooded, safely widowed woman all of my own, accessible to me all day and every day, and, more momentously, every night, too, a prized possession that I might show off boldly to the world, whenever and wherever I pleased. So now I sharpened my ears and listened keenly to whatever else she might have to add on the subject of her husband's prospective demise. Alas, she would say nothing more, and seemed abashed, indeed, by what she had already said, and short of asking straight out how long the doctors had given the purblind optician I could get nothing further out of her.

But what was I doing there, in her living room, in my scratchy suit, on a Sunday, in the dying days of that summer — what? So often the past seems a puzzle from which the most vital pieces are missing.

Although I grew up in that world of transience and hidden presences, and married a woman who grew up there, too, I still find hotels uncanny, not only in the stillness of the night but in the daytime, too. At mid-morning, especially, something sinister always seems to be afoot under cover of that fake, hothouse calm. The receptionist behind the desk is one I have not seen before, and gives me a blank look as I drift past and does not smile or offer a word of greeting. In the deserted dining room all the tables are set, the gleaming cutlery and the sparkling napery laid out just so, like an operating theatre where multiple surgical procedures will presently be carried out. Upstairs, the corridor buzzes with a breathless, tight-lipped intent. I pass along it soundlessly, a disembodied eye, a moving lens. The doors, all identical, a receding double procession of them, have the look of having been slammed smartly shut one after another a second before I stepped out of the lift. What can be going on behind them?

The sounds that filter out, a querulous word, a cough, a snatch of low laughter, seem each the beginning of a plea or a tirade that is cut short at once by an unheard slap, or a hand clapped over a mouth. There is a smell of last night's cigarettes, of cold breakfast coffee, of faeces and shower soap and shaving balm. And that big trolley thing abandoned there, stacked with folded sheets and pillow-cases and with a bucket and a mop hooked on at the back, where is the chambermaid who should be in charge of it, what has become of her?

I stood outside Dawn Devonport's door for fully a minute before knocking, and even then I barely brushed my knuckles against the wood. There was no response from within. Was she sleeping again? I tried the knob. The door was not locked. I opened it an inch and waited again, listening, and then stepped into the room, or insinuated myself, rather, slipping in sideways without a sound, and closed the door carefully behind me, holding my breath as the catch caught. The curtains were not drawn, and although the air was chill, there was more brightness than I had expected, almost a summer radiance, with a broad beam of sunlight angling down from a corner of the window, like a spot, and the net curtain a blaze of gauzy whiteness. Everything was tidied and orderly — that missing maid had been in here, anyway — and the bed might not have been slept in. Dawn Devonport lay on top of the covers, on her side again, with a hand under her cheek and her knees drawn up. I noticed how shallow an indentation in the mattress her body made, so light is she and how little of her there is. She still had her coat on, the fur collar making an oval frame for her face. She was looking at me from where she lay, those grey eyes of hers turned up to me, larger and wider than ever. Was she frightened, had I alarmed her by sliding into the room in that sinuous and sinister way? Or was she just drugged? Without lifting her head she extended her free hand to me. I clambered on to the bed, shoes and all, and lay down, face to her face, our knees touching; her eyes seemed larger than ever. "Hold on to me," she murmured. "I feel as if I'm falling, all the time." She drew back the wing of her coat and I moved closer and put my arm over her, inside her coat. Her breath was cool on my face and her eyes were almost all I could see now. I felt her ribs under my wrist, and her heart beating. "Imagine I'm your daughter," she said. "Pretend I am."

So we remained for some time, there on

the bed, in the cold, sunlit room. I felt as if I were gazing into a mirror. Her hand lay lightly, a bird's claw, on my arm. She talked about her father, how good he had been, how cheerful, and how he would sing to her when she was little. "Silly songs, he sang," she said, " 'Yes, We Have No Bananas,' 'Roll Out the Barrel,' that sort of thing." One year he had been elected Pearly King of the Cockneys. "Have you ever seen the Pearly King? He was so pleased with himself, in that ridiculous suit — he even had pearls on his cap — and I was so ashamed I hid in the cupboard under the stairs and wouldn't come out. And Mum was Pearly Queen." She cried a little, then wiped at the tears impatiently with the heel of a hand. "Stupid," she said, "stupid."

I withdrew my arm and we sat up. She swung her legs off the bed but remained sitting on the side of it, with her back turned to me, and lit a cigarette. I lay down again, propped on an elbow, and watched the lavender smoke curling and coiling upwards into the shaft of sunlight at the window. She was crouching forwards now, with her knees crossed and an elbow on her knee and her chin on her hand. I watched her, the slope of her back and the set of her shoulders and the outline of her shoulder-blades folded like wings and her hair wreathed in smoke. A drama coach I once took lessons from told me a good actor should be able to act with the back of his head. *"Roll out the barrel,"* she sang softly, huskily, *"we'll have a barrel of fun."*

Had she really intended to kill herself, I asked. Had she wanted to die? She did not answer for a long time, then lifted her shoulders and let them fall again in a weary shrug. She did not turn when she spoke. "I don't know," she said. "Don't they say the ones who fail weren't serious in the first place? Maybe it was just, you know, what we do, you and I." Now she twisted her head and looked at me at a sharp angle over her shoulder. "Just acting."

I said we should go back, that we should go home. She was still regarding me from under her hair, her head on one side and her chin resting on her shoulder. "Home," she said. Yes, I said. Home.

Somehow it seems to me it was the thunder-clap that did it, I mean I think it was by some dark magic our undoing. Certainly it presaged the end. The storm caught us at Cotter's place. There is something vindictive about that kind of rain, a sense of vengeance being wrought from above. How relentlessly it clattered through the trees that day, like artillery fire showering down on a defenceless and huddled village. We had not minded rain, before, but that was the gentler kind, mere grapeshot compared to this barrage. At Cotter's place it even used to give us a game to play, running here and there to set a pot or a jam-jar on the floor under each new leak in the ceiling as it sprang. How Mrs. Gray would squeal when a plummeting cold drop fell on the back of her neck and slithered down along her bare skin under her flowered dress. By happy chance the corner where we had set out our mattress was one of the few dry places in the house. We would sit there together contentedly side by side, listening to the susurrating rain among the leaves, she smoking one of her Sweet Aftons and I practising jackstones with the beads from a necklace of hers the string of which I had broken unintentionally one afternoon in the course of a particularly energetic bout of love-making. "Babes in the wood, that's us," Mrs. Gray would say, and grin at me, displaying those two endearingly overlapping front teeth.

It turned out she was terrified of thunder. At the first crash of it, directly overhead and at what seemed no higher than the level of the roof, she went ashen-faced on the instant and crossed herself rapidly. We had been just short of the house when the rain came on, sweeping down on us through the trees with a muffled roar, and although we had sprinted the last few yards along the track we were thoroughly wet by the time we tumbled in at the front door. Mrs. Gray's hair was plastered to her skull, except for that irrepressible curl at her ear, and her dress was stuck to the front of her legs and moulded around the curves of her belly and her breasts. She stood flat-footed in the middle of the floor with her arms out at either side and flapped her hands, scattering drops from her fingertips. "What'll we do?" she wailed. "We'll catch our deaths!"

The summer had drawn to an end almost without our noticing — the storm was a brusque reminder — and I was back at school. I had not called for Billy on the first morning of the new term, and did not on any subsequent morning, either. It was harder than ever to look him in the eye now, not least because that eye was so like his mother's. What did he imagine had happened, that I should shun him like this? Maybe he thought of that day in Rossmore when I bumped into him with his tennis friends and his two rackets in their fancy new presses. In the school yard we avoided each other, and walked home by separate ways.

I was in trouble elsewhere, too. I had done badly in my exams, which was a surprise to everyone, though not to me, whom love had kept busy throughout that previous spring when I should have been at my studies. I was a bright boy and much had been expected of me, and my mother was sorely disappointed in me. She reduced my pocket money by half, but only for a week or two — no moral tenacity, that woman — and, much more seriously, threatened to make me stay indoors and apply myself to my schoolwork from now on. Mrs. Gray, when I told her of these punitive measures, sided against me, to my astonishment, saying my mother was quite right, that I should be ashamed of myself for not working harder and for putting in such a poor academic performance. This led at once into the first real row we had, I mean the first that was caused by something other than my unresting jealousy and her amused disregard of it, and I went at her, bald-headed, as she would have said, which is to say, just like an adult — I was very much older now than I had been before this summer began. How darkly she glowered back at me, how defiantly, from under down-drawn brows, as I thrust my face close up to hers and snivelled and snarled. A fight like that is never forgotten, but goes on bleeding unseen, under its brittle cicatrice. But how tenderly we made up afterwards, how lovingly she rocked me in her embrace.

It had not occurred to us, in the golden glare of that long-lasted summer, that sooner or later we would have to look for somewhere more resistant to the elements than the old house in the woods. Already there was an autumnal crispness in the air, especially in the late afternoons when the sun had declined sharply from the zenith, and now with the rains it was chillier still — "We'll soon be doing it in our overcoats," Mrs. Gray said gloomily — and the floorboards and the walls were giving off a dispiriting odour of damp and rot. Then came the thunder-clap. "Well, that," Mrs. Gray declared, her voice shaking and the raindrops dripping from her fingertips, "that puts the tin hat on it." But where else were we to find shelter? Desperate speculation. I even toyed with the thought of requisitioning one of the disused rooms under the attic in my mother's house; we could come through the back garden, I said eagerly, seeing us there already, and in by the back door and up the back stairs from the scullery and no one would be the wiser. Mrs. Gray only looked at me. All right then, I said sulkily, did she have a better suggestion?

As it turned out, we need not have worried. I mean, we should have worried, but not about finding a new place for ourselves. That day, even before the last grumbles of thunder had settled and ceased, Mrs. Gray in her fright was off, scampering in the rain along the track through the streaming wood, with her shoes in her hand and her cardigan pulled over her head for an ineffective hood, and was in the station wagon and had the engine started and was moving off before I caught up and scrambled in beside her. By now we were both thoroughly soaked. And where were we going? The rain was battering on the metal roof and dishfuls of it were sloshing back and forth across the windscreen before the valiantly labouring wipers. Mrs. Gray, her hands white-knuckled on the wheel, drove with her face thrust forwards, the whites of her eyes glinting starkly and her nostrils flared in fright. "We'll go home," she said, thinking aloud, "there's no one there, we'll be all right." The window beside me was awash, and quavering trees, glassy-green in that electric light, loomed in it an instant and were gone, as if felled by our passing. The sun, improbably, was managing to shine somewhere, and the washes of rain on the windscreen now were all fire and liquid sparks. "Yes," Mrs. Gray said again, nodding rapidly to herself, "yes, we'll go home."

And home we went — to her home, that is. As we were drawing into the square there was an almost audible swish and the rain stopped on the instant, as if a silver bead curtain had been drawn peremptorily aside, and the drenched sunlight crept forwards, to re-stake its shaky claim on the cherry trees and the sparkling gravel under them and the pavements that had already started to steam. The air in the house felt damp and had a wan, greyish odour, and the light in the rooms seemed uncertain, and there was an uncertain hush, as if the furniture had been up to something, some dance or romp that had stopped on the instant when we entered. Mrs. Gray left me in the kitchen and went off and came back a minute later having changed into a woollen dressing-gown that was too big for her — was it Mr. Gray's? — and under which, it was plainly apparent, to my avid eye, at least, that she was naked. "You smell like a sheep," she said cheerfully, and led me down — yes! — led me down to the laundry room.

I have a suspicion she did not remember our previous encounter there. That is to say I do not think it occurred to her to remember it, on this occasion. Is it possible? For me this narrow room with the oddly lofty ceiling and the single window set high up in the wall was a holy site, a sort of sacristy where a hallowed memory was stored, whereas for her I suppose it had reverted to being just the place where she did the family's washing. The low bed, or mattress, I noticed at once, was no longer there, under the window. Who had removed it, and why? But then, who had put it there in the first place?

Mrs. Gray, humming, took a towel to my wet hair. She said she did not know what to do about my clothes. Would I wear one of Billy's shirts? Or no, she said, frowning, perhaps that would not be a good idea. But what would my mother say, she wondered, if I came home soaked to the skin? She did not seem to have noticed that, under cover of the towel she was so vigorously applying to my head — how many times in her life had she dried a child's hair? — I had been edging ever closer to her, and now I reached out blindly and seized her by the hips. She laughed, and took a step backwards. I followed, and this time got my hands inside the dressing-gown. Her skin was still slightly damp, and slightly chilled, too, which somehow made her seem all the more thoroughly, thrillingly naked. "Stop that!" she said, laughing again, and again stepped back. I was out from under the towel, and she made a wad of it and pushed it at my chest in a halfhearted attempt to fend me off. She could go back no farther now for her shoulder-blades were against the wall. The belted gown was agape at the top where I had been fumbling at it, and the skirts of it, too, were parted, baring her bare legs to their tops, so that for a moment she was the

Kayser Bondor lady to the life, as provocatively dishevelled as the original was composed. I put my hands on her shoulders. The broad groove between her breasts had a silvery sheen. She began to say something, and stopped, and then — it was the strangest thing — then I saw us there, actually saw us, as if I were standing in the doorway looking into the room, saw me hunched against her, canted a little to the left with my right shoulder lifted, saw the shirt wet between my shoulder-blades and the seat of my wet trousers sagging, saw my hands on her, and one of her glossy knees flexed, and her face paling above my left shoulder and her eyes staring.

She pushed me aside. Of all the things that were about to start happening, I think that push, the shock of it, although it was not violent or even ungentle, is the thing I have remembered of that day with the keenest clarity, the acutest anguish. Thus must the puppet feel when the puppeteer lets the strings fall from his fingers and ducks out of the booth, whistling. It was as if in that instant she had sloughed a self, the self I knew, and stepped past me as a stranger.

Who was it that was standing in the doorway? Yes, yes, I need not tell you, you know already who it was. The lank plaits, the thick specs, the knock-knees. She was wearing one of those dresses that little girls wore then, vaguely Alpine, dotted all over with tiny flowers, pleated, and with a crimpled, elasticated front to the bodice. In her hand she was holding something, I do not remember what — a fiery sword, perhaps. Marge was there, too, her fat friend from the birthday party, the one who took a shine to me, but I paid her scant heed. They just stood, the two of them, looking at us, with curiosity, it seemed, more than anything else, then turned aside, not hurriedly, but in that dull blank way that spectators turn aside from the scene of an accident when the ambulance has driven off. I heard their clumsy school shoes clattering on the wooden steps up to the kitchen. Did I hear Kitty snicker? Mrs. Gray went to the doorway and put her head into the corridor, but did not call out to her daughter, did not say anything, and after a moment came back again, into the room, to me. She was frowning, and nibbling at her lower lip. She looked as if she had misplaced something and were trying hard to think where she might have left it. What did I do? Did I speak? I remember her looking at me for a second as if puzzled, then smiling, distractedly, and putting a hand to my cheek. "I

think," she said, "you should go home now."
It was so strange, the simple, utter, incon-
testable finality of it. It was like the end of
an orchestral performance. All that had held
us suspended and rapt for so long, all that
violent energy, that tension and concentration, all that glorious clamour, suddenly in
that moment stopped, leaving nothing but a
fading gleam of sound upon the air. I did
not think to protest, to plead or weep or
shout, but did as she bade me and stepped
past her meekly without a word, and went
home.

What happened after that happened with
bewildering swiftness and dispatch. By
evening Mrs. Gray had fled. I heard — from
whom? — that she had gone back to the
town where she and Mr. Gray had come
from, to the grand boulevards and the
worldly sophisticates about which and
whom she had so liked to tease me. It must
have been where she was born, for she was
staying there in the care of her mother, it
was said. The news that Mrs. Gray had a
mother was so amazing as to divert me for
a moment from my anguish. She had never
mentioned a mother to me, unless she did
and I was not listening; it is possible, but I
do not think even I would have been that

inattentive. I tried to picture this fabulous personage and saw an immensely aged version of Mrs. Gray herself, wrinkled, stooped and for some reason blind, leaning at a wicket fence in a sunlit cottage garden profuse with summer flora, smiling in sad forgiveness and holding out her hands in that vaguely beseeching way that blind people do, welcoming home her disgraced and penitent daughter. So strange, so strange even now to think of a previous Mrs. Gray — no, she would have been a Mrs. someone else. That is another thing I never knew, my maiden's maiden name.

The next day, auctioneer's signs sprouted on the front of the house in the square, and in the window of the shop in the Haymarket, too, and Miss Flushing's nostrils and the rims of her eyes were redder than ever. Do I recall the station wagon pulling out of the square packed with household things, and Mr. Gray and Billy and Billy's sister crowded together in the front seat, that seat on which Mrs. Gray and I had so often bounced together as on an enchanted trampoline, Mr. Gray looking pained but with his jaw juttingly set, like Gary Fonda in *The Grapes of Noon*? Surely I am inventing again, as so often.

Yet come to think of it their going cannot

374

have been that precipitate, for days were to pass, a week, even, or more than a week, before I had my final encounter with Billy Gray. In my memory the seasons have shifted yet again, for although it was still September I see our confrontation acted out in raw winter weather. The place was called the Forge, near the square where the Grays lived; a blacksmith must have worked there, long ago. The surroundings were appropriate, for the Forge was always associated for me, and still is, with a nameless disquiet. Yet it was an unremarkable enough place, where a hill road leading up to the square broadened and turned in an odd, lopsided way, and another, narrower road, little used, led off at a sharp angle into the countryside. Where this road started there was an overhang of heavy dark trees, underneath which was a well, or not a well, but a broad-mouthed metal pipe protruding from the wall, through which poured a constant flow of water, smooth and shiny as moulded zinc and thick as a man's upper arm, that plunged into a mossed-over concrete trough that was always full yet never overflowed. I used to wonder where so much water could be coming from, for it did not slacken off even in the driest months of summer, and was, I thought, uncanny in its unrelenting dedication to its one, monotonous task. And where did it go to, the water? Must have run off underground into the Sow River — can that really have been its name? — a meagre dirty stream that ran along a culvert at the foot of the hill. What do they matter, these details? Who cares where the water came from or went to, or what the season was or how the sky looked or whether the wind was blowing — who cares? Yet someone must — someone has to. Me, I suppose.

Billy was walking up the hill and I was walking down. I cannot say why I was there or where I was coming from. I must have been in the square, even though I distinctly recall making every effort to avoid the sight of that cardboard For Sale sign displayed outside Mrs. Gray's bedroom window like a flag on a plague ship. I might have crossed to the other side of the road, or Billy might have, but neither of us did. My memory, with its lamentable fondness for the pathetic fallacy, sets a raw wind skirmishing about us, and there are dead leaves, of course, scraping along the pavements, and those dark trees shake and sway. Details again, you see, always details, exact and impossible. Yet I have not remembered what Billy said to me, except that he called me a dirty fucking bastard and suchlike, but I do see his tears, and hear his sobs of rage and shame and bitter sorrow. He tried to hit me, too, wildly swinging those sheaf-gatherer's arms of his, while I retreated in little skips and hops, bent halfway over backwards like a contortionist. And I, what did I say? Did I attempt to apologise, did I try to explain myself and my base betrayal of our friendship? What explanation could I have offered? I felt peculiarly detached from the moment. It was as if what was happening were something that was being shown to me, a particularly violent sequence from a morality play, illustrating the inevitable consequence of Unchastity, Lust and Lewdness. Yet at the same time, and I know it will provoke jeers of contempt and disbelief when I say it, at the same time I had never felt such care, such compassion, such tenderness — such, yes, such love for Billy as I felt there on that hill road, with him flailing and sobbing and me bobbing backwards, ducking and weaving, and the cold wind blowing and the dead leaves scrabbling and that thick skein of water crashing and crashing into its depthless trough. If I had thought he would allow it, I believe I would have embraced him. What was enacted there, in cries of pain and wildly aimed blows, was, I suppose, some version, for me, of the parting scene that had not played itself out between me and Mrs. Gray, so that I welcomed even this poor simulacrum of what had been withheld and what I so piercingly missed.

In the days immediately following Mrs. Gray's flight I think what I felt most strongly was fear. I found myself abandoned and astray in a place that was alien to me, a place I had not known existed, and in which I suspected I had not the experience or the fortitude necessary to survive without suffering grave damage. This was grown-up territory, where I should not have to be. Who would rescue me, who would follow and find me and lead me back to be again among the scenes and the safety I had known before that bewitched summer? I clung to my mother as I had not done since I was an infant. I should say that although I thought it impossible for her not to have heard the scandalous news of Mrs. Gray and me — it might have been put about by a town crier, such was the instantaneity and volume of the gossip as it flew from street corner to church gate to kitchen nook and back again — she uttered not a single word about it, to me, and surely not to anyone else. Perhaps she also was afraid, perhaps for her also it was a strange and terrifying territory my salacious doings had landed her in.

Oh, but what a good son I was now, attentive, grave, studious, dutiful far beyond the call of duty. How prompt I was to run a household errand for my mother, with what patience and sympathy did I listen to her complaints, her grievances, her denunciations of our lodgers' laziness, venality and neglect of personal hygiene. It was all a sham, of course. If Mrs. Gray had bethought herself and come back as suddenly as she had gone, a thing that seemed to me not at all impossible, I would have flung myself upon her with all the old ardour, the old recklessness. For it was not discovery and disgrace, not the town's gossips or my mother's unspoken accusations, that made me tremble with fear. What I was afraid of was my own grief, the weight of it, the ineluctable corrosive force of it; that, and the stark awareness I had of being, for the first time in my life, entirely alone, a Crusoe shipwrecked and stranded in the limitless wastes of a boundless and indifferent ocean. Or rather say a Theseus, abandoned on Naxos while Ariadne hastened off about her uncaring business.

What was striking, too, was the silence that I felt around me. The town was humming with talk and I was the only one nobody spoke to. I welcomed Billy's onslaught that day in the Forge, for it made a noise, at least, and was aimed at me, uniquely. There will have been those in the town who were genuinely shocked and scandalised, but those, too, who will have secretly envied Mrs. Gray and me, the one lot not necessarily exclusive of the other. And everyone, to be sure, must have been vastly entertained, even those few who might have sympathised with us, disgraced, bereft and wounded as we were. I fully expected Father Priest to come calling again, this time to recommend that I be incarcerated among the Trappists on some sheep-flecked mountainside in remotest Alpland, but even he kept his distance, and his peace. Perhaps he was embarrassed. Perhaps, I ask myself uneasily, they were all embarrassed, even as they rubbed their hands in relish at the scandal? I would have preferred them to be outraged. It would have seemed more — what shall I say? — more respectful of the great thing Mrs. Gray and I had made between us and that was now no more.

I waited, confidently at first but then with deepening bitterness, for Mrs. Gray to send me something, a word, a valediction from afar, but nothing came. How would she have communicated with me? She could hardly have sent a letter through the post to me, to my mother's house. But wait — how did we communicate before, when our affair was still going on? There was a telephone in the overflowing cubby-hole beside the kitchen that my mother called her office, it was an antiquated model with a handle at the side that had to be cranked to get a connection to the operator, but I would never have called Mrs. Gray on it, and she would never have dreamed of calling me, for apart from anything else the operator always listened in, she could be heard on the line, making curious shiftings and excited, mousy scrabblings. We must have left notes for each other somewhere, at Cotter's place, maybe — but no, Mrs. Gray did not go there alone, she was afraid of the woods, and on those occasions when by chance she got there before me I would find her cowering anxiously in the doorway and on the point of flight. So how did we manage? I do not know. Another unsolved mystery, among the many mysteries. There was an occasion when through some mix-up she did not come when she was supposed to, and I waited for her through an agonised afternoon, increasingly convinced that she would appear no more, that she was lost to

381

me for ever. That was the single occasion I can recall when the lines of communication between us broke down — but what lines were they, and where were they laid?

I did not dream about her, after she was gone, or if I did I forgot what I had dreamed. My sleeping mind was more merciful than the waking one, which never tired of tormenting me. Well, yes, it did tire of its sport, eventually. Nothing so intense could last for long. Or might it have, if I had truly loved her, with selfless passion, as they say, as people are said to have loved in olden times? Such a love would have destroyed me, surely, as it used to destroy the heroes and the heroines in the old books. But what a pretty corpse I would have made, marbled on my bier, clutching in my fingers a marble lily for remembrance.

My my, talk about trouble. Marcy Meriwether says she is going to sue me. She telephones half a dozen times a day, demanding to know what I have done with Dawn Devonport, where I have hidden her, her furious voice on the line swooping from operatic trills and warbles to a gangster's guttural muttering. I imagine her, a disembodied Medusa-head suspended in the ether, threatening, bullying, cajoling. I insist

382

repeatedly that I do not know the where-abouts of her star. At this she does her harsh and phlegmy laugh, followed by an interval of heavy wheezing as she lights up another cigarette. She knows I am lying. If filming is disrupted for one more day, *one more day,* she will terminate my contract and set her lawyers on me. This she has been saying every day for a week. I will not be paid another cent, she squawks at me, not another red cent, and furthermore she will move to seize back from me the pay I have received up to now. Behind all the blare and bluster I seem to detect a note of relish, for she enjoys a fight, that much is plain. When she slams down the phone, it leaves a whirring sensation for some seconds in my ear.

Toby Taggart invited me to lunch at Ostentation Towers the day after my return from Italy. I found him in the Corinthian Rooms, in a plush-lined booth, squirming and sighing and sitting on his hands to keep from biting his nails. What an aggrieved and wounded look he gave me. He was drinking a martini with an olive in it, he said it was his third; I have never seen him drink before, it is a mark of his distress. Look, Alex, he said, softly, patiently, this is serious, his shaggy head lowered and his square hands joined before him over his martini as if to consecrate it — this could jeopardise the whole movie, do you understand that, Alex, do you? Toby reminds me of a boy I knew at school, a shambling fellow with an enormous head that was made more massive still by a mop of glistening black hair coiled tight in wiry curls that tumbled over his forehead and his ears. Ambrose, he was called, Ambrose Abbott, nicknamed Bud, of course, or sometimes, ingeniously, Lou — yes, even in the matter of names he had no luck, no luck at all, poor chap. Ambrose could be heard coming from afar, for he was a keen collector of metal objects — blunt penknives, keys without locks, tarnished coins no longer in circulation, bottle-tops, even, in times of scarcity — so that as he walked he clinked and chinked like a Bedouin's loaded pack-camel. Also he was asthmatic, and carried on constantly a medley of sighs and soft whoops and faint, rasping whistles. He was immensely brainy, though, and took first place in every school test and State examination. I think, looking back, he had a crush on me. I imagine he envied my pose of insolent bravado — I was already rehearsing for those future roles as dashing leading men — and my proclaimed disdain for study and hard work. Perhaps, too, he sensed the musky aura of Mrs. Gray about me, for it was in the time of Mrs. Gray that I came to know him well, or well-ish. He was a tender soul. He used to press gifts on me, gems from his collection, which I accepted with ill grace and swapped for other things, or lost, or threw away. He was killed, later, knocked off his bike by a lorry on his way home from school. Sixteen, he was, when he died. Poor Ambrose. The dead are my dark matter, filling up impalpably the empty spaces of the world.

We had a pleasant lunch, Toby and I, and spoke of many things, his family, his friends, his hopes and ambitions. I really do think him a fine fellow. When we had finished and I was leaving, I told him he should not worry, that I was sure Dawn Devonport had simply gone underground for a time and would soon return and be among us again. Toby is staying at the Towers, and insisted on seeing me out. The doorman tipped his top-hat to us and drew open the tall glass door — *boing-g-g!* — and we stepped out together into the late-December day. Re-markable weather we are having, clear and crisp and very still, with delicate Japanese skies and a sense in the air of a continuous far faint ringing, as if the rim of a glass were being rubbed and rubbed. The poet is right, midwinter spring is its own season. Toby, fuddled after those martinis and further glasses of wine, had begun again earnestly to entreat me in the matter of Dawn Devonport and the need for her to return to work. Yes, Toby, I said, patting him on the shoulder, yes, yes. And back inside he shambled, I hope to sleep off all that alcohol.

I walked across the park. There was ice on the duck pond and on the ice a crazed glare of reflected, warmthless sunlight. All at once, ahead of me, I spied a familiar figure, shuffling along the metalled pathway under the black and glistening trees. I had not had a sighting of him for some while, and had begun to worry; someday surely he will fall off the wagon finally and do for himself at last. I caught up with him and slowed my pace and walked along close behind him. I did not detect the usual fug that he trails in his wake, which was encouraging. In fact, as soon became clear, he has undergone one of his periodic metamorphoses — that girl of his must have taken him in hand again and given him a thorough going-over. He does not seem as perky as in previous resurrections, it is true — his feet in particular, despite the plush boots, seem permanently beyond repair — and he has developed a distinct hump above his right shoulder-blade. All the same he is a new man, compared to what the recent old one was like. His pea-coat had been cleaned, his college scarf washed, his beard trimmed, while those desert-boots looked brand-new — I wonder if the daughter works in a shoe shop. By now I had drawn level with him, though I kept myself at a discreet remove on the far side of the path. He was fairly surging along, despite the infirmity of his feet. He had his hands up, as usual, half clenched into fists in their fingerless gloves; now, though, in his resuscitated state, he might have been some champ's favoured sparring partner rather than the punch-drunk staggerer of previous times. I was trying to think of something I might do for him, or give him, or just say to him, to mark the little miracle of his return yet again from the lower depths. But what could I have done, what said? Had I tried to engage him in even the most bland exchange, about the weather, say, it would surely have resulted in embarrassment for us both, and who knows, he might even have taken a poke at me, sobered and jauntily pugnacious as he seemed. But it cheered me to see him in such fine fettle, and when a little farther on he veered off along the path around the pond I went on my own way with a measurably lightened step.

I must remember to tell Lydia I have seen him, in all his renewed, Lazarine vigour. She knows of him only by repute, through my reports; nevertheless, she takes a lively interest in his successive declines and recoveries. She is that sort of soul, my Lydia, she worries about the lost ones of the world.

In the long and troubled years of Cass's childhood there were certain moments, certain intermittences, when a calm descended, not solely on Cass but upon all our little household, though a doubtful calm it was, heartsick and anxious at the core. Late at night sometimes, when I was at her bedside and she had lapsed at last into a sort of sleep after hours of turmoil and mute, inner anguish, it would seem to me that the room, and not just the room but the house itself and all its surroundings, had somehow dipped imperceptibly beneath the common level of things into a place of silence and imposed tranquillity. It reminded me, this languorous and slightly claustral state, of how as a boy at the seaside on certain stilled afternoons, the sky overcast and the air heavy, I would stand up to my neck in the warmish, viscid water and slowly, slowly let myself sink until my mouth, my nose, my ears, until all of me was submerged. How strange a world it was just under the surface there, glaucous, turbid, sluggishly asway, and what a roaring it made in my ears and what a burning in my lungs. A kind of gleeful panic would take hold of me then, and a bubble of something, not just breath, but a kind of wild, panicky joyfulness, would swell and swell in my throat until at last I had to leap up, like a leaping salmon, twisting and gasping, into the veiled, exploded air. Whenever I come into the house in these recent days I stop in the hall and stand for a moment, listening, antennae twitching, and I might be back, at night, in Cass's room — sickroom, I was about to write, since that was what it most often was — so poised and hushed is the air, so shaded and dimmed the light, somehow, even where it is brightest — Dawn Devonport by a negative magic has wrought permanent twilight in our home. I do not complain of this, for to tell the truth I am glad of the effect — I find it a calmative. I like to imagine, standing there excitedly on the mat just inside the front door, submerged and breathless, that if I concentrate hard enough I will be able to locate by mental exertion alone the exact whereabouts in the house of both my wife and Dawn Devonport. How I am supposed to have developed this divinatory power I cannot say. In these latter days they reign like twin deities, the two of them, over our domestic afterworld. To my surprise — though why surprise? — they have come to be fond of each other. Or so I believe. They do not discuss this with me, needless to say. Even Lydia, even in the sanctuary of the bedroom, where such matters are meant to be aired, says nothing of our guest, if that is what she is — is she our captive? — or nothing that would suggest what her feelings or opinions are in regard to her. I suppose it is none of my business. When Dawn Devonport and I returned from Italy, Lydia took her in without a word, I mean without a word of protest, or complaint, as if the thing had been ordained. Is it that women naturally accommodate each other when trouble comes? Do they, any more than men accommodate men, or women accommodate men, or men accommodate women? I do not know. I never know about these things. Other people's motives, their desiderata and anathemas, are a mystery to me. My own are, too. I seem to myself to move in bafflement, to move immobile, like the dim and hapless hero in a fairy tale, trammelled in thickets, balked in briar.

One of Dawn Devonport's favourite roosting places about the house is the old green armchair in my attic eyrie. She passes hours there, hours, doing nothing, only watching light change on those ever-present hills far off at the edge of our world. She says she likes the feeling there is of sky and space up here. She has borrowed a jumper of mine that Lydia knitted for me long ago. Lydia, knitting, I cannot imagine it, now. The sleeves are too long and she uses them as an improvised muff. She is always cold, she tells me, even when the heating is set to its highest. I think of Mrs. Gray: she, too, used to complain of the cold as our summer waned. Dawn Devonport sits in a huddle in the chair with her legs drawn up, hugging herself. She wears no makeup and binds her hair back with a bit of ribbon. She looks very young with her face bare like that, or no, not young, but unformed, unshaped, an earlier, more primitive version of herself — a prototype, is that the word I want? I treasure her presence, secretly. I sit at my desk in my swivel chair, with my back turned to her, and write in my book. She says it pleases her to hear the scratching of the nib. I recall how Cass as a little girl used to lie on her side on the floor while I paced, reading my lines aloud from a script held up before me, reading them over and over, getting them into my head. Dawn Devonport has never acted in the theatre — "Straight to screen, that was me" — but she says the mountains look like stage flats. She intends to give up acting altogether, so she insists. She does not say what she will do when she stops. I tell her of Marcy Meriwether's threats, of Toby Taggart's heartstruck appeals. She looks out again at the hills, ash-blue in the afternoon's unseasonal sunlight, and says nothing. I suspect it pleases her to think herself a fugitive, sought by all. We are in a conspiracy together; Lydia is in it, too. I try to remember what loving Cass was like. Love, that word, I say it and it makes my poor old heart run fast, tickety-tock, its little flywheel fairly spinning. I see nothing, understand nothing, or little, anyway; little. It seems not to matter. Perhaps comprehension is not the task, any more. Just to be, that seems enough, for now, up here in this high room, with the girl in her chair at my back.

Today there was a letter waiting for me on my desk, a letter in a long, cream-coloured envelope embossed with the blazon of the University of Arcady. That rang a cracked bell. Of course — Axel Vander's safe haven off there on the sunny side of America, where Marcy Meriwether hails from. I love expensive stationery, the rich crackle of it, the shiny roughness of its surface, the gluey aroma that is for me the very smell of money. I am invited to attend a seminar the sobering title of which is *Anarch: Autarch — Disorder and Control in the Writings of Axel Vander.* Yes, I, too, was compelled to consult the dictionary; the result was not enlightening. All expenses paid, though, first-class flights, and a fee, or honorarium, as the letter's signatory, one H. Cyrus Blank, delicately has it. This Blank is the Paul de Man — him again! — Professor of Applied Deconstruction in the English Department at Arcady. He seems a friendly type, from his tone. Yet he is vague, and does not say in what capacity I am being invited to join in these arcadian revels. I might be required to come as the old fraud himself, with limp and ebony walking stick, eye-patch and all — I would not put it past them, Professor Blank and his fellow deconstructionists, to have thought of hiring me as an impersonator, a sort of moving wax-work representation of their hero. Shall I go? JB is also invited. It might be a pleasant jaunt — think of all those oranges fresh off the trees — but I am wary. People, real people, expect actors to be the characters they play. I am not Axel Vander, nor anything like him. Am I?

Blank. I have come across that name in JB's life of Vander, I am sure I have. Was there not a Blank involved somehow when Vander's wife died, in suspicious circumstances, as they say? I must look up the index. Could my Professor Blank be this other Blank's father, or his son? These spidery strands of connection, stretching across the world, their clinging touch gives me the shivers. Blank.

I think it is time Dawn Devonport was returned to the world. I am not sure how to put this to her. Lydia will help, I know. They spend a great deal of time together down in the kitchen, smoking and drinking tea and talking. Lydia has become an inveterate tea drinker, like my mother. I approach the kitchen door but when I hear their voices from the other side, an undulant blended buzz, I stop, and turn, and tiptoe away. I cannot think what things they talk about. Voices behind a door always seem to me to be coming from another world, where other laws obtain.

Yes, I shall ask Lydia to aid me in persuading our auroral guest, our star of the morning, to reassume her role, to step back into her part, to be in the world again. The world? As if it were the world.

I met JB for a drink, not sure why, and now wish I had not. We went at the cocktail hour to a place of his choosing, a sort of gentlemen's club up a side street, a curious establishment, unremarkable on the outside but gloomily palatial within, pillared and porticoed and sunk in a somnolent hush. The pillars were white, the walls Athenian blue, and there were many oil portraits of indistinct staring figures with high collars and mutton-chop whiskers. We sat on either side of a vast fireplace, in buttoned leather armchairs that squeaked and groaned in weary protest under us. The fireplace was deep, and disturbingly black in its depths, with an ornate brass fender and a brass coal scuttle and gleaming firedogs, but no fire. An ancient attendant in bow-tie and tails brought us our brandies on a silver tray and set them down wheezingly on a low table between us and went away without a word. I thought we were the only ones in the place until I heard someone unseen in the far depths of the room clearing his throat with a long, hawking rasp.

JB is distinctly odd, and grows odder each time I encounter him. He maintains a furtive, anxious air, and gives the impression always of being in the process of edging nervously away, even when he is sitting still, as now, in his high, winged armchair with his legs crossed and a brandy glass in his hand. Toby Taggart tells me it was JB who recommended me for the part of Vander. It seems he was there in the audience that disastrous night years ago when I dried on stage, a tongue-tied, goggling Amphitryon, and was impressed. I wonder what impressed him. What would he not be prepared to do for me had I dragged my way through to the final curtain? Now he sat there, at once glazed and alert, watching my lips intently as I spoke, as if he thought to read from them a different and darkly revealing version of the altogether too innocent-sounding matters that my words were meant to convey. No, he said hastily, interrupting me, no, he was sure there had been no one with Axel Vander in Liguria. This gave me pause. If I wished he would look up his notes, he went on, with a vehement gesture of the hand that was not holding the brandy snifter, but he believed he could say with certainty that Vander had been alone in Portovenere, quite alone. Then he looked away, frowning, and making a faint distressed humming noise at the back of his throat. There was a pause. So Vander, then, I said, had been in Portovenere, in fact. I felt like one who has been discharged from hospital with a clean bill of health but who arrives home only to find the ambulance waiting outside the house, its back doors wide open and two bored attendants standing in the street holding ready the stretcher, with its blood-red blanket. At my question JB turned back, I could almost hear the cogs in his neck grinding, and stared at me pop-eyed, opening and closing his mouth as if to test the mechanism before trusting himself to speak. He did recall, he said, the Nebraskan savant Fargo DeWinter, when he spoke to him in Antwerp all those years ago, mentioning something about an assistant who had worked with him on the Vander papers. I waited. JB blinked, gazing at me now in what seemed a fixed, faint torment. He had the impression, he said, with the wincing look of one trying in desperation to hold on to some fragile thing he knows he is about to let drop, and it was only an impression, mind, the merest hint of a suspicion, that it was this assistant and not DeWinter himself who had unearthed the goods, the real, that is the bad, goods on Vander and his questionable, to say the least, past. I waited again. JB went on staring and twitching. It was I now who felt I was about to let fall that breakable thing. When Cass was a little girl she used to say that as soon as she was grown-up she would marry me and we would have a child just like her so that if she died I would not miss her and be lonely. Ten years; she has been dead ten years. Must I set off in search of her again, in sorrow and in pain? She will come no more to my world, but I go towards hers.

Billie Stryker telephoned. I have come to fear these calls. She tells me there is someone I should speak to. I thought she said this person was a nun and I assumed I had misheard. I really must have my hearing seen to. My hearing, seen to — ha! There it is again, language playing with itself.

I have begun to look at Billie under a new light. Languishing for so long in the shadow of my inattention she seemed herself a shadow. But she, too, has her aura. She is, after all, the link between so many of the figures that most closely concern me — Mrs. Gray, my daughter, even Axel Vander. I ask myself if she might be more than merely a link, if she is, rather, in some way a co-ordinator. Co-ordinator? Odd word. I do not know what I mean, but I seem to mean something. I used to think, long ago, that despite all the evidence I was the one in charge of my own life. To be, I told myself, is to act. I missed the vital pun, though. Now I realise that always I have been acted upon, by unacknowledged forces, hidden coercions. Billie is the latest in that line of dramaturgs who have guided from behind the scenes the poor production that I am, or am taken to be. Now what new twist of the plot has she uncovered?

The Convent of Our Sacred Mother stands on a bleak rise above a windy confluence where three ways meet. Here we are in the suburbs, yet I felt as though I had ventured on to a trackless wilderness. Do not mistake me — I am fond of spots like this, bleak and seemingly characterless, if that is the word, fond, I mean. Yes, give me an unconsidered corner any day over your verdant vales, your sparkling, majestic peaks. My scenic detours will lead you down littered streets where washing hangs from windows and slippered old parties with their dentures out stand in front doorways watching you. There will be slinking dogs going about their business, and children with dirt-smeared faces playing behind barbed wire on waste ground under a charred sky. Young men will put their heads far back and flare their nostrils and stare truculently, and girls in high heels and piled-up hairstyles will preen and flounce, pretending not to be aware of you, and screech at each other with the voices of parrots; it is always the girls who know there is an elsewhere, you can see them yearning for it. There are dustbin smells, and smells of mouldering plaster and rotting mattresses. You do not want to be here yet there is something here that speaks to you, something uneasily half remembered, half imagined; something that is you and not-you, a portent out of the past.

Why would the canny Sisters build their mother house — their mother house! — on such a spot? Maybe the building, painted mantle-blue and many-windowed, as commodious as one of Heaven's promised mansions, was designed originally for some other purpose, was a barracks, maybe, or maybe a madhouse. The sky seemed impossibly low this day, the bellied clouds as if resting on the ranks of chimney pots and the rooks skimming down in deep, long arcs on to the wind-polished grass, seeming pressed upon by the weight of that sky and steering themselves by the ragged tips of their wings.

Sister Catherine was a brisk little body with a smoker's cough. I would not have taken her for a nun at all. Her hair, grizzled like mine but cut shorter, was uncovered, and her habit, such as it was, square-cut from grey serge, looked to me like the kind of outfit that librarians and businessmen's dowdy secretaries used to wear in my young days. When exactly was it that nuns stopped dressing the part? One must go far to the south, nowadays, to the Latin lands, to find the true original: the heavy black skirts to the ground, the hood and wimple, the big wooden rosary slung about the non-existent waist. This person's legs were bare, her ankles thick. Strain though I might, I could not see in her a likeness of her mother. She was home, she told me, on vacation, her word, from the mission fields abroad. At once I pictured a vast sandy tract under a white and pitiless sun, all scattered about with skulls and bleached bones and bits of glass and glittering metal lashed with thongs to painted sticks. She is a doctor as well as a nun — I remembered that coveted microscope. Her accent has a New World edge. She chain-smokes, Lucky Camels being her brand. She still wears those thick-lensed specs; they might have been from her father's shop. I told her that Catherine was, had been, my daughter's name. "Called Kitty, too, like me?" she asked. No, I said: Cass.

There was an inner cloister where we

walked, a stone-flagged, arcaded corridor around four sides of a gravelled courtyard with an open sky above. On the gravel there were palms growing in tall Ali Baba pots, and a trellis trailing some variety of winter-flowering climber with a pallid and despondent bloom. Despite my overcoat I was cold, but Sister Catherine, as I suppose I must go on calling her, in her thin grey cardigan, seemed not to notice the raw air and the wind's insidious, icy fingers.

It seems I was mistaken about everything. Nobody knew about her mother and me. She had told no one what she had seen in the laundry room that day. She was lighting a cigarette, and had her hands cupped around a match, and now she looked up at me sideways with a glint of the Kitty of old, scornful and amused. Why, she asked, had I imagined that everyone knew? But I thought, I said in bewilderment, I thought the town was rife with talk of how her mother and I had carried on so disgracefully throughout that summer. She shook her head, detaching a flake of tobacco from her lip. But her father, I said, had she not told him? "What — Daddy?" she said, spluttering on a mouthful of smoke. "He'd have been the last one I would tell. And even if I had told him he wouldn't have believed me

— in his eyes Mumser could do no wrong."
Mumser? "That's what we called her, Billy and I. Don't you remember anything?" Evidently not.

We walked on. The wind moaned among the stone arcades. I was suffering the same constraint that used to take hold of me in the old days in face of Kitty's mockery and sly merriment. And how peculiar it felt, being here with her, after all these years, this tough little person giving off puffs of smoke like an old-fashioned steam train and shaking her head in happy wonderment at my ignorance, my deludedness. They used to say she was delicate; obviously they were wrong. Even if, she was saying, even if it had been proved to her father that for months his wife had been up to monkey business with a boy of — what age had I been then, anyway? — he would have done nothing about it, for he loved Mumser so desperately and held her in such helpless awe that he would have let her get away with anything. Saying these things, she displayed no rancour against me, the me of now or the me of then. She did not even seem to feel I had done wrong. I, on the other hand, was in a sweat of shame and embarrassment. Monkey business.

But Marge, I said, stopping short as I sud-

403

denly remembered, her friend Marge, what about her? Well, she said, stopping too, what about her? Surely, I said, she would have told what she had seen. She frowned, peering up at me as though I had lost my senses. "What do you mean?" she said. "Marge wasn't there." This I could not take in at all. I had seen them in the doorway of the laundry room, I remembered it distinctly, the two of them standing there, Kitty in her pigtails and her round glasses and lardy Marge breathing through her mouth, both staring in that dull and slightly puzzled way, like a pair of *putti* who had lighted by mistake upon a crucifixion scene. But no, the nun said firmly, no, I was wrong, Marge was not there, it had been she alone at the open door.

We had come to a corner of the rectangular courtyard where there was an unglazed arched narrow window, an arrow-loop, or loop-hole, I think it is called, affording a view down the hillside to where those three roads converged. We could see cramped housing estates with serried roofs, and parked cars like so many coloured beetles, and gardens, and television masts, and mushrooming water-towers. The wind was streaming steadily through the stone slit, forceful and cold as a cascade of water, and we stopped and leaned into the deep embrasure to get the unexpectedly fresh feel of it on our faces. Sister Catherine — no, Kitty, I shall call her Kitty, it feels unnatural not to — Kitty was shielding her cigarette in her fist and still smiling to herself in bemusement at the enormity of my misconceptions, my misrememberings. Yes, she said again cheerily, I was wrong about everything, everything. The day that she happened upon us in the laundry room was not the day that Mrs. Gray left to go back to her mother, that was a month later, more than a month, and Mr. Gray had not shut the shop and put the house up for sale until long afterwards, at Christmas time. By then her mother, who had been ill throughout that summer, our summer, hers and mine, was failing fast; everyone had been surprised that she had held on for so long. "Because of you, probably," Kitty said, tapping a finger on the sleeve of my coat, "if that's any comfort to you." I put my face close up to the narrow window and looked down into that populous vale. So many, so many of the living!

She had been mortally sick for a long time, my Mrs. Gray, and I without an inkling. The child who had died had torn something in her insides when it was being born, and in that fissure the mad cells gathered and bided until their hour came. "Endometrial carcinoma," Kitty said. "Brr" — she gave herself a shake — "to be a doctor is to know too much." Her mother died, she said, on the last day of that year. By then my heart had healed, and I had turned sixteen, and was about other business. "She was cold, all the time, that September," Kitty said, "though remember how hot it was? Every morning Pa would build a fire for her and she would sit in front of it all day wrapped in a blanket, looking into the flames." She gave a sort of soft little angry laugh through her nostrils and shook her head. "She was waiting for you, I think," she said, shooting me a glance. "But you never came."

We turned and walked back across the courtyard. I told her how Billy had flung himself at me in the Forge that day, shouting and weeping and swinging his fists. Yes, Kitty said, she had told him, he was the only one she had told. She had felt she had owed it to him. I did not ask why. Now we were pacing again under the arcades, our footsteps sharp on the flagstones. "Will you look at those," she said, stopping, and pointing with her cigarette, "those palms. What sort of a thing are they, to have here?" Billy died three years ago, of something in the brain, an aneurysm, she supposed. She had not seen him for a long time, had hardly known him any more. Her father outlived him by a year — "Imagine that!" Now they were all gone, and she was the last of the line, and the name would die with her. "Oh, well," she said, "the world will hardly lack for Grays."

I would have liked to ask her why she became a nun. Does she believe it all, I wonder, the crib and the cross, the miraculous birth, sacrifice, redemption and resurrection? If so, in her version of things, Cass is eternally alive, Cass, and Mrs. Gray, and Mr. Gray, and Billy, and my mother and my father, and everyone else's father and mother, back through all the generations, even unto Eden. But that is not the only possible or highest heaven. Among the wonders that Fedrigo Sorrán told me of that snowy night in Lerici was the theory of the many worlds. Some savants hold that there is a multiplicity of universes, all present, all simultaneously going on, wherein everything that might happen does happen. Just as on Kitty's thronging paradisal plain, so, too, somewhere in this infinitely layered, infinitely ramifying reality Cass did not die, her child was born, Svidrigailov did not go to

America; somewhere, too, Mrs. Gray survived, perhaps is surviving still, still young and still remembering me, as I remember her. Which eternal realm shall I believe in, which shall I choose? Neither, since all my dead are all alive to me, for whom the past is a luminous and everlasting present; alive to me yet lost, except in the frail afterworld of these words.

If I must choose one memory of Mrs. Gray, my Celia, a last one, from my overflowing store, then here it is. We were in the wood, in Cotter's place, sitting naked on the mattress, or she was sitting, rather, while I half lay in her lap with my arms loosely draped about her hips and my head on her breast. I was looking upwards, past her shoulder, to where I could see the sun shining through a rent in the roof. It must have been hardly more than a pinhole, for the beam of light coming through it was very fine, yet intense, too, radiating outwards in spokes in all directions, so that at every tiniest adjustment of the angle of my head it made a shivering, fiercely burning wheel that spun and stopped and spun again, like the gold wheel of an enormous watch. It struck me that I alone was witness to this phenomenon sparked at this one insignificant point by the conjunction of the great spheres of the world — more, that I was its maker, that it was in my eye it was being generated, that none but I would see or know it. Just then Mrs. Gray shifted her shoulder, dousing the beam of sunlight, and the spoked wheel was no more. My dazzled eyes hastened to adjust to her shadowy form above me, and quickly the moment of eclipse passed and there she was, leaning down to me, holding up her left breast a little on three splayed fingers and offering it to my lips like a precious, polished gourd. What I saw, though, or what I see now, is her face, foreshortened in my view of it, broad and immobile, heavy-lidded, the mouth unsmiling, and the expression in it, pensive, melancholy and remote, as she contemplated not me but something beyond me, something far, far beyond.

Kitty let me out at a corner of the cloisters, through a postern gate, or sally-port — ah, yes, how I love the old words, how they comfort me. I was fiddling with my hat, my gloves, a fussed old party suddenly. I did not know what to say to her. We shook hands quickly and I turned and seemed to reel down that hillside, and was soon among those paltry, blemished streets again.

I am going to America. Shall I find Svidrigailov there? Perhaps I shall. JB and I are to travel together, an ill-assorted pair, I know. We have put our faith in the largesse of Professor Blank, our putative host at the Axelvanderfest in Arcady, where I am told there are no seasons. Our passage is booked, our bags are packed, we are eager to be off. All that remains is to shoot our final scene, the one in which Vander comes to bid farewell to Cora, his tragic girl who died of love for him. Yes, Dawn Devonport is back on set. In the end it was Lydia, of course, who persuaded her to return and be again among the living. I shall not ask what deal was done down in that kitchen lair, amid the libations of tea and the sacrificial fumes of cigarette smoke. Instead, I shall wait on the fringes of light as they lay out the star in her shroud and apply the last touches to her makeup, and I shall think, lingering there, before walking forwards to lean down and kiss her cold and painted brow, that a film set resembles nothing so much as a nativity scene, that little lighted space surrounded by its dim, attentive figures.

Billie Stryker, too, will shortly set out on a journey, to Antwerp, Turin, Portovenere. Yes, I have commissioned her to retrace whatever slime-trail Axel Vander may have left along that route ten years ago. More unfinished business. What things she will unearth I do not care to think but yet would know. I fear there is much that is buried. She is eager to be off, looking forward to getting away from that husband of hers, I do not doubt. I have signed over to her what I have been paid for playing Vander these past weeks. To what better use could I have put such a tainted bounty? Billie, my sleuth.

When I was a child I, too, like Cass, suffered from insomnia. I think in my case it was that I deliberately kept myself awake, for I had bad dreams, and was prey to an abiding fear of sudden death — I would not lie on my left side, I remember, convinced that if my heart should fail while I was asleep I would wake up and feel it stopping and know I was about to die. I cannot say what age I was when I suffered this affliction; probably it was about the time of my father's death. If so, I added to my bereaved mother's torment by tormenting her with my wakefulness, night after night. I would beg her to leave her bedroom door open so that I could call out to her every few minutes to make sure she, too, was still awake. Eventually, exhausted no doubt by her own grief and my merciless importunings, she would fall asleep, and I would be left alone, wide-eyed and with scalding eyelids, crouched under the night's stifling black blanket. I would stay there like that, in terror and anguish, for as long as I could bear it, which was not long, and then I would get up and go into my mother's room. The convention was, and it never varied, that I had been asleep and had been wakened by one of my nightmares. Poor Ma. She would not allow me to get into bed with her, that was a rule she enforced, this least forceful of souls, but she would pass something to me, a blanket or an eiderdown, to put on the floor beside the bed to lie on. She would reach out a hand, too, from under the covers, and give me one of her fingers to hold. In time, when this ritual had become the norm, and I was spending a part of every night on the floor beside her bed, clutching her finger, I devised my own arrangement. I found a canvas sleeping bag in the attic — it must have been left behind by a lodger — and kept it in a cupboard, and would drag it with me into my mother's room and wriggle into it and lie down in my place on the floor by her bed. This went on for months, until in the end I must have surmounted some barrier, crossed into a new and sturdier phase of growing up, and began to keep to my own room, and to sleep in my own bed. And then, years later, one night in the immediate, agonised aftermath of Mrs. Gray's departure, I found myself scrabbling in the cupboard for that old sleeping bag, and finding it I crept with stifled sobs into my mother's room and spread it on the floor, as I used to. What did my mother think? I believed she was asleep, but presently — did she know I was weeping? — I heard a rustling sound and her hand came out from under the sheet and she touched me on the shoulder, offering me her finger to hold on to, as in the old days. I went rigid, of course, and shrank back from her touch, and presently she withdrew her hand and turned over with a heave and a sigh, and soon was snoring. I watched the window above me. The night was ending and the dawn was coming on, and light, uncertain as yet, a faint effulgence, was seeping in around the edges of the curtain. My eyes ached from weeping and my throat was swollen and raw. What I thought could not end had ended. Whom now would I love, and who would love me? I listened to my mother snoring. The air in the room was stale from her breath. One world was ending, without a sound. I looked to the window again. The light around the curtain was stronger now, a light that seemed somehow to shake within itself even as it strengthened, and it was as if some radiant being were advancing towards the house, over the grey grass, across the mossed yard, great trembling wings spread wide, and waiting for it, waiting, I slipped without noticing into sleep.

ABOUT THE AUTHOR

John Banville was born in Wexford, Ireland, in 1945. His first book, *Long Lankin,* was published in 1970. His other books are *Nightspawn, Birchwood, Doctor Copernicus* (which won the James Tait Black Memorial Prize in 1976), *Kepler* (which was awarded the *Guardian* Fiction Award in 1981), *The Newton Letter* (which was filmed for Channel 4), *Mefisto, The Book of Evidence* (which was short-listed for the 1989 Booker Prize and winner of the 1989 Guinness Peat Aviation Book Award), *Ghosts, Athena, The Intouchable, Eclipse, Shroud, The Sea* (which was awarded the Man Booker Prize in 2005), and *The Infinities.* He has received a literary award from the Lannan Foundation and was nominated for the Man Booker International Prize in 2007. He lives in Dublin.